"One of the earliest autho1
described as writing hard
Booth must have had an
he made it in Hollywood
winning the Academy Award for best story for
The House on 92nd Street in 1945."
—Steve Holland, *Bear Alley*

"There is a real atmosphere of mystery and
romance in Charles G. Booth's "Sinister
House"... It is set in the charming scenery of
Southern California, and the noise of the surf
breaking on the beach in front of the "House
of Yesterday" is continually reaching the ears
of the reader... Mr. Booth's mastery of
characterisation and aptness in fitting his
characters for the positions allotted to them
and keeping them in these have combined to
produce a story which will be read at one
sitting." —*Dundee Courier*

"The three strongest characters are all female.
Not in the contemporary sense of strong
where they lecture, shame and beat up the
male characters, but they are the determining
forces that drive the story. An entertaining
read." —Bill Kelly

Charles G. Booth Bibliography
(1896-1949)

Novels:
Sinister House (1926)
Gold Bullets (1929)
Those Seven Alibis (1932; published in UK as *At Ten Paces*, 1933)
The General Died at Dawn (1937)
Mr. Angel Comes Aboard (1944)
The Excommunicated (with Ahmad Kamal; 1952)

Anatole Flique series:
Murder at High Tide (1930)
The Cat and the Clock (1935)
Kings Die Hard (1949)

Collections:
Murder Strikes Thrice (1946)

Film Work:
The General Died at Dawn (1936; based on a story)
The Magnificent Fraud (1939; based on a story)
Hurricane Smith (1941; based on a story)
Sundown (1941; co-scripted)
The Traitor Within (1942; co-scripted)
The House on 92nd Street (1945; co-scripted)
Johnny Angel (1945; based on *Mr. Angel Comes Aboard*)
Strange Triangle (1946; adaptation)
Behind the Green Lights (1946; co-scripted)
Fury at Furnace Creek (1948)
Moon Over Parador (1988; re-make of *The Magnificent Fraud*)

Sinister House

•••••••••••••••••••••

Charles G. Booth

Introduction by Steve Holland

STARK
HOUSE

Stark House Press • Eureka California

SINISTER HOUSE

Published by Stark House Press
1315 H Street
Eureka, CA 95501, USA
griffinskye3@sbcglobal.net
www.starkhousepress.com

SINISTER HOUSE
Originally published and copyright © by William Morrow & Co.,
New York, 1926; and Hodder & Stoughton, London, 1927.

"Charles G Booth: Hard-boiled Pioneer" © 2015 by Steve Holland,
originally published in *Bear Alley* and reprinted by permission of the
author.

ISBN: 979-8-88601-074-9

Text design by Mark Shepard, shepgraphics.com
Cover design by Jeff Vorzimmer, ¡caliente!design, Austin, Texas
Cover art: *View of the Artist's Home, Graycliff*, 1894 (Detail)
by William Trost Richards
Proofreading by Bill Kelly

First Stark House Press Edition: February 2023

Charles G Booth:
Hard-boiled Pioneer

By Steve Holland

One of the earliest authors who could be described as writing hard-boiled fiction is Charles G. Booth, who penned stories that relied on criminal argot for realism. Booth must have had an ear for dialogue as he had a successful career as a Hollywood scriptwriter, winning the Academy Award for Original Motion Picture Story for *The House on 92nd Street* in 1945. What is perhaps surprising is that Booth was an Englishman and had spent his early years in Canada.

Writing for the *Los Angeles Times*, Lee Shippey described a visit to Booth's home in Ocean Beach, portraying him as living modestly in a neighbourhood where few knew that he made his living writing. "Booth is a very pleasant chap, still not very robust, but Southern California has done a great deal for his health." Elsewhere he was described as having a slight, wiry physique, with sharply cut features; his early childhood deprivations stamped on him a zeal for helping others and a determination to succeed; he was passionate about writing and it was a serious business to be worked at; he would never offer less than his best, and would not compromise with what he thought was right. A friend, Lee Lockwood Bloomenshine, wrote of Booth: "He came to success the hard way. A hundred times his manuscripts were rejected before one was purchased. Nothing could deter or dissuade him. A story once started must be finished. For long hours through the days and years he slugged away, shaping words into marketable dreams. When he reached the top in his profession—as he did one exciting never-to-be-forgotten Hollywood night—the Academy Award he received was the symbol of a determination that would not be denied."

Charles Gordon Booth was born in Prestwich, an area of the bustling midlands city of Manchester, on February 12, 1896, the son of William Booth and his wife Emily Ada (née Hill).

William was a bricklayer and building contractor, still working at the turn of the century despite having reached his early seventies. He died in June 1905, aged 74. Emily, a Methodist thirty years her late husband's junior, decided that there might be better opportunities in Canada for her and her 10-year-old son and sailed to Montreal in 1907.

Having attending his first school in Manchester, Booth continued his education at public schools in Toronto, Ontario, and Winnipeg, Manitoba. Living in St. Boniface, a suburb of Winnipeg, he left school at the age of 14 in order to help support his mother. For a while he worked as a claims investigator for a railway firm, but found the experience unpleasant as it required him to be as heartless as possible. Booth was working as a stenographer for a lumber firm in Norwood, when, on March 3, 1916, he volunteered to join the Canadian Over-Seas Expeditionary Force. Booth served in the 203rd Battalion (Winnipeg Rifles), which sailed to England in October 1916; Booth, unfortunately, had fallen ill and never made it overseas and was honourably discharged in 1917.

Booth spent the next seventeen months in hospital where he developed an interest in creative writing and also in the Isle of Pines, an idyllic island off the south coast of Cuba. Booth had read about the island and had the idea that he would knock out some short stories and sell them, making enough money to visit the island.

Booth began writing stories, sending out two or three at a time without success. He was almost crushed when four stories were returned on the same day, but kept churning them out until he had accumulated thirty unsold manuscripts and 105 rejection slips. His first sale was to *Saucy Stories*, although his story 'The Iron Mother' was anything but saucy. Other sales followed, including his first in print, 'Beyond the Code', to *Western Home Monthly*.

Sales to *Canadian Home Journal*, *MacLean's Magazine*, *Overland* and *Love Story Magazine* followed. Booth quit his job as a book keeper at a lumber mill and left Canada on April 4, 1922, taking his mother to Washington and from there to San Diego, California, where he made a living writing fiction. Stories began appearing in *Detective Story Magazine* in 1922 and *Black Mask* in 1923.

His career took off quickly and he sold tales to *Fawcett's Triple-X Magazine*, *Flynn's*, *Novelets*, *Excella*, *Weird Tales*, *Fighting Romances*, *Brief Stories*, *Mystery Magazine*, *Sunset*, *Top-Notch Magazine*, *Argosy All Story*, *People's Popular*

Monthly, Thrills, 20-Story Magazine, West and *Five Novels Monthly* over the next decade.

His first novel, a crime thriller entitled *Sinister House*, was serialised in *Mystery Magazine* in early 1926 and published by William Morrow in the USA and Hodder & Stoughton in the UK a year later, where it was positively reviewed:

> There is a real atmosphere of mystery and romance in Charles G. Booth's "Sinister House"... It is set in the charming scenery of Southern California, and the noise of the surf breaking on the beach in front of the "House of Yesterday" is continually reaching the ears of the reader. The story opens with a hold-up and develops suddenly into a murder mystery, the victim of which is an intrepid wanderer, Conniston, whose chief possessions are some intaglio gems. There are several reasons why Kerry O'Neil should be suspected, but these Gail Hollister, refuses to countenance, and the remainder of the story tells of her efforts to clear his name. Mr. Booth's mastery of characterisation and aptness in fitting his characters for the positions allotted to them and keeping them in these have combined to produce a story which will be read at one sitting, or reluctantly laid aside if necessity compels interruption. (*Dundee Courier*, 19 Apr 1927)

Elsewhere, other critics found nothing new in the plot but admitted that Booth had maintained the suspense and the solution came as a complete surprise.

In 1927, when he applied for naturalization, Booth was living at 4905 Del Mar Avenue, Ocean Beach, California. Three and a half years later – and now living at 4695 Coronado Avenue, Ocean Beach – he become a naturalized citizen, his application certified on September 22, 1930.

Booth's second novel, *Gold Bullets*, was serialised in *Holland's* in 1928-29 ahead of book publication and was as well received as its predecessor:

> A thrilling mystery is evolved by Charles G. Booth in "Gold Bullets"... which develops on unusual lines. In the first chapter a Californian millionaire is found murdered, and his son is suspected. The chief clue to the mystery is an old pistol with gold bullets owned by a close friend of the murdered man. Events move

dramatically to a deserted gold mine where a long-dead past is resuscitated, and the real criminal is brought to justice. This novel intrigues and baffles in an absorbing fashion (*Aberdeen Journal*, 17 Sep 1929)

Booth's stories began appearing in more prestigious titles, including *Life* in the US and in *Pall Mall*, *Premier* and *Pearson's Magazine* in the UK. His third novel, *Murder at the High Tide*, was another hit.

The title of this detective "thriller" means more than most such titles, for two murders were committed when the tide was at the maximum. First there is a shooting of a self-made man whose hobby, it appears, was to alienate everyone with whom he came into contact, and then comes the death from a similar cause of the only man who seems to have any clue to the perpetrator of the first crime. When a man is hated as Dan Parados, the victim of the first crime was, there are more motives than the average detective cares to cope with, but the reader will enjoy himself picking up the various clues and pursuing the false trails he is expected to follow. (*Aberdeen Journal*, 25 Aug 1930)

The detective in the case was a "comically suave French policeman," according to Steve Lewis (*The Mystery Fancier*, Jul/Aug 1979). "In his own words, he's the cleverest on the Paris Surete. He's also greatly given to twirling his moustaches and busily polishing the top of his head, all the while contemplating life's little mysteries."
Flique returned in *The Cat and the Clock* five years later:

A few hours before being found stabbed to death in her dressing-room, glamorous, heartless Stella Ghent swerved her car purposely into a kitten and killed it.
    You're puzzled—not sorry—when Charles G. Booth tells you of her death in his new thriller, "The Cat and the Clock". You're puzzled which of her enemies killed her. Was it her former dancing partner, red-haired Vivian Storm, or one of those she was blackmailing with a diary as a weapon?
    The other suspects are either connected with the stage or a politics racket—all sufficiently intelligent to put over a pretty fool-proof innocence plea.

Snowball, the dead kitten, is the clue with which the famous French detective, bald, bewhiskered Anatole Flique, solves the mysteries of a real-life drama in Hollywood's make-believe background.
Joe Irysh, Stella Ghent's Press manager tells the story briskly and convincingly. (*Lancashire Evening Post*, 20 Sep 1938)

It was around the same time he completed the above that Booth began his career as a Hollywood scriptwriter, his first success the sale of the story *The General Dies at Dawn*, adapted for the screen by Clifford Odets. It starred Akim Tamiroff as General Yang, whose vanity O'Hara (Gary Cooper), as a soldier of fortune in the ranks if the people's army in China, uses to save himself and a girl, Judy Perrie (Madeleine Carrol), a beautiful honey trap sent by the war lords O'Hara is engaged in annihilating.

The success of the film meant that Booth's play "Caviar for His Excellency" had three or four studios bidding for the rights, which were eventually picked up by Paramount who wanted George Raft for the lead role. Raft refused out of hand, which led to him being dropped by Paramount. The story became *The Magnificent Fraud*, about a group of politicians anxious to gain control of a South American country following the assassination of its president. To hide this fact, they hire a French actor Jules LaCroix (Akim Tamiroff), fleeing from a murder charge, to impersonate Señor Presidente, only to find that the actor takes the job seriously and eventually dies for his newly adopted country. The film was remade in 1988 as *Moon Over Parador* starring Richard Dreyfuss.

Hurricane Smith (1941, a.k.a. *Double Identity*), scripted by Robert Presnell for Republic from Booth's story, tells how rodeo rider 'Hurricane' Smith (Ray Middleton) is wrongly jailed for murder and robbery; he escapes and tracks down the real crooks, but after stealing the money he uses it to marry and start a new life. He is tracked down by 'Eggs' Bonelli (J. Edward Bromberg) and blackmailed.

Sundown (1941) was co-scripted with another escapee from England, Barré Lyndon (best known for his plays *The Amazing Dr Clitterhouse* and *The Man in Half Moon Street*), based on Lyndon's *Saturday Evening Post* story. The film was an odd war film set in East Africa starring Gene Tierney as the exotic Zia who Major Coombes (George Sanders) suspects is a Nazi sympathizer; however, along with district commissioner

William Crawford (Bruce Cabot) she swaps trading for helping guide British troops through the dark continent. The film had a mixed critical reception: the *New York Times* called it "ridiculous ... the whole film becomes so much banal nonsense" but it was nominated for three Academy Awards (cinematography, score, art direction); the bad reviews won out and it was a flop at the box-office.

Booth's next original screenplay, *The Traitor Within* (1942), co scripted with Jack Townley, concerned rival trucking firms; Sam Starr (Don Barry) resents his rival John Scott Ryder (Ralph Morgan) taking credit for wartime heroics, but accepts his generosity when Sam loses his truck. When he discovers that Ryder has been blackmailed into his actions by Molly (Jean Parker), his wife, he refunds the gift; Ryder, also being blackmailed by a crooked politician, is left with his guilt and decides to end his life... only for Starr to be suspected of his murder.

Booth was living in Sierra Vista Street, Grossmont, San Diego, when he registered for service in World War II at the age of 46. He was able to continue his screenwriting career, becoming a contract writer for Twentieth Century Fox, receiving an Academy Award for his picture story for *The House on 92nd Street* (1945). The film saw him team up again with his *Sundown* collaborators Barré Lyndon and director Henry Hathaway and was notable for successfully bringing a documentary style of storytelling to the screen, using locations in New York and Washington and using FBI personnel to play FBI agents. An American student, Dietrich (William Eythe) pretends to be working for the Nazi's whilst passing on information to the FBI. The story was based in part on the Duquesne Spy Ring case from 1941.

RKO's *Johnny Angel* (1945) was based on Booth's 1944 novel *Mr Angel Comes Aboard* and starred George Raft as the titular merchant ship captain who discovers his father's ship derelict and adrift. A survivor, stowaway Paulette (Signe Hasso), reveals that a shipment of gold has been stolen and Angel crosses swords with Lilah (Claire Trevor), his boss's wife, as he doggedly tracks down the missing bullion and his father's murderer.

Back at 20th Century Fox, Booth collaborated with Scott Darling on *Behind Green Lights* (1946), a story of political intrigue and murder. The body of a dead private detective is parked at the front of a police station and becomes central to Police Lieutenant Sam Carson (William Gargan)'s case.

Switched for another body, and then lost; but pressure is being put on Carson to arrest Janet Bradley (Carole Landis), who admits she was in his room; as does Nora (Mary Anderson), Bard's estranged wife.

Booth adapted Jack Andrews' story for *Strange Triangle* (1946) starring Signe Hasso as Francine Huber, whose husband, bank manager Earl (John Shepperd), is embezzling funds. Sam Crane (Preston Foster), a bank investigator, gets involved with Francine and is used to cover up her husband's crime and then as a fall guy in his murder.

Fury at Furnace Creek (1948) was Booth's only western, based on a story by David Garth and with additional dialogue by Winston Miller. Two brothers (Victor Mature and Glenn Langan) go undercover to prove that their father (Robert Warwick) was not responsible for the massacre of troops at Furnace Creek fort by Indian raiders hiding in a wagon train.

Booth died in Beverly Hills, Los Angeles, California, on May 22, 1949, aged 53. In 1937, he had married Lilian Lind, born in Newman Grove, Nebraska, on 18 Mar 1904, the daughter of Carl Edward Lind and his wife Emelia, née Nelson, and raised in Twin Falls, Idaho, where her father ran a garage. Lilian was living in California in 1930 and travelled at least once to Japan but had no recorded occupation.

Their son, Charles Rockwell (Rocky) Booth, was born in Los Angeles on 3 January 1947. Lilian subsequently remarried and, as Lilian Booth Foley, died in San Diego on 13 January 1996; she was later buried at Twin Falls.

Booth's novels were translated into most European and Scandinavian languages—Finnish, Swedish, Dutch, German, etc.—but despite his success he never did make it to the Isle of Pines. The nearest he came was his honeymoon, which was spent on the Virgin Islands.

—*Bear Alley*
October 26, 2015

Steve Holland is a British researcher of pulp and popular fiction, his books including *The Trials of Hank Janson* and *The Mushroom Jungle*. He publishes the results as Bear Alley Books and on his blog, which can be found at bearalley.blogspot.co.uk.

Sinister House

A Mystery Story of Southern California

By Charles G. Booth

CHAPTER I
The Man With the Tiny Ears

Early in life Mr. Conrad Gill, the diamond broker, had mastered the art of keeping one's disappointments to oneself. Good taste in all things, especially in those which pertained to the personal feelings, was one of the maxims by which he had governed his career. But while he attributed much of his considerable success to his self-restraint, it must not be inferred that he admired the quality for its commercial properties alone and that he did not pride himself on his appreciation of the graceful effect of a genial countenance in the face of defeat.

Whether in this matter of the Conniston intaglios his defeat was temporary or permanent, Mr. Gill did not know. Perhaps old Conniston might be induced to change his mind. He hoped so, for the intaglios were almost the finest he had ever seen, which really meant that they were almost the finest anybody had ever seen. But if Conniston stuck to his suddenly conceived determination to hang on, well—Mr. Gill shrugged his modish shoulders—he would accept defeat gracefully, as usual; so gracefully, indeed, that Conniston, a sentimentalist at heart no doubt, might be persuaded to relent and let him have them. If he didn't—Mr. Gill shrugged again—once more he would have demonstrated that his sense of values was not confined to the gems which, in the channels of trade, constantly passed through his sensitive fingers.

The beauty of the night and the tranquil motion of the limousine under the skillful pilotage of his son, Victor, who sat alone in the front seat, inclined Mr. Gill to reflection; he let his nimble mind run over the interview which had just terminated in old Conniston's library at the Casa de Ayer, and the one that had preceded it.

He had met Colonel Conniston in Los Angeles a month previously. The antiquary had expressed a desire to discuss with him the sale of the gems. Would he inspect them at the Casa de Ayer, just off the coast highway, at his convenience? Mr. Gill had seen the famous collection at the Panama-California Exposition in San Diego a decade or so before, and he had experienced some little difficulty in repressing his enthusiasm at the invitation to the point at which he could accept it without loss of dignity to himself. A definite date had not been fixed upon; however, Mr. Gill had allowed a reasonable interval to elapse before presenting himself in company with his son who, in a moderate way, was also his partner, at the Casa de Ayer. But only to find that the Colonel had suddenly changed his mind! That very evening, in fact! He would not sell at any price! And Mr. Gill had been prepared to go to three hundred thousand!

His disappointment was intense. He had not intended to keep the gems permanently, of course; but he had hoped to retain them for a little while before passing them on at a reasonable profit. But the old man was not to be moved, and after congratulating him on his collection and declining his offer of hospitality for the night, they had wished him good evening.

Perhaps they had been overhasty in taking their departure, Mr. Gill meditated. The Casa de Ayer had that charming Spanish-California atmosphere which he loved so well and encountered so seldom. And Colonel Conniston, notwithstanding his inexplicable obstinacy in this matter of the intaglio gems and an almost startling irascibility of manner, was as thoroughly a part of the picture as Don Silvestre Calderón must have been when he built the place nearly a hundred years before. There remained only some fifty acres of the original Mexican-California grant, but the old man had withstood the subdividers with their tempting offers, their hideous signboards, and their chattering free lunch excursionists, and Mr. Gill honored him for it.... Ah, well, they would be on their way to-morrow.

By now the limousine had left the Conniston estate several miles behind. They were on a rough dirt road which rose in a long sweeping curve, and as the car ascended the grade the poignant beauty of the night held Mr. Gill entranced. The moon was nearly full. A magic wand had waved and earth and sky and silver sea were a fairy universe in which Mr. Gill felt that he and his limousine had no right whatever. All too soon the car must top the slope and the architectural disharmonies of Ocean Strand on the other side would mar the matchless loveliness of the scene. Mr. Gill touched his son on the shoulder.

"Slow down, Victor. The night is precious. We must not miss it."

Physically, they resembled each other, Mr. Gill and his son. They were of middle height, though Mr. Gill had filled out comfortably, whereas Victor was still lean and wiry; their eyes were black and piercing, with Victor's a trifle the harder, perhaps; their noses were slightly aquiline, their lips were thin and bloodless, their fingers long and sensitive; and each had a striking pallor of countenance and a skin so flawless in texture as to suggest a bit of Chinese porcelain.

But here the resemblance ended. Victor Gill was dour, silent, inscrutable. He reminded his father of a river the source and the outlet and the depth of which are unknown. Mr. Gill regretted the existence of these qualities in his son, but he had given up trying to solve him years ago. Nevertheless, Victor could drive as shrewd a bargain as Mr. Gill himself, and there were moments when the latter had high hopes of him, though he realized that he would never be the man his father was.

The limousine had almost reached the crest of the slope now. Here the view was at its best and Mr. Gill abandoned himself to the beauty of the night. In spite of his bitter disappointment he was inexpressibly glad that they had driven down, for he had thought that with the coming of the subdivider and the hordes from the Middle West romance had perished in California, whereas here he found it rising on the breath of the sage, a rare incense that went to his head like old wine.

Had Mr. Gill found himself slipping back into a more spacious age, had his limousine by some forgotten magic turned itself into a stage coach of a hundred years ago, and had there suddenly appeared on the brow of the hill a lean dark figure in sombrero and silver spurs, pistol in hand, commanding them to stand and deliver, be would have accepted the situation unquestioningly. So it happened that when the latter part of his absurd fancy became actuality Mr. Gill, in a sense, was prepared for it.

On the top of the slope a solitary eucalyptus tree stood guard over the unfrequented road. As the limousine drew abreast of the tree a man leaped out of its shadow and ran swiftly toward the car. He wore a brown belted suit; a hat of the same color was pulled down over his eyes and a triangle of white handkerchief concealed the lower part of his face. The man sprang onto the running board of the limousine.

"Stop the car and stick up your hands!"

The muzzle of an automatic pistol pressed into Victor Gill's white cheek. The lean brown hand that held it was as steady as a rock, and the dark tempestuous eyes above the triangle of handkerchief were bright with anger and imperious with command. Victor Gill shot one swift look at the man; then he threw on the brakes. The car stopped suddenly, pitching Mr.

Gill forward on the cushions.

"Now—stick up your hands! Both of you!" The pistol swung from one head to the other. "And be sharp about it!"

There being nothing else to do, they obeyed him.

"Think of the devil!" Mr. Gill murmured unsteadily.

The masked man gave a short, hard laugh. "You'd better, or you may see him."

The broker shivered a little. "What do you want?"

"A good deal, Conrad Gill."

The latter grew a shade paler.

"Ah, you have the advantage of me!" The tremor in his tone denied his assumption of lightness.

"I propose to retain it, too! If you carry any weapons keep your hands off 'em!"

The threat was unmistakable.

"We don't! I can't bear firearms. What do you want?"

"The Conniston intaglios! Hand 'em over—quick!"

"Ah!" The exclamation was as much a gasp of relief as a cry of astonishment. Mr. Gill thanked his stars that Colonel Conniston had changed his mind. "What makes you think I have them?" he temporized.

"Never mind. I *know!*" There was something starkly emphatic about that last word. "Hand 'em over and be quick about it!"

"My dear sir—"

"None of that! Do as I say!"

"But we haven't got them!"

There came a leap of fury in the dark eyes above the triangle of handkerchief. The pistol jerked up, then down again, and advanced to within an inch of Mr. Gill's forehead. Never in all his well-nurtured life had the broker encountered death in any but a strictly impersonal sense, but now he was sure that he recognized it in the black muzzle of the pistol and in the furious stare of the dark eyes behind it.

"I'll give you thirty seconds." The voice was savage; otherwise it might have been pleasantly toned. Mr. Gill's blood ran cold.

"But I tell you we haven't got them!" he insisted, desperately. "Conniston wouldn't sell! Changed his mind at the last moment! Isn't that so, Victor?"

All this while Victor Gill had maintained a watchful silence, according the masked man so searching a scrutiny that no visible detail of the latter's person or attire could have escaped his piercing black eyes.

"Conniston would not sell the intaglios," Victor Gill said in his passionless voice, apparently undisturbed by any emotion whatever. "We have not got them. Better take yourself off," he added significantly.

The man did not move. "Twenty seconds, Mr. Gill."

The broker attempted bluster.

"This sort of nonsense passed out with the stage coach fifty years ago!" he shrilled, utterly abandoning his romantic illusions. "You can't get away with it, young man! There's a penalty that'll engage your attention for some time to come! Rank nonsense! Put that thing down!"

"Ten seconds, Mr. Gill."

The broker's suave composure now completely deserted him.

"We haven't got them!" he gasped, hysterically. "Conniston wouldn't sell, I tell you! Changed his mind—put that thing down!"

"Five seconds," the man said, coldly.

Mr. Gill's eyes protruded grotesquely. "For God's sake—don't shoot! Victor—do something! Tell him we haven't got them!"

"I have done so, father," the son said, impassively.

The collapse of Mr. Gill was pitiable and the masked man eyed him appraisingly for a moment. He seemed less sure of himself now, as if doubt had come upon him. The fury left his eyes. Suddenly he seemed to come to a decision. Stepping down from the running board, he opened the doors of the limousine, still covering the two men within, and indicated the road.

"Get out!" he commanded. "I'm going to search you!"

Victor Gill complied immediately, in silence, and without any manifestation of emotion whatever. The older man was too overcome by what he believed to have been a perilously narrow escape from destruction to alight without assistance from his son. They were driven in front of the glaring headlights of the machine and the masked man went through their garments and over their persons exhaustively and unceremoniously. Bewilderment rather than disappointment appeared to attend his failure to find the intaglios.

"No tricks!" he commanded curtly as he turned to the limousine.

There were compartments in each of the four doors; these he examined first. Then he poked around the gray upholstery of the seats and peered down onto the carpeted floor.

Suddenly Mr. Gill caught the hum of a car ascending the grade from Ocean Strand and saw the flare of its headlights on the curving road. His heart began to race. Had the man seen it? Apparently not. Mr. Gill glanced surreptitiously at his son. Victor responded with a scarcely perceptible nod and pursed his lips for silence. The ascending headlights grew enormously; their flares knit into the beams from the lamps of the limousine. Evidently the machine was traveling at a high rate of speed. Mr. Gill began to grow hot and cold by turns. How would the situation break? Would the man show fight or would he run? The latter, Mr. Gill devoutly hoped. He had a horror of the crack of firearms, the bite of lead in human flesh.

The car swooped up the grade, a purring monster with eyes of fire. Now it was a hundred yards below them ... now sixty! Still the man at the limousine did not see or hear it, the freshening southwesterly carrying off much of the *whir* of its swift approach. Mr. Gill began to tremble. He glanced at his son. Victor stood with arms folded, pallid face as inscrutable as ever, black eyes as hard and bright as bits of steel. Once again Mr. Gill realized the unfathomable qualities of his son.

And then, in a blinding flare of light, the monster was upon them. There came the scream of brakes, the grind of tires skidding on the dirt road, and the machine—a touring car—slid to a standstill nose to nose with the limousine. Mr. Gill saw the masked man leap back from the limousine and rush forward into the flare cast by the headlights. And then a singular thing happened. The man flung up his hand as if something had struck him in the face, and he stopped dead in his tracks.

A shabby person in a gray cap and a khaki shirt slouched behind the wheel of the touring car. He looked white around the lips, and his hands gripped the wheel convulsively as if he had just grasped the nature of the situation he had come upon. But it was not at him that the man who had concealed his face was staring, but at the girl in the seat behind. She had risen to her feet; her hands were gripping the back of the front seat for support. Her eyes met the man's dark reckless ones across the flare of light.

The girl was pretty—darned pretty, thought Mr. Gill. She had removed her hat and her bobbed hair stood out like a nimbus about her head. Its shade was that rare coppery-red which is more copper-colored than red and the clear white of her skin set it off like a flame. Her eyes, he felt sure, would be that deep luminous blue—as if a light were burning behind them—which made one doubt one's materialism.

But as Mr. Gill continued to stare at the girl there swept across her charming face such a tempest of emotion—bewilderment and horror and contempt—that he held his breath in expectation of thunder and lightning. The lightning played in the girl's eyes, but there was no thunder; not so much as a tiny whisper of it. The purr of the automobile engine, the sigh of the breeze, the wild music of the surf below grew remote and meaningless. One could have heard a leaf drop. Still neither of them spoke and Mr. Gill, whose sense of situation was always immoderately strong, knew that he had stumbled upon drama, the tension of which nothing could enhance.

Suddenly the man who had covered his face staggered back, dropping his pistol. Then he turned swiftly, and with a low cry that was either a sob or a moan, plunged down the slope, crackling through the sage, and disappeared from sight.

Mr. Gill quickly recovered himself and ran forward.

"My dear young lady!" he exclaimed in his soft voice. "You have saved us from a nasty situation! That rascal meant business!"

The girl's face was drawn and colorless. Instead of looking at Mr. Gill she touched the chauffeur on the shoulder.

"Oh, do go on!" she cried in a tense voice. "It can't be far now."

The man shifted uneasily.

"I don't figure on runnin' into no holdup, ma'am!" he said. "I gotta wife and family. Better come out in the morning."

The girl's eyes flashed, and she put her hand on the door.

"Go back if you want to. I'll walk."

"My dear young lady!" Mr. Gill exclaimed again, his voice almost a caress now. "You shall do nothing of the sort! My car is at your service. Where do you wish to go?"

But here the chauffeur cut in sullenly, "Aw, I'll take a chance! Can't be more'n a couple of miles, anyhow. He'll have to jump some to stop this baby once she gets a-goin'!"

The girl sank back in the seat, and before Mr. Gill could voice a protest the powerful car leaped forward and roared down the slope. He stared after the diminishing tail light with a flush of mortification mantling his pallid face. Turning, he saw his son examining the pistol the man had dropped.

"Dangerous-looking weapon," he commented casually.

"Oh, I don't know," Victor responded, coolly.

"You would if it had gone off!"

"It isn't loaded."

"Not loaded!" Mr. Gill echoed blankly. When a crisis has passed it is always disappointing to learn that one hasn't been in danger, after all. "It might have been," he stated, defensively.

"Of course," Victor agreed, dispassionately.

They got into the car. Victor Gill started the engine. There was a curious intent expression in his remarkable eyes as he stared down the slope at the twinkling lights of Ocean Strand. His thin, slender fingers curled around the wheel.

"I wonder if she is going to Conniston's place," Mr. Gill mused.

"It looked that way."

"She certainly recognized him."

"Yes.... So did I."

"What!"

"He was the man we ran into at Conniston's."

Mr. Gill whistled. "How do you know? His face was covered."

"His ears weren't."

"What about his ears?"

"The smallest I ever saw."

"Those eyes of yours, my boy!" Mr. Gill exclaimed admiringly. "You see more than the Lord ever intended man to see!"

He leaned back on the cushions.

"That girl knew him, and she's on her way to Conniston's," he muttered. "Queer! I suppose we shall have to report to the police."

Victor nodded. "Soon enough in the morning. They won't catch him anyhow."

The car moved forward and, gaining momentum, swept down the slope towards the twinkling lights of Ocean Strand.

Mr. Gill, ever a "connoisseur of situations," let his nimble mind run back over the affair. Why was the girl going to the Casa de Ayer? What did she know of this young man who had stopped them? What had he been doing at Conniston's? Had the man and the girl anything to do with Conniston's refusal to sell the intaglios? There was something queer behind it all, and Mr. Gill wished he knew what it was.

However, a minute or so later Victor drew up before the nondescript hotel which was to shelter them for the night, and faced with the probability of an unaired bed and doubtful eggs for breakfast, Mr. Gill let the affair recede to the back of his mind.

CHAPTER II
The House of Yesterday

The original estate of Don Silvestre Calderón, gentleman of quality, patron of the arts, and former subject of the King of Spain, had comprised many thousands of acres of that picturesque peninsula of the southern California coast locally known as Point Almo. The site of Ocean Strand, the rocky shoreline from the village to the end of the point seven miles south of it, the western slope and much of the crest of the rise which forms the backbone of the peninsula had been well within it.

There were fiestas in those days and love and life and laughter. Too many and too much, perhaps, for the material prosperity of those children of the sun. Lean-faced cowboys, fantastic in spur and sash and sombrero, performed prodigious feats with the half-wild cattle which roamed the plains and mesa land on which the coast cities were presently to stand. Dark-eyed senoritas gave color and unfulfilled promise to the land. Courtly dons wondered a little and doubted a little and strove bravely to perpetuate their charming adaptation of an old-world feudalism already in decay.

This was before the coming of the conquering Americans, men with colder blood and hands of iron. Their advent heralded the collapse of the empire of the padres and the dons and the gradual breakup of the great estates.

As these unexploited areas fell into the hands of a more practical if less sensitive race there came a vast inpouring of eastern capital; development commenced on a huge scale. Bankrupt ranches became commercial successes; towns sprang up overnight; irrigation projects flourished; the prune and the peach, the fig and the walnut, the orange and the grape turned desert waste and mesa into orchard and vineyard. Later, came the more blatant subdivider and the oil driller; then the camera man, the booster, and the Middle West invasion.

Of the kingdom of the padres and the dons there remains but an echo as from a remote and distant past: a fragrance as of the evening jessamine in the early hours of morning. Presently, that too will be gone.

The Calderón estate had fared somewhat differently. Of the original grant there remained but fifty acres, and these were now in the possession of Colonel Conniston. The rest of the property had fallen into less sympathetic hands. But apart from that section of it upon which stood the village of Ocean Strand most of it had escaped exploitation of any sort. Held for speculation purposes, it was still in that state of virgin primitiveness in which Don Silvestre had found it a hundred years before.

A paved road which branched off the coast highway—El Camino Real—skirted the shore of the east side of the peninsula and ran out to the lighthouse at the extreme end of the point. Here an enterprising caterer by the name of Jim Beasley operated a fast roadhouse known as the Green Crocodile.

At the end of the point the pavement stopped. The road continued on around the west shore of the peninsula, past the Conniston grounds and on into Ocean Strand; but it was ungraded and in wretched condition and that steady stream of traffic whose destination was the Green Crocodile went along the east road. A sojourn at the notorious roadhouse made imperative a return by the same route. There had been a time when occasionally tipsy parties got on the west road. One such had gone over the cliff. The Green Crocodile had then enjoyed one of its periodical raids and the highway commission had closed the dirt road at that end.

Some five miles north of the Green Crocodile were the Conniston grounds; they lay between the road and the edge of the cliff. A drive branched off from the road and wound its way through a grove of cypress and eucalyptus trees to the edge of the cliff upon which, a hundred years before, Don Silvestre Calderón had built the Casa de Ayer, one of the most pretentious houses of the Spanish-Mexican era. It is not known why he called his home the House of Yesterday. Perhaps, with keener insight than that of most of his fellow-countrymen, he foresaw the inevitable dissolution of the empire of the padres and the dons and realized with an exquisite bitterness that his home could never be anything but a house of yesterday.

Shortly after the coming of the Americans the body of Don Silvestre was found in one of the deeper caves up the shore. It was not known whether he had *permitted* the tide to trap him or not, but the tragedy occurred the day after the greater part of his estate was taken away from him. Colonel Conniston had set a door over the narrow mouth of the cave and fitted into it a brass plate in memory of the man who had died there....

A minute or two after her encounter with Mr. Gill and the man who had concealed his face, the girl, Gail Hollister, found herself entering the historic grounds of the Casa de Ayer. She caught her breath and clasped her hands together as the beauty of the parkland cast its spell upon her. She had not thought it would be just like this.

There were eucalyptus trees, tall and melancholy, and stiff-boughed cypresses; date palms with fronds like bayonets and boles like pineapples; and feather peppers through which the moon etched delicate silver traceries on the cinder drive. It was like entering a fairyland in shadow. The sweet serenity of the scene soothed the hurt she had received.

Great trees enshrouded the house in shadow, but as the headlights of the car flared upon it she saw that it was of adobe, cream in color, and that the roof was of red tile. She got a glimpse of a lawn grown rank, of a red-tiled terrace, and of a balcony hung with wisteria, honeysuckle, and bougainvillea. The scent of evening jessamine met her like an incense. The place was perfect! If only Colonel Conniston were a part of it!

"Isn't it wonderful!" she whispered, as the car stopped in front of the door.

"Not so worse," the chauffeur admitted. He put her suitcase down on the steps. "That'll be seventy-five cents, ma'am.... Thank you."

The man fumbled with his cap.

"About that holdup. I s'pose them fellers in the limousine will report it! D'you want me to phone in; or will you?"

Gail whitened a little. For a moment the sensuous beauty of the garden had driven the fantastic encounter to the back of her mind. If only it might prove some horrible nightmare!

"I don't know," she faltered. "The two men ... it's really their affair. Colonel Conniston will know what to do."

The man nodded. "It's up to you then, ma'am."

The car moved on.

Gail found herself wielding a knocker which was fixed to the great copper-studded oak door before her. It was an ivory tusk weighted with metal and reverberations of sound poured out upon her. She hastily let it go and waited. A minute or so passed; and then the door opened some seven or eight inches and in this space there appeared the gray head and puckered face of a little brown gnome of a man with black button eyes and an air of suspicious inquiry about him.

"What is it?" he demanded in a thin, faraway voice.

Gail smiled. "I am Miss Hollister. Colonel Conniston expects me."

"To be sure! To be sure!" the little man exclaimed, and flung the door open. "Come right in! Come right in!"

He picked up her suitcase and Gail saw that the suspicion had died away in his eyes. Their expression was wistful and there was something that was remote in them, as if this strange little man lived largely in the past, occasionally in the present, and never in the future. He led her through a spacious hall finished in a darkish wood against which Gail caught the glint of light on old armor. They came to a door which he opened, in his thin voice announcing:

"Miss Hollister."

His eyes followed her inquiringly as she entered.

The room was distinctive. Time had mellowed it as it does some lovely thing come up from antiquity. Great dark beams spanned the murky ceiling. From one of them hung a bronze electric lamp which spilled colorful light upon the center of the floor and over the old and massive furniture. Dark and mysterious tomes lined two of the walls, reaching up to the ceiling. A steel vault was set into one of the walls. Oriental draperies concealed a window and a bright Oriental rug covered the floor. There was a library table of antique design and a fireplace with an elaborately carved mantel. A eucalyptus log blazed in the grate, faintly scenting the room with its pungent odor.

And with his back to the fireplace, legs apart, stood a little round oldish man with pink cheeks, an obstinate chin, and an abundancy of white mustache. His blue eyes were adventurous and twinkling, and they examined Gail from her smart shoes to her copper-red head with frank admiration.

He was altogether delightful, was Gail's swift conclusion.

"Red!" he chuckled.

Gail smiled. "Copper!" she corrected him firmly.

"To be sure!" the little man boomed. "A rarity, Miss Hollister. Treat it as such, my dear—and forgive me. I never could keep a still tongue in my head."

They shook hands. The colonel regarded Gail a trifle doubtfully.

"McEwan said he was sending me an authority on antiques. One who thoroughly understood catalog work, Miss Hollister. My stuff is in a frightful mess. Frightful! Never had any head for bookwork!"

"I am Dr. McEwan's assistant," Gail reminded him gently.

"Of course you are!" he agreed heartily. "So it follows that you must be competent. We shall work together delightfully, I am sure. But I rather expected—" The colonel paused.

"An antique," Gail suggested.

He chuckled. "Something of the sort. Sensible shoes—last year's hat—"

"And horn-rimmed glasses."

"To be sure! Instead he sends me youth and beauty—"

"And red hair!"

"A charming combination, Miss Hollister."

The colonel struck a little Chinese gong which stood on the mantel.

"You must be famished!" he exclaimed, rubbing his hands together. "I could do with a snack myself."

The little brown gnome of a man appeared.

"See what Mrs. Wessels has for us in the icebox, Dimity."

The old man bobbed his head and with a sharp glance at Gail hurried out.

"Another of my antiques," the colonel chuckled. "You mustn't mind him looking at you that way. He has a trick of watching folk with those button eyes of his. Watching and listening and coming upon one unexpectedly out of all sorts of corners! But you'll like Dimity for all of that. I've had him with me for thirty years. Been all over the world with me. He saved my life once and ever since he's had the notion in his queer old head that he was bound to look after me. Deuced embarrassing at times. He lost his wife years ago; he thought the world of her and it seems to have touched his brain a little. Well, many of us are none too sane when it comes to that."

Dimity returned, bearing a tray set for two. There were delicious ham and chicken sandwiches, a salad, fruit and cream and cake and tea. Colonel Conniston disclosed a hearty appetite and since Gail had dined indifferently that evening they cleared the tray between them.

"I'll have Mrs. Wessels take you to your room," he announced when they had finished.

"I'd love to see your collection first, if it's not too late," Gail said.

The colonel slapped his thigh. "Splendid! You shall."

He took a bunch of keys from his pocket and unlocked a stout oak door near the fireplace. Opening it he switched on lights and stood aside for Gail to enter.

She found herself in a long, narrow room with drawn shades. Glass cases extended down each side of it and along the middle. They were crammed with a multitude of antiques, curios, and relics from almost every age in the history of man and representative of nearly every race on the face of the earth. A superficial attempt at classification had been commenced, but apparently the colonel had given it up in despair.

Accustomed as Gail was to the method and order which prevailed at the Westcoast museum, in Los Angeles, her place of employment, this bewildering and not infrequently absurd disorder was an affront to her critical sense. The colonel enthused incessantly over his really comprehensive collection, but he had no illusions about his instincts for classification.

"An awful mess, isn't it?"

"Anarchy!" Gail cried with a shudder. "English pewter caressing that darling Ming vase! And those gold-mounted French dueling pistols rubbing shoulders with an Australian boomerang! And look at that little jade god!" she whispered, as they passed on to the next case.

Conniston lifted the cover and Gail deftly extracted from a disorder of small bronze temple gongs the little Chinese figure that had caught her eye. Barely three inches in height, the figure, nevertheless, was carved with an exquisite attention to detail. The toes and fingers were perfect. Gail was charmed with it.

"Isn't it lovely!" she cried.

Conniston stroked his abundant mustache.

"It is! There's a yarn goes with it, too. I must tell it to you some day. John O'Neil and I got it in Northern China years ago."

Gail's heart seemed to stop beating.

"Who did you say?" she whispered.

"John O'Neil, the explorer. I was with him in China. He died ten years ago. Poor John! He was one of the best! You couldn't have known him!"

"No," said Gail. "I didn't know him."

There was silence for a moment.

The colonel's face had saddened as he spoke of his dead friend. But now there came a flash of fire in his blue eyes as if the name had recalled some recent unpleasant experience. In a moment he was himself again and they passed on to the next case.

It contained the most comprehensive collection of idols that Gail had ever seen. There were gods of jade and ivory, of wood and ebony and stone; even a little silver god. And they were from India and China and the Islands; from Persia and Japan and the old Mexico of the Aztecs and the Mayas. Some of them were ugly, most of them were absurd; a few were lovely. Behind all of them ran a tale of fantasy and terror. Somehow, a little Chinese snuffbox, exquisitely done, had got into their midst.

"Snuff for the gods," chuckled Colonel Conniston.

"I want everything straightened out, numbered, and catalogued," he declared when, a little later, they had passed out of the room. "Dates, historic interest, value, fabric, and so forth."

"You have notes?" Gail asked, startled a little at the largeness of his desire.

"To be sure! Millions of them. But I can't make head or tail of most of 'em! Are you good at reading indifferent handwriting?"

"Yours?"

The colonel colored. "Er, yes. I am rather careless at times."

Gail smiled. "I'll do my best. I've been helping Dr. McEwan with a Maya tablet the Ellison Expedition brought up from Yucatan."

"Splendid!" the colonel exclaimed. "Mine isn't that bad." He glanced at his watch. "Bless my soul! It's eleven o'clock! How we old chaps talk! You'd better be off to bed!"

Gail hesitated for a moment; then she said: "You haven't shown me the intaglios, Colonel. I'd love to see them!"

Again there came a flash of fire in his twinkling eyes. Then he gave his genial chuckle.

"The emeralds, eh?" he cried. "They all want to see our emeralds. And so you shall, my girl! So you shall!"

He went to the vault, spun the dial, and set the indicator to the combination. Opening the door he entered the vault and reappeared with two shallow, covered trays which he impressively placed on the antique table.

Gail caught her breath as the dazzling beauty of the incised gems leaped up at her. They lay on beds of white satin arranged in the form of crescents, the larger stones towards the apex of each crescent. On the white satin they gleamed like green fires on fields of virgin snow. Two-thirds of the gems were heraldic in design, the rest were classic.

There was something hypnotic about their fiery beauty. Gail, ever imaginative, wondered if they might not so fascinate a beholder as to arouse in him an uncontrollable desire to possess them; if there might not be an affinity between their cold, green fires and some enslaved human heart. The thought was absurd, of course, and she put it out of her mind.

"Intaglio work," Conniston was saying, "is incised engraving—

the opposite of the cameo process, engraving in relief. The ancients practiced the art. It has been revived many times, but it is almost unknown now. The Italians did clever work—some of it is there.... I was offered three hundred thousand for them—as lately as to-night!" he suddenly declared in a dry voice.

His tone compelled Gail to look up at him.

"You did not take it?"

"I did not!"

So passionate was his utterance that Gail was amazed.

"I'm so glad!" she cried, in a moment. "They are too lovely to sell! You are going to keep them?"

The question was unfortunate in its effect upon the colonel.

"Sell them!" he rapped out in a sudden flare of fury. "Sell them! That young pup stood up and told me I'd have to—told me—" His extraordinary fury choked him; he grew incoherent; his pink cheeks crimsoned; then he raged on again. "Young fools! With their new ideas and their new morals and their contempt for age and authority! 'Don't give a damn for this' and 'Don't give a damn for that!' Telling me what I should do! In my own house! Impudence! Sell them—"

He broke off sharply and clapped his hand to his heart. His face went deathly white and he lurched forward.

"Colonel! You are ill!" Gail ran to his side and put her arm about him. She could feel his body trembling against her own. For a moment she held him; then he shook her off.

"All right! All right!" he whispered. "Nothing—only this fool heart of mine!" He gulped a glass of water which stood on the tray. His color slowly returned. "All right, now!"

"You are sure?" Gail cried distressfully. "Shall I ring for Dimity—"

"No, no!" he exclaimed vehemently. "I'm all right, I tell you!" His eyes fell on the intaglios; he straightened. "Sell them! Of course I'll sell them. But I'll make that young pup wait a while first." He took another gulp of the water. "What an old fool I am going off like that! Never could keep a still tongue! You'll forgive me, won't you, my dear?"

He returned the intaglios to the vault, locked it, and glanced at his watch again. "Eleven thirty! Time old dogs were in their beds!"

He picked up the little gong beater. But instead of striking the gong he put it down again and crossing unsteadily to the door which led into the hall jerked it open. Dimity tottered into the room, recovered himself, and stood blinking owlishly at them, apparently not greatly concerned at his discovery.

"Listening again, eh, Dimity!" the colonel railed. "What is it this time?"

"I thought you might be needing me, sir," the little man said in his thin voice. "I just came!"

Conniston seemed on the verge of losing his temper again; he laughed shortly, instead.

"Have Mrs. Wessels come here."

The little man hurried off, shaking his head. Gail stared after him in bewilderment; but the colonel made no further comment on the odd behavior of his old servant. Rightly indeed had this place been called the House of Yesterday! she reflected.

A minute or so later, as Gail followed the housekeeper up the great dark staircase she remembered that she had not mentioned her encounter on the highway to the colonel. And then, because she was always honest with herself, she admitted in the secrecy of her own mind that she never had intended to. A sense of foreboding took possession of her, tightened itself around her heart like threads of steel.

"Kerry!" she whispered to herself, "why did you do it?"

CHAPTER III
The Man in the Moonlight

Mrs. Wessels was an ample, rosy-cheeked woman of middle age. She was addicted to tight lacing and voluminous skirts and she was the widow of a pork butcher whose memory she deeply revered. Mrs. Wessels was English and looked it and Gail fell in love with her at once.

"These stairs do puff me!" she panted, as she joined Gail on the landing above. "Here's your room. The colonel 'ad me make it real nice for you. I do 'ope you'll like it, Miss 'Ollister."

She led Gail into a room finished in walnut. A bright rug covered the floor. There were roses on the dressing table and books on a writing desk. A bathroom adjoined, for much as the colonel appreciated the charming old-world atmosphere of the Casa de Ayer he did not despise the modern conveniences.

"It's dear of you to go to so much trouble!" Gail said gratefully. "The room is lovely!"

Mrs. Wessels smiled happily and flung open the French window. Through it Gail stepped onto a small balcony and beheld the gardens softly mysterious in moonlight and shadow below. Beyond them were the orchards, and to the west was the ocean with a silver scarf across its dark and troubled breast.

"It's like fairyland!" Gail whispered ecstatically.

"'Eaven," Mrs. Wessels said piously.

Gail ran her eyes along the coast to the end of the point and there she caught the twinkling gleam of a green light minute with distance. There was something cold and sinister about it as if it were the eye of some malevolent monster brooding over the tranquility of the night.

"What is that green light?" she asked.

The housekeeper stiffened. "That's the Green Crocodile, Miss 'Ollister!"

"A roadhouse?"

"Yes. And no better than it ought to be, neither. Fine goings on they have from all one 'ears! I 'ope you'll never see the inside of it!"

Gail smiled absently. Her eyes were troubled and her thoughts were elsewhere. For a moment longer they stood on the balcony; then they went inside.

"We 'ave breakfast at eight," the housekeeper said, as she closed the window. "Eight sharp, if you please. The colonel likes it prompt. What kind of a stummick 'ave you, Miss 'Ollister?"

Gail looked at her, startled.

"Why, I don't know, Mrs. Wessels. Just an everyday sort of a stomach, I suppose."

"What I mean is this," the housekeeper hurried on, "I 'ave three kinds of stummicks to set up for. Take the colonel, now. 'E's American. 'Ot cakes and waffles and syrup. Nice but indigestible. Then there's me. I'm English. Toast and marmalade and tea with cream in it, and roast beef and Yorkshire pudding for dinner. Good enough for Royal George, as poor Wessels used to say. And there's Dimity—'e likes 'ot stuff. Chili con carne! 'Ot tamale! And *peppers!* 'Orrible! You see 'ow it is, Miss 'Ollister."

Gail pondered gravely for a moment.

"Mine is just a plain sort of stomach, Mrs. Wessels. Cereal and fruit and toast and coffee for breakfast. But some day you shall bake me a Yorkshire pudding and smother it with gravy, and one of Dimity's hot tamales—perhaps."

"That I will!" Mrs. Wessels assured her, vastly relieved.

"Surely Dimity isn't a Mexican?" Gail inquired.

Mrs. Wessels pursed her lips.

"Not 'e! As American as you are! And a queer one at that! What with 'is peeping and watching and listening and 'is carrying around of 'is dead with 'im—"

"His—what!"

"In 'er corfin, Miss 'Ollister! Cross my 'eart, I do!"

"Mrs. Wessels!" Gail was aghast.

"It amounts to the same thing! His wife died years ago and 'e's been a bit off it ever since. Burned 'er body, 'e did, poor thing—"

"Cremated it, you mean!"

"That's it. And 'e's carried it around in a box ever since—"

"An urn?"

"An urn, to be sure. 'As it on 'is dressing table where 'e can see it. It isn't 'ealthy, Miss 'Ollister. And it isn't *right.* What's a body going to do on the last day? Now Wessels! I put 'im away decent—" Mrs. Wessels broke off sharply. "Here it's twelve o'clock and me keeping you up with my talk! And you *that* tired! I do 'ope you'll sleep well. Is there anything else I can get you?"

"Nothing, thank you, Mrs. Wessels."

"Good night, then, my dear!"

Mrs. Wessels took her departure.

Gail undressed slowly and got into bed. She was dead tired and her eyes ached for sleep; but she knew that she could not rest. The colonel's volcanic personality, his remarkable collection of antiques and intaglios, and Mrs. Wessels' stream of chatter had soothed her. But now that she was alone her memory of that unfortunate encounter on the road again leaped into the forefront of her mind. Sleep! She felt as if she could never sleep again.

A month before Kerry O'Neil had dropped like a meteor into the calm serenity of her life and, unmeteorlike, there he had stayed. He was engaged in a mining venture in Mexico and he had come north with an exceptionally fine collection of rock crystals which Dr. McEwan, the director of the Westcoast museum, had purchased for his institution. Kerry O'Neil had dark hair and tempestuous eyes that could kindle or chill with extraordinary swiftness, and a knack of blundering his way out of the near-catastrophes his impulsive nature was forever getting him into. There was romance and color and life and an amazing audacity in Kerry O'Neil. One sensed it as one senses heat in a flame. He had done everything, seen everything, been everywhere.

There was nothing definite between them. Gail had not even admitted to herself that there ever would be anything definite between them. But Kerry had a way of looking at her with those reckless eyes of his that thrilled her as she had never thrilled before. Her life had been cast in sheltered places; merely the grandeur of the past colored her work at the museum and constantly she had asked herself if there was in her that which could match the clean white flame that was Kerry O'Neil.

But as she tossed on the bed and stared into the darkness which pressed like leaden weights on her eyeballs she wondered if the flame were as clean and white as she had believed. That incredible scene on the highway: Kerry, with a handkerchief over his face and a pistol in his hand, and that suave, plump little man at his mercy! What madness had driven him to it?

A clock somewhere in the house struck two.... And then the half hour. Still sleep eluded her! Her nerves were on fire. The booming of the surf, magnified by the stillness of the night, rolled up to her charged, it seemed, with sullen threat.

Three o'clock.

The room was stifling. She felt as if she was suffocating.
Heat passed over her in waves. Then her body chilled and a
sense of dread, arising she knew not whence, took possession
of her. The atmosphere of the room, the very stillness of the
night, seemed alive, tingling with it. Her body was drenched
with sweat. Barely could she repress an impulse to scream.
Trembling, she fumbled for the switch and snapped on the
light.

The friendly glow comforted her. She slipped out of bed, got
into a robe and slippers, and looked at herself in the mirror of
the dressing table. Her cheeks were flushed, her eyes were
leaden. She opened the French window and passed out onto
the balcony.

A cool breeze freshened her. She shivered a little. The gardens
were almost entirely in shadow now, the moon having
descended far in the west. The front of the house, too, was
enshrouded in darkness and as she stared along the lean
facade her fevered imagination found it strangely altered.
Something cold and sinister lay upon it, like the shadow of a
malign hand. Within her breast stirred again that dread which
had come upon her in the bedroom.

Suddenly, her body grew tense and still. On the circular
driveway which surrounded the lawn near where it entered
the main drive there yet remained a pool of moonlight. Across
this pool of light had darted the figure of a tall, heavily built
man. In a flash he had vanished down the tree-bordered drive.

Gail shrank back against the adobe wall in the grip of a
dread she could not understand. It seemed to encompass her
as a swamp miasma rising up at her feet would have done. It
was on her lips, in her throat, choking her, pressing around
her pounding heart. Who could the man be? What was he
doing on the grounds? His movements had been highly
suspicious. Should she rouse the household?

Perhaps her overwrought imagination had deceived her.
Certainly she had seen the man, but might not he be connected
with the place and have the right to be down there even at
that hour in the morning? She did not know what to think,
what to do.

In perplexity Gail reentered the bedroom. Sleep was farther
away from her than ever. The room stifled her again and that
unaccountable dread tightened in her breast. Some inward
sense impelled her to action. She must do *something!* What?
Opening the door she peered up and down the landing, light
from the bedroom streaming past her. There was no sound:

merely that oppressive stillness which was like a knife blade on her raw nerves.

Gail went to the head of the stairs and peered down into the darkness below. She could see nothing, hear nothing. The house was like a tomb. She forced herself to descend the carpeted staircase. On the bottom step she stopped and listened. No sound! And then, to her horror, she saw a tall figure standing motionless in the hall. Her legs threatened to collapse beneath her. A scream rose to her lips; she suppressed it. By an immense effort of will she compelled herself to whisper:

"Who's there?"

No response. She waited, sick with terror. The figure did not move. And then she gave a little hysterical laugh of relief. It was one of the suits of armor she had noticed upon entering the house.

The clock struck four. Its strokes were like the strokes of doom.

Gail crept around the newel post and beheld a thin line of light against the floor towards the lower end of the hall. The library door was there, she remembered. What did the light mean? Was the colonel in the room? Or had he and Dimity retired, leaving the light on? Either theory was easily conceivable; but there was also the theory that someone who had no right there was responsible for the light. Had she the courage to find out?

Nerving herself for the ordeal Gail crept forward. She came to the door, opened it, and peered into the room.

The center of the library was flooded with light from the hanging lamp; the walls were in shadow. There seemed to be no one in the room. Yes, there was! A cry smothered in her throat. She took a step forward, stopped; her blood was like ice in her veins.

A man lay on the floor with his head and body in the shadows beyond the hearth and his feet in the light in front of it. His legs were bound with a curtain cord. Gail ran forward. A little scream broke from her lips. She dropped onto her knees beside the still figure on the floor.

It was Colonel Conniston, and he was dead.

CHAPTER IV
The Unknown Hand

Gail shrank away from the body with horror written in her face. She put her hands to her eyes to shut out the sight of it. Nearly a minute passed before she could bear to look at it, to touch it.

The body was cold. There were dark marks on the throat. The face had a swollen, purplish appearance. Pajamas and quilted silk dressing gown covered the body. A leather slipper was on the right foot; the other lay nearby. The eyes were fixed and staring, and they were a little amazed in their expression as if, in his last moments, Colonel Conniston had solved the riddle of life and death. The curtain cord which bound his legs was tightly knotted.

A passionate indignation swept over Gail. She had met Colonel Conniston for the first time only a few hours before, but notwithstanding his extraordinary outburst of temper she had sensed in him qualities which had endeared him to her. And now he was dead! Gail got up, white-lipped and trembling. She must rouse Dimity and Mrs. Wessels. And then? The police, of course! Her eyes ran round the room, rested upon the vault door. It was shut. Were the intaglios safe?

Just then she heard a tinkle of sound at the door which led into the hall. It stopped. Gail hesitated for an instant; then she sprang forward, caught the handle, and jerked the door open. To her astonishment Dimity tumbled headlong into the room.

"Dimity!" she cried. "Colonel Conniston"—she indicated the still figure on the floor—"he's dead! Somebody—has been here!"

The little man's precipitous entrance into the room had sent him to his knees. He crouched there, staring fixedly at his dead master. There was a queer, inarticulate agony in his puckered face. Terror crept into his eyes and he crawled forward until he could touch the still face, run his hands over the cold body. Gail could not bear to look upon his grief.

Then he stood up. His brown button eyes were hard with suspicion.

"You found him?" he whispered. "Like this?"

"Yes. Just now, Dimity. I couldn't sleep. I came down. What were you doing out there? Why didn't you come in?"

He stared at her piteously for a moment. The suspicion died away in his eyes.

"Listening ... watching," he whispered. "I thought I heard something and I came down." He seemed to address some inward accusing voice rather than the girl who was studying him so closely.

"Do you know—who did this?"

He gave her an odd, terrified look.

At that moment there came a step in the hall, the door opened, and Mrs. Wessels, huge and fantastic in hair curlers and muddy gray dressing gown, rolled in. She looked at the figure on the floor and screamed. Her body rocked to and fro and thinking she was going to fall Gail ran to her side and put her arm around her.

"He's dead, Miss 'Ollister!" the woman moaned.

Gail nodded. Her own eyes were blurred with tears. She led Mrs. Wessels out of the room, into the kitchen, and deposited her in a chair. Hurrying back to the library she found Dimity still staring at his master with terrified eyes.

"Is there a telephone?" she asked, sharply.

"We are too far out, Missie."

"Had the colonel a car?"

"Yes."

"You must drive in to Ocean Strand and get the police."

"Yes."

"At once, Dimity!"

Gail's peremptory tone had the desired effect. He bobbed his head, hurried across the room, and drew aside the Oriental draperies which concealed the French window. The window was bolted. He drew the bolt, opened the window, and vanished into the darkness.

Gail went to the window. It opened upon a small ornamental iron balcony. Across the balcony blew a stiff breeze from the ocean and Gail was reminded of the scantiness of her attire. She drew her gown more closely around her and as she did so she remembered that Dimity had been fully dressed. Did this mean that he had not yet retired for the night? It must! What was he doing up?

Just then a car whizzed past the window, swung sharply to the left. Evidently, Dimity knew how to drive.

Gail was about to close the window when she heard a rustle in the small shrubbery outside. Instantly she was on the alert.

"Who's there?" she cried apprehensively.

There was silence for a moment. And then a man rose up out

of the shadows below, set his lean brown hands upon the balcony rail, and grinned up at her. "Hello, Gail!"

"Kerry!" For a second or so Gail's heart seemed to stop. "What are you doing here?" she whispered.

"Nosing around," was the casual reply. "Anything wrong? You look kind of peaked."

She could not answer him.

"Are you alone?"

"Yes."

He vaulted the rail and stood before her, tall and lithe and brown. His crisp hair was uncovered and twinkling lights were in his dark eyes. There was something about him that suggested a finely tempered sword. His ears lay close to his well-shaped head. Their delicate smallness was distinctive. He sobered when he saw the terror in Gail's eyes.

"What's wrong?"

He pushed past her into the room.

"Good God!" she heard him cry.

He dropped onto his knees and ran his hands over the body. Gail compelled herself to watch him. The swift movements of his hands fascinated her. Then they grew still and he stared down at the set face beneath him. Gail edged nearer. His mouth was white and hard; his hands were clenched. Suddenly, he whipped out a knife and slashed at the cord that bound the legs of the dead man.

"Kerry! You shouldn't have done that!"

He looked up at her. "Why not?"

"Dimity has gone for the police. They'll want everything left as it was when I found him. I haven't touched a thing."

Kerry stood up. "I am always doing the darn-fool thing. I didn't think. It hurt me to see him lying there—like that! Poor old chap! What happened? Who did it?"

Gail shuddered. "I don't know. He must have heard someone and come down."

Kerry nodded. "And tackled the man, I suppose—just like him to do it—and his heart stopped. I wonder who it was! I'll bet a dollar he was after the intaglios!" Kerry wheeled excitedly towards the vault.

"Kerry!"

"What's wrong?"

"Don't touch that vault!"

"You talk like Sherlock Holmes!" he grinned. "Fingerprints, eh? I ought to have known *that!*"

Gail quietly closed the hall door.

"Why did you do that?" His voice had sharpened.

"The housekeeper is in the kitchen."

"What about her, Gail?"

She looked at him steadily. "What are you doing here, Kerry?"

"I heard someone scream."

"Mrs. Wessels, I suppose. What were you doing on the grounds?"

He grinned sheepishly. "I followed you."

"You followed me!" Incredulously.

"Yes. I wondered what you wanted with old Conniston—you didn't tell me you were coming down here. I figured on seeing him myself again this morning, too. There's a summer house along the cliff, the night was dry, and I thought I might as well bunk out there—since the colonel hadn't offered me a bed," Kerry glanced sadly at the still figure. "Poor old chap! I believe he meant to, but we were raging at each other and I left in a hurry."

Gail sighed. It was these irrationalities of his that drew him to her.

"Will you be serious, Kerry?" she cried distressfully. "You are all mixed up in this affair, yet you don't seem to realize your position. You've simply got to explain things: your presence here; that dreadful holdup on the road. I can't understand you!"

The distress in her voice touched him. He caught her hands in his and drew her near to him.

"I've got a bushel of things to explain, Gail," he said earnestly. "You must think me every kind of a fool. A crook, maybe; everything that's rotten. I certainly made an ass of myself last night—in more ways than one. But I can't tell you about it now. I heard someone in the grounds a while ago. Didn't think much of it, then—none of my business—but I'd better take a look around."

Gail nodded slowly. "Perhaps you had, Kerry. You'll be careful, won't you?"

He pressed her hands and vanished through the window.

Gail stood thinking. She was capable of an immense faith in those who were dear to her and she recklessly placed all of it in Kerry O'Neil, whose antecedents were as vaguely spectacular as a comet's tail. She was sure that he would explain everything to her: the holdup, his interview with Colonel Conniston, their quarrel, and his connection with the famous intaglios. But would the police believe him? Kerry had a way of making the fantastic sound reasonable, but to expect

him to account for his quarrel with Conniston, the holdup
(should he by any chance be identified as its perpetrator), and
his presence in the grounds at the time of the murder, without
rousing the suspicions of the police, was to expect the
impossible.

Indeed, if the two men Kerry had held up should recognize
him the case against him would be regarded as complete. That
would mean a charge of murder. Gail could not see it any other
way and she went sick with horror at the thought. There was
but one thing to do: Kerry's presence in the grounds and his
return to the library must be concealed at all costs!

Having come to this decision Gail passed into the hall,
intending to go upstairs and dress; but the light in Mrs.
Wessels' kitchen suggested the housekeeper to her as a fertile
source of information and she went there instead. Mrs. Wessels,
still white-faced and shaky, was sitting at the table with an
innocent-looking glass in her hand. She set it down with a
bang.

"Only a drop o' peppermint, Miss 'Ollister," she explained. "It
always settles me up. Will you 'ave some?"

Gail shook her head. For the moment she was at a loss for
words.

"Poor Colonel Conniston!" Mrs. Wessels went on, sorrowfully.
"'E was *that* good to me! A bit sharp of his tongue, mebbe, but
a gallant gentleman for all that! 'Oo do you think did it?"

Gail ignored the question. "Had the colonel any visitors last
night?"

"'E had that! Three of 'em. A young, dark, tallish chap come
first. Dimity let 'im in. And a nice way 'e talked to the colonel,
too!"

Gail's heart gave a leap. "What do you mean, Mrs. Wessels?"

"Well, I was a-coming downstairs and I heard them 'aving
'igh words. The colonel told the young chap to get out; and the
young chap up and told 'im 'e'd see 'im in the 'ot place first."

Gail shuddered. "Who were the other two?"

"Parties by the name of Gill, Miss 'Ollister. Just as I got to
the bottom of the stairs there came a rapping at the front
door. I went myself and just as I got the door open if this
young chap didn't come running out of the library and shove
past me, 'is face as red as a beet, and rush off down the drive!
I showed the other two in to the colonel. And nice gentlemen
they was, too—though one of 'em looked as if 'e never 'ad much
to say for 'imself."

Gail pondered these revelations pessimistically. Suddenly, a thought struck her.

"Is there anybody else attached to the house but you and Dimity?"

"No, Miss 'Ollister. We manage nicely, Dimity and me. 'E's real 'andy for all of 'is queer ways."

"Is there anybody living or camping on the grounds?"

"No, indeed!"

This was relieving to Gail. It meant that the man she had seen slinking across the pool of moonlight had no business to be there. And since it was not Kerry whom she had seen—he was heavier in build than O'Neil—it was extremely probable that it was the man who had killed Colonel Conniston and whom Kerry had heard in the grounds.

While Gail was dressing in her room she continued to ponder upon what Mrs. Wessels had told her. Who were these two men, the Gills, whom the housekeeper, had admitted into the colonel's library? Gail furrowed her brow and paused, chamois in hand. Colonel Conniston had said he had been offered three hundred thousand for the intaglios that very night! The Gills? Of course! Now she remembered. Conrad Gill was the well-known Los Angeles diamond broker. And who were the two men Kerry had stopped on the road? The Gills, of course! Kerry, then, had been after the intaglios!

Gail glanced at her wristwatch. A quarter of five! Dimity should be back with the police any minute. Suddenly, her heart grew cold with fresh terror. The reflection had presented a new angle of the situation. Kerry was searching the grounds. He would never think of the danger he was in. He almost certainly would run into their arms! Why hadn't she thought of this before? She must find him! Warn him! Had she time?

Flying downstairs, she rushed into the library. Apparently, everything was as she had left it. As she passed through the window onto the ornamental balcony she saw the flush of dawn on the crest of the ridge. Trees and shrubbery were taking on definite forms and outlines. Presently, it would be light. In the meantime she must find Kerry. But the grounds were extensive and thickly wooded and she hadn't the slightest idea where or how to begin.

"What shall I do?" she whispered.

She thought of calling to him. No! that would be courting disaster. Panic began to unnerve her and she stared wildly into the dimness ahead. She was on the point of climbing over the rail when her problem was suddenly solved by the appearance of Kerry from behind a hydrangea bush.

"Hello, Gail!" he greeted her. "Nothing doing. Couldn't find a thing."

She motioned to him to be silent.

"What's wrong, honey? Still sleuthing?"

Before she could stop him he had vaulted the rail and was standing before her.

"Kerry! Be serious—please!" she pleaded. "The police are here—will be any minute! They mustn't suspect that you came back! You've *got* to get away!"

He looked at her incredulously. "To hear you talk anyone would think I killed old Conniston!"

"The police will say you did—unless you get away—now! Don't you understand the position you are in?"

He caught her hand in fingers of steel. "Good God! *You* don't think *I* did it?"

"Don't be absurd! Just think for a moment! You quarreled with Colonel Conniston?"

"Yes."

"Mrs. Wessels overheard you. Perhaps Dimity did, too—"

"He did. If you mean that little old manservant. He was listening outside the library door when I rushed out. I tumbled over him. Queer chap!"

"Very well. Think of the rest of it. You have spent the night in the grounds—uninvited—and you stopped the Gills with a pistol on a public highway."

"It wasn't loaded."

"You must have been mad."

"I was. I am. There's madness in my blood. My father lost his life in Tibet. My grandfather died under Garibaldi. Uncle Dick perished on Everest. A Kerry O'Neil fought the Spaniards under Drake. Mad blood, Gail! Go on."

"Hero blood, Kerry. Why did you stop the Gills?"

"I thought they had the intaglios. Half of 'em happen to be mine."

"Yours!"

"It's a long story."

"Will the police believe it?"

Kerry meditated. "Probably not," he admitted, seriously. "I guess you are right. You are—always. I'm an ass and I'm in a devil of a mess! It all depends on whether the Gills recognize me or not."

"They are not going to recognize you, Kerry!"

"How do you know?"

"You are going away—now! You are going straight back to

Los Angeles! When the police look you up you will admit your interview with Colonel Conniston and nothing else. *Nothing else!* Not a word about the holdup or your coming back here!"

Kerry grinned down at her. "You talk like a slick lawyer, Gail! But I guess I'll stay and face it out—"

She caught him furiously by the arm. "You shall not! You are going—now!"

"And leave you to face it—alone! I guess not!" His dark eyes sparkled.

Gail was desperate. She seized the lapels of his coat and tugged at them in a frenzy. "Kerry, you must! I ask you—for my sake—I can't bear the thought—of them taking you!"

He caught her hands almost savagely. "Golly! Does it matter—that much? Do you really care whether they take me or not?"

She tried to draw away from him, but he held her hands fast. The poignant look in her eyes must have given him his answer. Just then they heard the roar of a car in the drive. Gail pushed him towards the rail.

"Kerry!" she sobbed. "They are here! Oh, do go!"

"No—"

"You can't help me by staying—they'll arrest you!" Her voice rose hysterically. "If you don't—you'll make it all the worse—for me! They'll say—dreadful things!"

There came an authoritative hammering on the front door. Mrs. Wessels' slippered feet clap-clapped up the hall. Gail's face was piteous in its distress.

"If you put it that way," he cried in an agony of indecision.

"I do, Kerry! I do!"

He made up his mind suddenly. "All right! But I'll stick around here—I won't go up north. Don't worry! They'll not catch me unless I want 'em to!"

Gail had to be content with this. "If it is safe I'll come down to the beach tonight—"

"Better not!"

"I shall! Go, Kerry!"

He slipped over the rail and vanished. Voices sounded in the hall. Heavy feet hurried towards the library. Gail drew back into the room. The half of the window which was closed rattled in the breeze and Gail was moved to shut and bolt the window lest Kerry in a fit of reckless obstinacy should take it into his head to return. She drew the curtains to, steadied them, dropped into a chair, and composed herself.

The door opened and three men entered the room.

CHAPTER V
Bolted Door

Gail never had encountered the police in their official capacity before and her heart was thumping mightily as she rose to her feet. Nevertheless, she met the three men with a coolness that astonished herself. One of them, a thin dark bearded man with a satchel, dropped onto his knees beside the body and began to examine it with the swift competence of the physician. The other two had an air of grim authority about them which Gail had not expected to encounter in Ocean Strand.

The senior of the two was a thickly set man with a square chin and hard and cold humorless eyes that constantly endeavored to estimate the potentialities of everything and everyone they rested, upon. Even as at this moment they were endeavoring to estimate the potentialities of Gail Hollister and to determine her relation to the sequence of events which had terminated in the death of the man on the floor. The other was somewhat nondescript in type. He had a long, narrow face and sullen eyes; and while his bearing was official and authoritative it seemed less instinctive than reflected.

There was no sign of Dimity. Mrs. Wessels hovered uncertainly in the background.

The senior officer stared at the body for a moment; then he addressed Gail curtly.

"I am Bartlett of the sheriff's office. We got a long-distance call to the effect that a Colonel Conniston had been killed at the Casa de Ayer. Did you call us?"

"Why, no!" Gail exclaimed in surprise. "Aren't you from the village?"

"The village? Certainly not! We are from the sheriff's office at St. James. Who called us?"

"I don't know," Gail said, in bewilderment. "Dimity—Colonel Conniston's servant—drove into the village. Perhaps the officer there phoned you."

"No, he didn't." Bartlett indicated the body. "Who found him?"

Gail shuddered. "I did."

"What time?"

"About four."

"How long after that was it before your man left for the village?"

Gail thought. "About fifteen minutes."

Bartlett pondered this. "Four-fifteen," he muttered. "What time did we get that call, Decker?" addressing the other deputy.

"Four-five—exactly," the man returned with impressive promptness.

Gail looked at her wristwatch. "It's four-fifty-five now," she said suggestively.

"Four-fifty-six," Bartlett corrected her. His cold blue eyes scanned her narrowly. "Are you Conniston's daughter?"

"No. I was sent down by the Westcoast Museum at Los Angeles to help Colonel Conniston catalogue his antiques. I only got here late last night."

"Antiques, eh! Your name?"

Gail told him.

The doctor looked up just then, having finished his examination of the body.

"He has been dead about four hours, I should think," the doctor stated. "He had a valvular lesion of the heart. There are finger marks on his throat. He must have been in violent struggle with someone—it finished him."

Bartlett nodded and turned to Gail again. "Tell me everything you know about it."

Gail faced him coolly. "I don't know anything about it," she said steadily. "I came down from my room about four o'clock and found him lying there."

Bartlett was silent for a moment, but he did not remove his eyes from Gail. She grew uneasy beneath their steady scrutiny.

"Why did you come down from your room?"

"I couldn't sleep. I had a feeling there was something wrong and I got up. I just had to get up. It was this sense of something being wrong that brought me down." Bartlett looked unconvinced and Gail added hurriedly, "And I saw a man in the garden."

"A man!" Bartlett appreciated the definite. "When? Where?"

Gail described the relation of the balcony to her rooms and the gardens below and explained how she had seen the figure of a man flit across the pool of moonlight.

"Can you describe him?"

"He was tall and fairly heavily built. I might recognize him if I saw him again."

"Hm! You might! Why couldn't you sleep?"

Gail felt her color rising. "What are you driving at, Mr. Bartlett?"

The cold eyes flickered a little. "The truth. Did you leave

everything as you found it?"

"I did!"

Just then a car whirred up the drive and stopped in front of the house. Someone pounded on the front door and Mrs. Wessels bustled out to answer the summons. A moment later a stoutish, red-faced man in a semi-official khaki uniform entered the room, followed by Dimity. The officer's optimistic countenance fell at sight of the deputy and his man, Decker.

"Hello, Bartlett!" he grumbled. "Beat me to it, eh? I was out rounding up a couple of drunks in Dillon's pool hall. Bad business, this! Great old scout, the colonel! Get onto anything?"

"Peters," Bartlett acknowledged briefly.

He shrugged grimly and into his hard, cold eyes there came an expression as near to humor as Gail was ever to see in them. Then he stated the situation as he understood it and repeated the little that Gail had told him. Incidentally, he made it clear that the case was a county affair, that it was in his hands, and that Deputy Sheriff Bartlett was unaccustomed to interference of any sort.

Bartlett knelt by Conniston's body and examined the finger marks in the fleshy neck. Then he looked at the hands, felt in the pockets of the dressing gown, and contemplated the severed curtain cord which had bound the legs. He did not speak. A minute passed. The atmosphere of the room grew taut, like a violin string. Gail felt as if it were tightening around her throat, cutting into the flesh, strangling her. Mrs. Wessels rolled her vast head uncertainly. Terrified bewilderment haunted Dimity's brown button eyes.

Suddenly, the deputy looked up at Gail.

"Was this cord around his legs when you found him?"

"Yes," Gail admitted, unthinkingly.

"Why did you cut it?"

The question came like a shot. Gail trembled, but she held her head up. No sooner had she made the admission than she realized the consequences of Kerry's thoughtless act. Bartlett had assumed that *she* had cut the cord! She dare not contradict herself. She must maintain the assumption.

"You knew he was dead," Bartlett went on, sternly.

"Why didn't you leave him alone?"

Gail dropped her eyes. "I am sorry. He looked so pitiful lying there ... like that. Does it matter?"

Bartlett grunted and stood up as if it were of no great consequence. But Gail had the uneasy feeling that she hadn't heard the last of it.

The deputy crossed to the vault. It was immersed in shadow. An electric globe hung in front of it and he turned it on, flooding the door with light. He inspected the handle and the door closely for a minute or so; then he tried the handle. The door was locked.

Moving to the window, he drew back the Oriental draperies which concealed it, and the early morning sunlight poured into the somber room. The glass and the bolt held his thoughtful attention for several minutes; he then drew back the bolt, opened the window, and stepped onto the balcony. His eyes dropped to the rail, to the earth below. There were no footprints. Decker followed him onto the balcony and Bartlett spoke to him in low, curt tones. They reentered the library, but Decker continued on into the hall and disappeared.

Bartlett now turned his attention to the library table. It was long and narrow, of oak, and dark with age, and its massive legs were exquisitely carved. Gail had placed it as seventeenth century French. Upon the table lay a small Venetian hand mirror, a lens such as jewelers and antiquaries use, a bronze inkstand by Cellini, writing materials, and a writing pad with bronze corners.

Behind the table stood a swivel chair upholstered in leather. Two other chairs were drawn up in front of the table. Behind, and a little to the right of these two chairs, was the door of the vault. Later on, the setting of the room as it was at that time was to become vivid in the memory of everyone there.

Bartlett dropped into the chair behind the table and pointed to one of the other two.

"Sit there, Miss Hollister."

Gail resented his tone; she obeyed, nevertheless. The sunlight streamed full upon her copper-red head. Her heart was thumping furiously, but she eyed the deputy coolly.

He lit a cigar.

"Have you any idea who killed Conniston?"

"Certainly not."

"Care to take a guess at the motive?"

Gail stiffened. "Why do you question me?" she demanded. "I met Colonel Conniston for the first time last night. I don't know any more about his affairs than you do."

"Answer the question."

Gail's dark eyes flashed. "I don't know of any reason why anyone should kill Colonel Conniston. I thought him a delightful old gentleman."

Bartlett drew on his cigar thoughtfully. "If you were a crook," he went on, "would you call this a likely looking crib?"

"I might," Gail admitted.

"Why?"

"Well, there's the Conniston intaglios."

"What are they?"

Gail explained.

"Conniston showed them to you, eh? Did he tell you what they are worth?"

"Colonel Conniston said he was offered three hundred thousand dollars for them last night."

Bartlett whipped out his cigar. "Who by?"

"Conrad Gill, the Los Angeles broker, I believe."

"Old Gill, eh? Well, he's the boy with the money. You saw Conniston return the stones to the vault?"

"I did."

"And lock it?"

"Yes."

Bartlett grunted. "My bet is they are not there now. Do you know if anyone else called on Conniston last night?"

Gail's hands clenched beneath the table. This was the question she had dreaded more than any other. She wondered if the color were receding in her cheeks, if those cold eyes read her distress.

"I believe Mrs. Wessels said there was someone else. A young man, wasn't it?" she calmly inquired of the housekeeper.

"A young man, Miss 'Ollister, and a queer one at that, as I told you!"

"Queer—what do you mean?" Bartlett rapped out.

Finding herself the center of interest Mrs. Wessels instantly became conscious of her nightdress, her dressing gown, and her hair curlers, and threatened to become inarticulate. Bartlett was relentless, however.

"Come, come!" he said curtly. "What about this young man?"

Mrs. Wessels drew her robes around her and after one or two false starts repeated substantially what she had said to Gail.

"Ever see this man O'Neil before?"

"No, sir, I 'aven't."

"Have you?" addressing Dimity.

The little man's brown button eyes widened fearfully. He stared at Bartlett as if he did not understand the question. There was tragedy in his puckered face and the conviction that he knew something of the death of his master entered Gail's mind.

"No," he said in his thin voice, "I never saw him before."

Bartlett looked at him narrowly. "Sure?"

Dimity seemed surprised at the question.

"Yes, I'm sure," he said, gently.

Bartlett meditated. "Had Conniston any relations?"

"There's Mr. Norman Stark, his nephew, sir," Dimity went on, vaguely. "He lives in Los Angeles. He's the only one as I know of."

"Me, too," Mrs. Wessels echoed.

"How long have you been with Colonel Conniston, Dimity?"

"How long?" The little gnome-like face grew more puckered than ever. "I can't remember things the way I used to. It must be a matter of thirty, mebbe forty years. I ain't sure. Things are dim—misty. I was all over the world with the colonel: India, China, Tibet, the South Seas—I can't remember them all." His voice seemed to die away into nothing; his brown eyes were humid with tears. "I loved the colonel like a brother!" he whispered.

There was silence for a moment.

"Any idea who killed him?" Bartlett pursued.

"Would I be holding it back if I had?" the little man cried. Then, with astonishing vigor: "If ever I get my hands on him!" His bony fingers curled expressively until they were like talons and a look of ferocity twisted his little nub of a face.

Bartlett seemed satisfied, but again Gail had that impression of depth in Dimity.

Just then Decker reentered the library. Gail had taken an instinctive dislike to the man and his reappearance troubled her vaguely. He bent confidentially over Bartlett's shoulder and spoke to him at length in tones so low that Gail could not catch a word of what he said. Bartlett started suddenly, whipped the cigar out of his mouth, vehemently replaced it. Then he pushed Decker aside and looked at Dimity again.

"When you left the house an hour ago which way did you go out?"

"That way," Dimity said gently, and he pointed to the French window through which streamed the morning sunlight.

"Was it bolted?"

"Yes, sir."

"Are you sure?"

"Oh, yes. The colonel was always very particular about having all the doors and windows locked and bolted, 'count of his antiques. All the outside doors have bolts as well as locks on 'em."

"And so far as you know all the other outside doors and windows were bolted on the inside at that time."

"Yes, sir."

"Including the front door?"

"Yes."

Bartlett's eyes darted to Gail again.

"Have you any idea how the man who killed Conniston got in and got out?"

"No," said Gail.

"You haven't thought about it, eh?"

Bartlett leaned over the desk towards her. There was something in his expression that terrified the girl.

"Did you bolt that window before Dimity unbolted it?"

Gail's heart grew cold, but she answered steadily,

"Certainly not! Why should I?"

"You saw Dimity unbolt it?"

"Yes."

"You bolted it after he left?"

"Yes."

"Why?"

Gail began to tremble. "The window—rattled." Thank heaven it had!

"Rattled, eh!" The inflection was sardonic. "Very well. Now this is important. You have heard Dimity's statement to the effect that all the doors and windows were fastened last night and that each outside door is fitted with a bolt as well as with a lock. This statement is correct. Decker has been through the house and examined every door and window in it, including those in the cellar. All are bolted with the exception of that one there which I unbolted myself a few minutes ago. If Conniston's murderer got in and then got out of the house how do you account for every window and door in it being bolted on the inside at the time and since you found the body?"

Gail did not grasp what lay behind the question. Her mind merely seized upon the absurdity of the statement that *every* means of exit from the house was bolted on the inside when someone had certainly passed through one of them.

"There must be a door or window open or broken in somewhere," she said, positively. "A man can't pass through a bolted door or window without first unbolting it. Mr. Decker must be mistaken."

"Not on your life," Decker said, doggedly. "I've been all over the house. You know me, chief!"

Bartlett said nothing. He merely lit another cigar and waited, his eyes still on Gail. Decker began to grin: a queer, lip-curling grin with a malevolent significance hidden behind it. The room was tense and still. And then, in a flash, Gail perceived that they were waiting for her to speak. What had she to tell them? The answer came with a terrible swiftness and she grew numb with horror. They suspected those who were in the house. Dimity, Mrs. Wessels, herself—especially herself! Panic threatened her; she fought it down. How *had* that man got out? He couldn't have passed through a bolted door. That was absurd—insane. They were waiting for her to speak. She must say something.

"Perhaps he got out—after Mrs. Wessels let you in. He may— he *must* have been in hiding—somewhere—"

"Mrs. Wessels rebolted the front door after admitting us and again after admitting Peters and Dimity," Bartlett stated, dispassionately. "It is bolted now."

"Force of 'abit," Mrs. Wessels whispered. "The colonel would 'ave it bolted."

"It won't do, Miss Hollister," Bartlett drawled.

There was silence for a moment.

"What do you mean?"

The deputy leaned nearer. "Conniston may have been killed by someone in the house, but I figure that the man who did the killing was let in and then let out—"

"By someone in the house?"

"Exactly."

Gail was white to the lips. "You think—I let him in?"

"I mean just what I said—no more—yet."

Gail felt as if she would faint; desperately she fought for clear-headedness. "I am under suspicion, then—more so than the others!" Her mind grasped the single weakness in Bartlett's theory. "You have forgotten one thing. If I—or anyone else let this man in would I have bolted the door or window after he had gone?"

Bartlett's eyes flickered a little. "The crook always slips up somewhere. I never knew it to fail. Don't miss the main point: A man cannot pass through a bolted door or window without first unbolting it. We have got to be logical in my business."

He suddenly got up, picked up the severed curtain cord which had bound Conniston's legs, and thrust it into Gail's face.

"Did you cut this?"

Gail stared at the cord in terror. This meant a lie!

How many more would she have to utter before she and Kerry were safely out of this dreadful morass! The strength was ebbing from her body. She could not hold out much longer. She was in a net and Bartlett was dragging her in.

"Yes—I cut it."

"What with?"

What had Kerry used? His knife, of course.

"A knife."

"Where is it?"

She was trapped. "I don't know! I don't know!"

"You must know."

The last thread of her self-control snapped. "I don't know, I tell you! I don't know!" she sobbed hysterically. "It's around— somewhere! I don't know anything about it—can't you leave me alone!" She buried her face in her hands.

There was silence in the room again. Decker laughed; an unpleasant, nasal sound. And then Mrs. Wessels shuffled forward with the light of battle in her eyes and protectingly encircled Gail's slim shoulders with one of her mighty arms.

"Yes, dearie, 'e's going to leave you alone, 'e is! That for you, Mr. Detective!" And Mrs. Wessels snapped her fingers beneath Bartlett's blunt nose. "Treating a poor girl this way! And 'er that 'adn't a thing to do with it! And throwing mud on them as 'ave served the colonel as long as Dimity and me! A fine detective you are! Shame on you! Come on, dearie!"

Mrs. Wessels drew Gail to her feet and with a fiery glance at the unruffled deputy who uttered not a word of protest led her out of the library and into the white-enameled sanctuary of her kitchen. She placed her tenderly in a very dilapidated and very comfortable rocking chair and put her feet on a footstool.

"There you are! A cup of 'ot tea and a bit of toast and you'll be as right as ninepence! The idear of that man saying the things 'e did! Just give me a minute to get dressed."

Mrs. Wessels rolled out of the kitchen. She returned shortly clad in a cotton dress, a clean apron, and minus her curling pins, and began to bustle around the kitchen in a flurry of accomplishment. Just as the kettle began to boil, Dimity crept in and quietly sat down at the table.

"After 'is stummick, as usual!" Mrs. Wessels commented bitterly. "'E'll 'ave to eat like a Christian this morning, 'e will!"

Dimity had nothing to say for himself. Gail had recovered her composure if not her peace of mind and she began to study the little man covertly. He seemed to be laboring under a burden of fear and grief and bewilderment. Dimity knew something, she was sure. How was she going to get it out of him? Perhaps he would come to her of his own accord.

"What sort of a man is Mr. Stark, the colonel's nephew?" Gail asked Mrs. Wessels, as the latter put the buttered toast on the table.

Mrs. Wessels started, nearly upsetting a pitcher of cream.

"Oh, 'im!" she said, with obvious reluctance. "'E's all right for them as likes 'em that way!"

Gail smiled and pressed for more definite information.

Mrs. Wessels shot a doubtful look at Dimity, who had not opened his mouth since coming into the kitchen. "'E's one of them as knows wot 'e wants," she proceeded diffidently, "and doesn't care 'ow he gets it—so they say!"

"So who says?"

"People, Miss 'Ollister," Mrs. Wessels said vaguely. So vaguely indeed that Gail got the impression that she was keeping something back. And then, more volubly: "Stuck-up and not so much as a good morning to you, that's 'im! 'E 'asn't been here for a goodish bit, the colonel and 'im 'aving 'ad words the last time he was out."

"Words—what about?" Gail asked quickly.

"'Eaven knows! Mr. Norman's one of them as 'ud quarrel with their false teeth."

"That is true," Dimity agreed unexpectedly, in his thin and distant voice.

They had breakfast, then, at the kitchen table. Dimity added nothing to his single comment, and Mrs. Wessels fell into a silence as profound as it was uncharacteristic. When the meal was over Gail escaped to her room.

CHAPTER VI
Cathedral Rock

Gail went to her room to think—to answer, if she could, the swarm of questions that buzzed in her mind like bees in a hive.

Who was the man she had seen in the moonlight? Assuming that it was Conniston's murderer how had he got in and out of this sinister house of bolted windows and doors? Had Dimity or Mrs. Wessels let him in? No! Dimity's knowledge of the affair was innocent, whatever else it might be, and Mrs. Wessels was out of the question. Had the safe been opened? Were the intaglios gone? Who had telephoned the sheriff's office at the county seat? And, above all, Kerry O'Neil—was he safe?

But when, some two hours later, there came a knock on the door Gail was no nearer enlightenment on these matters than when she had come up. With visions of Bartlett waiting outside she went to the door and opened it. Merely Mrs. Wessels stood there, however.

"'E's come!" the housekeeper whispered.

"Who?" Gail inquired with a smile.

"'Is 'Ighness!"

"Mr. Stark?"

Mrs. Wessels nodded. "And he wants to see you. Mebbe you'd better come down."

Gail shivered. Had she to go through that dreadful ordeal again?

"All right. Tell them I'm coming."

Mrs. Wessels hesitated. "Keep your eye on 'Is 'Ighness, Miss 'Ollister! 'E's a tricky one, 'e is!" And having delivered herself thus, Mrs. Wessels rolled on.

Gail entered the library shortly afterwards. She saw that the body had been removed to a couch which stood against the wall near the door. Bartlett was sitting in the chair behind the antique table talking to a tall, solidly built man who stood by the window. He stopped abruptly when he saw Gail. There was no one else in the room.

Norman Stark came towards Gail with his hand out and a mirthless smile on his lips. His eyes were gray green in color and arrogant in expression, but they gave a little leap of interest as Gail entered the sunlight which streamed through the window. He was rather handsome in a dark, heavy, sensual way.

"I am sure you are shocked at this terrible affair, Miss Hollister," he said, in his husky voice after he had introduced himself.

Gail nodded sadly. "I met Colonel Conniston for the first time last night, Mr. Stark. I thought him delightful. You are bound to miss him."

"Yes," said Norman Stark. "I am." But there was no feeling in his voice; his expression did not change. "Bartlett here tells me you came down to straighten out my uncle's antiques. Lord knows they need it!" He looked at her curiously. "I suppose you are—"

"Competent?" Gail suggested, a trifle acidly. She had suddenly decided that she didn't like Stark.

"Well, yes," Stark admitted.

"Colonel Conniston seemed to think so. But you may telephone Dr. McEwan if you wish. Or I will go back. I would much rather."

"No, you won't, my girl!" Bartlett cut in grimly. "You'll stop right here until I say you can go!"

Gail flushed. She had expected something like this. However, she respected the deputy's honesty of purpose, much as she feared and disliked him.

Stark she distrusted. There was something false and untrue about him, she told herself. He had neither pity nor affection for the dead man; merely a cold-blooded self-interest inspired him. She was struck by something vaguely familiar in the heavy set of his shoulders, in his catlike quickness as he moved across the floor. Gail looked at him keenly, but his face was strange to her. She didn't like the meaning way in which his gray-green eyes rested on her though.

"I want you to go on with the catalogue work," he told her. "We'll go through the museum later."

He said this with an anticipatory air that infuriated Gail. Ugh! She detested him.

"Stark got a long-distance call at his flat in Los Angeles telling him what has happened," Bartlett went on. "He doesn't know who phoned."

"I got the call just after four o'clock," Stark put in. "I started at once."

Gail looked at Bartlett. "At least you can't accuse me of that— there isn't a telephone in the house."

"I don't accuse you of anything—yet," Bartlett snapped. "But

I must consider the evidence: A man cannot pass through a bolted window or door. And they were all bolted!—I examined every one of them immediately after Mrs. Wessels took you away. That is the important point. Get around it if you can. But you can't."

"There may be a secret exit of some kind," Gail said, faintly.

"Nonsense! I'll be perfectly frank with you, Miss Hollister. I don't believe you or Mrs. Wessels or Dimity actually killed Conniston, but I do believe one of you let in the man who did—and let him out again. And I suspect you more than the other two because Mrs. Wessels isn't the type for that sort of thing and Dimity is half baked."

"You have forgotten the man I saw in the moonlight!"

"Oh, you probably saw a man, all right! The man you let in."

"And the motive for all this?" Gail inquired calmly.

"The intaglios, of course. Three hundred thousand in gems would tempt a pretty big crook. If his ears were keen enough and his fingers were sensitive enough the lock of that vault wouldn't bother him long. Or you may have pried the combination out of the old man."

Gail looked at the detective steadily. "I have been with the Westcoast Museum for five years, Mr. Bartlett. I am Dr. McEwan's confidential assistant. Doesn't that count for something?"

"Not a darned bit! Probably that is how you got onto the gems."

Gail's dark eyes flashed. "Am I permitted to go into the grounds?" she asked.

"Uh-uh!" Bartlett grunted. "Better not go far, though."

She was to be watched! was Gail's thought as she left the room.

There was a door at the lower end of the hall. Gail passed through it and found herself in a patio which extended from the rear of the house to the edge of the cliffs. The patio was like an anteroom of paradise. Much red tile, many singing birds, a pool with gold fish, old seats embowered with honeysuckle, wistaria, and bougainvillea, tempted her to linger.

Gail was reacting with astonishing calmness to the web of circumstance chance had spun around her. She realized that her position was dangerous, but her panic had passed and she refused to regard it as seriously as she had done at first. Once the means of entrance and exit used by Conniston's murderer had been determined she would be clear of suspicion. Her chief concern was to keep Kerry out of the affair. Where had he got to? she wondered anxiously.

She thought of going through the house and examining the doors and windows herself as Bartlett and Decker had done. Then she looked up and saw that most of the windows had been flung open to the morning breeze. It was too late to do anything in that respect now—unless there was a secret exit, as she had suggested to Bartlett. Her fertile imagination refused to let go of the idea.

Instead, she determined to familiarize herself with the beach and an approach to it so that she might keep her appointment with Kerry that night—presuming that it was safe to do so, of course. Her heart pounded mightily at the thought of seeing him. In the meantime her mood demanded vigorous expression. She must walk—quickly—until the blood raced in her veins.

A cinder walk led to the edge of the cliff where it joined a path which ran along the cliff in each direction. For a moment Gail let her eyes rest on the brilliant blue of the ocean a hundred feet below. Then she continued along the sun-drenched path in the direction of the end of the peninsula. A line of cypress trees extended along the cliff several yards from the extreme edge, forming a windbreak for the palms and peppers, the olive, the fig, and the citrus trees beyond. Some of the figs were ripe. Gail plucked several, peeled and bit into the luscious fruit, and cast the skins over the cliff.

A minute or two later she came to a little summer house perched on the edge of the cliff. It was round and thatched with palm fronds, and it looked like a huge mushroom. Wire screen enclosed the upper part of it and there were rustic benches inside. The door stood open and Gail entered. Cigarette butts were scattered around. This, then, was where Kerry had spent most of the night.

Suddenly, Gail saw a man dart from behind the thick foliage of one of the olive trees and vanish behind that of another. It was Decker! He had seen her! He was following her! Gail was determined to go down to the beach, but there appeared to be no way of leaving the summer house without Decker seeing her. She stood quite still for a moment, wondering what she should do. Then her eyes fell on one of the benches, and she began to smile delightedly.

"I wonder if I can do it!" she whispered.

Gail sat down on the bench.

Near the summer house a trail ran down the cliff to the beach below. The descent appeared to be fairly easy and Gail believed that she could get down it unseen by Decker, provided she could lead him to believe that she had not left the summer house. Now Gail was wearing her hat, a flimsy affair of green straw, which she had unthinkingly put on before coming out of the house. The lower part of the summer house was of wood, so the hat was the only part of her attire which Decker could now see.

She dragged one of the smaller benches towards her, upended it, and with a single quick movement ducked her head and transferred her hat to the uppermost end of the bench. She waited for a moment—breathlessly. Not so much as a rustle in the trees behind. Splendid! Doubling up, she dived out of the summer house, scurried towards the head of the trail and swiftly dropped below the edge of the cliff. Again she waited, her limbs tense and her heart going like a mill race. Nothing happened. Delighted with herself, she fled down the trail and reached the sandy beach.

The character of the cliffs fascinated her. Near the top they were of closely packed brown sand, but towards the bottom they were of sandstone of varying texture marvelously and fantastically sculptured by time and tide. As she trudged through the yielding sand, hugging the steepening walls closely, the lip of the cliff began to overhang and Gail saw that she was hidden from the sight of anyone who might be on the top.

Caves penetrated into the cliff. Some of them were mere niches in the scarred and pitted rock; others ran darkly and dankly back into the heart of the cliff; a few, more fissures than caves, rent the face of the cliff from bottom to top. Gail peered into some of the darker caverns and drew back, shivering, into the warm and brilliant sunlight.

She saw nothing of Kerry.

Presently, Gail found herself approaching a mighty pillar of rock which rose a hundred feet above her. At one time it must have been a part of the cliff wall, but the hungry tides had eaten around it until, at high water, the rock was an island separated from the cliff by a dozen yards of white-capped breakers.

So impressive was the rock from this angle that Gail was urged to inspect it from its seaward side. Cautiously she picked her way over a slippery wetness of small boulders and green seaweed to a smooth flat rock sunk, as by design, in the floor of the beach directly in front of the pile.

As Gail looked up at the facade of the rock its extraordinary character quite took her breath away. Never had she seen anything like it before. It was slaty blue in color and stratified in formation. The lower strata, an inch or two thick, mounted in the form of tiny steps from the flat rock upon which she stood to a sort of platform some two feet above it. The platform was arched over by the contour of the rock, roughly giving it the effect of a theater stage, or of the entrance to an ancient pagan temple, or of an altar consecrated to the sea gods.

Its resemblance to the latter grew more pronounced as Gail approached the tiny steps, for she found a font-like basin filled to the brim with seawater sunk in the rock platform. Gail was enchanted by the weird beauty of her discovery. Had some priestly figure in the robes of his office stalked out of the shadowy niche behind the font and proceeded to incant his rituals over her head she would have been prepared to accept him unquestioningly. It seemed beyond belief that merely wind and wave and time had sculptured out this austere beauty.

"Cathedral Rock!" she whispered. "I'm going to call it that!"

The cliffs behind the pillar of rock were perpendicular and the lap, lap of the turning tide warned Gail that she had better be getting back before she found herself cut off. She started back along the beach.

Presently, Gail was ascending the cliff trail again. At the top there was no sign of Decker and she entered the summer house. Her hat was gone! For a moment she stood there, troubled by a premonition of disaster. Then she made her way slowly back to the house.

Gail entered the Casa de Ayer by way of the patio door and passed into the hall with the intention of going up to her room. But to reach the stairs she must first pass the door of the library which was open; and in there was Bartlett—she could hear his voice. If he saw her she would be called in to explain the matter of the hat, and Gail was weary of explanations. She wanted to go to her room and think things out for herself. Well, she must risk it. Noiselessly, she tiptoed past the door, reached the staircase, started up it.

"Miss Hollister!"

Bartlett's voice cracked like a whip. Gail's hands dropped to her sides, the color fled from her cheeks. Decker appeared at the door of the library and favoring her with a sour grin jerked his thumb over his shoulder.

"Chief wants yer!" he said unpleasantly.

Gail dragged herself down the stairs and along the hall to the library door. She paused for an instant; and then, with a toss of her copper-red head, she entered the somber room. Again she stopped. A hand of ice seemed laid on her heart.

Bartlett still sat in the chair behind the library table, stiff and erect and cold of eye. On the table lay her bright green hat, soiled and crushed. Stark lounged by the window. And in the two chairs which were drawn up in front of the table sat Conrad Gill and his son, Victor, the diamond brokers, whom Kerry O'Neil had stopped on the road the night before.

CHAPTER VII
Accused!

From the first, Gail had dreaded the entrance of the Gills into the affair, but she had realized that it was almost inevitable and she was upset less by their presence in the library than by the suddenness with which she had come upon them. Fortunately she had the happy faculty of being able to adjust herself quickly to a difficult situation and almost at once she had her feelings well in hand again. She went forward into the room with the emotions of an actor who comes upon a theater stage at the highest point in the drama. Things were expected of her.

There were several other men in the room whom Gail took to be newspaper reporters. Keen-eyed, youngish men they were, and they regarded her with interest and frank admiration. Mr. Gill looked at her as if he wanted to pat her on the shoulder with his plump white hand. His son, Victor, merely glanced at her carelessly, nodded his hawk-like head, and returned to a study of his immaculate finger nails. Gail thought that she liked Victor Gill less than she liked his father and that she disliked him almost as much as she disliked Norman Stark. The latter still lounged by the window and there was something in his eyes as they rested on her that made Gail think of ice on hot flesh.

"Your hat, Miss Hollister," Bartlett said dryly. Gail picked up the bit of milliners' confectionery and regarded it critically.

"It was so nice of Mr. Decker to bring it up," she murmured.

"Why did you evade him?" Bartlett snapped.

Gail smiled engagingly. "He was so terribly in earnest it seemed a shame to disappoint him."

Decker's long face darkened, the reporters tittered and got out their notebooks, and Mr. Gill regarded Gail with interest that was more sympathetic than ever. Bartlett sprang to his feet.

"You were down on the beach!"

"I was."

"What were you doing there?"

"Looking at the scenery."

"It wasn't scenery that took you there."

"Very well, Mr. Bartlett."

"Answer the question!"

"I have done so."

Bartlett resumed his seat and lit a cigar. Gail watched him and waited. Outwardly, she was calm, but inwardly she was on fire. How much did the Gills know? What had passed between them and Bartlett while she was down on the beach? Had Bartlett connected Kerry with the holdup? The deputy's cold eyes rested on her again.

"Why didn't you report that holdup last night?"

Gail shivered a little. It had come—at last!

"I suppose I should have," she replied. "But—this awful affair"—her face saddened and she glanced at the still figure on the couch—"finding him like that—the holdup seemed trivial in comparison."

"And I suppose it seemed *trivial* before you found Conniston dead," Bartlett drawled. "Last night, I mean?"

Gail's eyes were the essence of candor; desperately she was fighting to keep her self-control. "Kerry!" she whispered to herself. The name seemed to give her fresh courage.

"I realize that I should have got word to the man in the village," she went on. "But Colonel Conniston was so charming and his antiques were so interesting that I didn't!" It sounded unconvincing and she added hurriedly: "Besides, there is no telephone in the house."

Suddenly, a happy thought struck her and she looked at the diamond broker.

"You were the one to have notified the police, Mr. Gill, not me!" she cried, warmly. "You *are* Mr. Gill, aren't you?"

With a nod the latter assured her that he was.

"You did notify them, didn't you?" Gail's tone implied that she took it for granted that he had.

Mr. Gill spread his white hands regretfully. "To tell you the truth, we neglected to. We were staying in the village overnight and my son thought we might as well wait until morning—and we did. Isn't that so, Victor?"

"Quite so," Victor Gill responded dispassionately.

"We got in touch with the local office an hour ago," Mr. Gill went on smoothly, "and they told us of the terrible affair up here. We came at once, of course."

"Your responsibility was greater than mine," Gail went on. "But surely it doesn't matter, Mr. Bartlett. They didn't lose anything—"

"How do you know they didn't?" Bartlett rapped out.

Gail caught her breath. "They couldn't have or they would

have called the police last night," she made quick response. He almost had got her that time!

A little mutter of appreciation ran around the group. Bartlett slowly got out of his chair and perched himself on the corner of the table in front of Gail who was still standing.

"How long have you known this man O'Neil?" he demanded, emphasizing every word.

Gail felt weak and ill. She could hardly stand on her feet. Bartlett's question could mean only one thing; her efforts on Kerry's behalf had been of no avail. The Gills had recognized the man who had held them up as the man whom they had seen hurriedly depart from the Casa de Ayer. "Kerry! Kerry!" Gail did not know what to do, what to say.

She stared around the group, desperately searching for sympathy in the circle of faces that hemmed her in. Mr. Gill was appraising her as he would an uncut gem. His son, Victor, betrayed no interest in anything but his finger nails. Stark had a look in his eyes that sickened her. How she detested the man! The reporters, a hard-boiled crew at first glance, were impersonal in their attitudes and their expressions of interest. And then Gail encountered the eye of the youngest of the reporters. It was anything but hard-boiled; there were humor and a twinkling warmth in it and she felt her strength and courage revive.

"O'Neil," she said steadily. "I know a Mr. O'Neil. I met him in Los Angeles. Surely you don't mean—"

Bartlett cut her short. "I mean that this man O'Neil, who called on the colonel last night, is the man who held up the Gills—and you know it, my girl! The Gills recognized him— and so did you!"

"The man was masked," Gail whispered. "They couldn't have!"

Mr. Gill spread his white hands again. "To be sure he was masked, Miss Hollister. But—er—haven't you noticed his ears?"

"His ears," Gail repeated tonelessly.

"Victor noticed them as O'Neil came out of the house, and again on the highway. Quite the smallest ears you ever saw, weren't they, Victor?"

"Quite," Victor Gill said calmly.

"Victor has remarkably keen sight," Mr. Gill went on. "Miss Hollister recognized the man, of course."

Gail was silent. Kerry's ears had betrayed him! Many a time had she teased him about them for they were the smallest she had ever seen on a man; small and delicately made. And the black eyes of Victor Gill had picked them out! The man must have the eyesight of a hawk! The thing was fantastic, incredible; and yet it was true. There was nothing she could say. She looked at Bartlett and waited, her face white and pitiful. He came to the point quickly.

"I want you to consider the evidence, Miss Hollister. O'Neil called on Colonel Conniston last night. Evidently he didn't get what he wanted, they quarreled, and he left in a rage. Later, he stopped the Gills and demanded the Conniston intaglios. Cool, eh? You came along and recognized him. O'Neil then dropped his gun and ran. Probably he figured the Gills hadn't the intaglios as he had thought. Later, Conniston is found dead.

"Very well. Now look at the rest of it. You neglected to report the holdup, you know this man O'Neil, and your replies to my questions have been evasive and contradictory. Add all this to the fact that every door and window in the house was bolted on the inside at the time Conniston was killed, and that you were in the house, and we have a pretty conclusive case against you. As for O'Neil, it is clear that he wanted the intaglios and that he didn't care how he got 'em. So he came back, killed Conniston, opened the vault, and took them—for I'll bet my last dollar they are not in the vault now. You let him in and let him out—through that window there, probably. But you slipped up on the job by bolting the window behind him. They always do. Get your things together—I'm going to take you along with me."

Gail recoiled from the man in horror. Take her with him! he had said. Take her where? What did he mean? But she knew very well what he meant and the knowledge harrowed her soul. In despair she searched the circle of faces around her. Every one of them accused her—except that of the young reporter. There was a look of bewilderment in his eyes as if he couldn't make up his mind. Kerry! Dear Kerry! He would be with her if he knew! Perhaps she had done wrong in urging him to go. Well, she would stick to her guns. They shouldn't drag a word about him out of her! Suddenly, a ray of hope pierced the darkness of her despair.

"You have forgotten about that man I saw in the moonlight last night!" she cried desperately. "You can't accuse Kerry O'Neil, or me, or anyone else until you know that he isn't the man who killed Colonel Conniston! He is the man! You've *got* to find him!"

"That would be O'Neil if it was anyone," Bartlett said casually. "Get yourself ready!"

"It wasn't!" Gail cried hysterically. "I know Kerry O'Neil too well to be mistaken!"

Bartlett nodded ironically. "You should," he said. Then he looked at the girl narrowly as if her desperate earnestness had made some slight impression on him. "The evidence is clear against you, my girl. If you had someone to support this yarn I'd consider it, but you haven't."

"And that's all you know about it, Mr. Detective, for I saw the man myself!"

It was Mrs. Wessels who had so dramatically substantiated Gail's declaration. She had come into the room unnoticed by the girl and now she was advancing upon Gail and Bartlett with her hands on her hips and a heightened color in her cheeks. The room was very quiet. So quiet indeed that it might have been empty. And then Bartlett's voice cracked sharply.

"What's that you say?"

Mrs. Wessels' eyes darted fire at the deputy. "'Alf past three it was that I saw 'im—"

"How do you know it was?"

"Because I'd got up, and while I was up I remembered I'd gone and forgotten to wind my alarm clock. And the colonel liking his breakfast at eight sharp—"

"You go up—why?"

"My 'ead," Mrs. Wessels explained succinctly.

"Your what?"

"My 'ead. It was aching fit to split. I wanted a hasparin. I keep them in a bottle in the bathroom. The bathroom 'as a east window; I looked through it and saw—'im!" Mrs. Wessels paused dramatically. "'E 'opped across a bit of moonlight on the drive and vanished before you could say Jack Robinson!"

Again that tense stillness in the room.

"You saw him," Bartlett snapped. "This man, O'Neil?"

Mrs. Wessels' attitude changed curiously. Her hands dropped from her hips, she shrank back as if she were afraid, and Gail, who was watching her with hope leaping in her heart, got the impression that she had said more, much more, than she had intended to. Gail slipped her hand into Mrs. Wessels' and the latter seemed to find courage in the contact. Her head went up with a jerk.

"No, and it wasn't this Kerry O'Neil, Mr. Detective!"

"Ah! you didn't recognize him, eh?"

"That I did!"

"Who was it?"

Gail felt Mrs. Wessels' hand tremble in hers. "Go on!" she

whispered.

The housekeeper stiffened again. Her eyes ran around the tense-faced group, rested on Norman Stark.

"It was you as I saw, Mr. Stark," she said, in a low tone. "And I don't care if I do lose my place."

And in that instant Gail knew where she had seen Stark's thickly set figure before!

CHAPTER VIII
Ten Thousand Dollars Reward

Mrs. Wessels had never played the role of leading lady before; nevertheless, she carried it off with credit to herself, facing the cold fury of Stark and the sharp suspicion of Bartlett without so much as the tremor of an eyelid.

Stark did not move away from the window, but into his gray-green eyes leaped so malevolent an expression that Gail, who was breathlessly watching him, drew back in alarm. His heavy lips trembled with passion and a moment had passed before he could control his speech.

"The woman is lying!" he said thickly. "I was in my apartment in Los Angeles until four-thirty this morning!"

He said this with his eyes on Bartlett and with the ring of truth in his voice. But Gail knew that he was lying, not Mrs. Wessels. She had seen Stark herself the night before, and while it had required Mrs. Wessels' evidence to make her realize that it was he, she had not the slightest doubt now that the man she had caught a glimpse of as he slunk across the pool of moonlight was indeed Conniston's nephew, and no one else. Stark's heavy physique and the set and swing of his body were those of the man she had seen. Her mind was quite made up on this point. It could mean but one thing and she recoiled from it in horror: Stark had killed Colonel Conniston and got out of the house by some secret exit. Probably he had the intaglios. She regarded the man with fresh loathing.

But her heart was singing. Mrs. Wessels had saved her. Bartlett had a shrewd brain and even if he did not accept the housekeeper's statement as truth he could not leave it out of his calculations. *Her* job was to find some means of trapping Stark!

Mrs. Wessels had bristled at the latter's tone.

"I'm not in the 'abit of lying, Mr. Stark, sir," she said, indignantly. "It was you all right, and you know it!"

Mrs. Wessels said this bravely. Gail alone guessed what the effort had cost her, for Stark was now her employer, and Mrs. Wessels had an undemocratic appreciation of the difference in their respective stations.

"Miss 'Ollister 'adn't a thing to do with it!" she went on vigorously, addressing Bartlett. "And I don't care 'oo says she 'ad! And there's another thing, too," she went on, shrewdly, "until you can prove I am lying, like Mr. Stark says, you can't touch a hair of 'er 'ead!"

"Exactly where were you at four o'clock this morning, Mr. Stark?" Bartlett demanded curtly.

"Asleep in my apartment in Los Angeles. The telephone woke me."

"Can you prove that?"

Stark looked at him ironically. "Am I expected to?"

"You would dispose of this woman's evidence if you could."

"I can't. I live alone and I was asleep in my room. A man doesn't take an alibi to bed with him. Surely you don't believe this fool yarn, Bartlett! The housekeeper has taken a fancy to this girl and they've made it up between them!"

"No one saw you leave the apartment house?" Bartlett cut in brusquely.

"Not so far as I know."

Bartlett drummed on the table with his fingers. Then he addressed Mrs. Wessels.

"Why didn't you report this before?"

"You didn't ask me," Mrs. Wessels said, with suspicious stupidity.

"How could you have made out the face of the man at that distance?" Bartlett went on sharply.

"I couldn't have."

"Then how do you know it was Stark?"

It was evident to Gail whose statement Bartlett inclined to. Mrs. Wessels aggressively set her hands on her hips.

"I knew 'im by 'is walk and 'is build and if that ain't enough for a body what's seen 'im off and on come fifteen year I'd like to know what is!"

There was silence again.

"All right," Bartlett snapped. "You can go!" With a look at Gail: "Both of you."

Gail went to the door with a smile on her lips and a song in her heart. Mrs. Wessels, whose genius had given her back her liberty, ambled ponderously and indignantly behind. Gail opened the door and passed into the hall—and nearly tripped over a man crouched there.

"Dimity!" she whispered, in astonishment.

The little man climbed to his feet and eyed her sullenly; then he backed down the shadowy hall and before Gail could utter a word of protest vanished from sight. She stared after him in bewilderment until, turning, she found Mrs. Wessels standing beside her, lips tight and hands still on her hips.

"Well, I'm blessed!" Mrs. Wessels said.

Gail glanced back into the library; then she put her fingers on her lips for silence. Mrs. Wessels nodded reluctantly and passed down the hall to the kitchen.

Thoughtfully, Gail went up to her room.

She drew a chair up to the window and resting her chin in her hand let her mind run back over the events of the last twelve hours. The effort to think calmed her and gave her a sense of mastery over herself which she had not had since her encounter with Kerry and the Gills on the highway.

More than ever was she inclined to the theory that Conniston's murderer had entered and left the house by some secret door or panel. The theory was quite in keeping with the romantic atmosphere of the Casa de Ayer. Might not the Spanish don who had built the place have provided it with a secret door to be used in case of emergency arising out of the unsettled condition of the country at that time? The idea was fascinating; it appealed to her tremendously.

If there was such an exit from the house knowledge of it on the part of Conniston's murderer implied considerable familiarity with the construction of the place. This, of course, presented to Gail again the problem of Norman Stark. She was convinced that he had killed Conniston and taken the intaglios.

He was Conniston's nephew and heir. Who, now living, would know more of the Casa de Ayer and its secrets—if it had any— than he?

But if Stark had got the intaglios, and provided the vault was not open already, how had the combination come into his possession? And why had he relocked the vault and left the house by means of this secret way, the existence of which she was assuming? To divert suspicion from himself and fasten it upon those within the house—this answered the last question. And certainly it seemed to be the true answer, for had not Mrs. Wessels caught a glimpse of Stark in the moonlight he would have been beyond suspicion and she, Gail Hollister, would have been on her way to jail.

And now Gail found herself contemplating the problem of Dimity. Where did the queer little man fit into the puzzle? A thought struck her. Had Dimity killed his master? It was shocking, but conceivable. Quite so, indeed! The little man's queerness, his vague replies, his peephole spying—all this counted tremendously against him. If it were Dimity her secret exit theory was disposed of. However, she still clung to her first conception. Stark had been in the grounds: he must be guilty.

And then her mind was seized by a fresh thought that drained the color from her cheeks. Were Dimity and Stark in the affair together? Dimity was listening at the library door, fully dressed, while she was examining the body. Mightn't he have let Stark in and let him out when the thing was done? Again was her secret exit theory disposed of. Perhaps Stark had some hold upon Dimity and the little man had been driven to a partnership in crime. Such an explanation would account for his surreptitious listening and watching.

On the other hand, Dimity's years of faithful service told against any theory that involved him in the crime. His mind was unbalanced, certainly, but according to Colonel Conniston his abnormality had driven him to an excess of tenderness for and watchfulness over his employer, to anything, indeed, but the taking of his life.

Automatically, Gail's mind swung back to her first theory: Stark! When a favorable opportunity presented itself she would make a tour of the house in the hope of coming upon this secret door or panel, in the existence of which her certainty of Stark's guilt inclined her to believe. Not that she would be likely to find it!

But Gail was weary of supposition and theory. They had brought her nowhere. She stood up, shook herself vigorously, and opened the window. The breeze freshened her and she stood there with her face to it, drinking in the warm salt air.

Suddenly, Gail saw half a dozen men with Decker in the lead break away from the house and advance upon the wooded grounds of the estate. Their vigilant attitudes puzzled her for a moment; then she guessed their purpose. Bartlett had brought up reinforcements. They were a search party and Kerry O'Neil was their quarry! Had Bartlett reason to believe that Kerry was still on the peninsula? Gail was in terror for a moment, but she comforted herself with the thought that they hadn't got him yet. Her confidence in Kerry equaled her faith in him.

A little later Gail had lunch with Dimity and Mrs. Wessels in the kitchen ...

Not for a moment had Gail forgotten her assertion to Kerry that she would go down to the beach that evening, provided she could do so without endangering his liberty. But much had happened since she had seen Kerry. She was under grave suspicion herself and her movements certainly would be watched. Had she not been sure that Kerry was in dire need of food she would have given up all thought of going; but her fertile imagination pictured him as starving to death if she failed him. Somehow, she must evade those who would be watching her and get food to him.

She reflected that if Bartlett had any suspicion of her intentions she might disarm it somewhat by commencing the classification of the Conniston antiques. At any rate, the work would occupy her attention until evening.

The museum was open but there was no one in it. Sunlight streamed in through narrow barred windows and motes of dust danced in the beams; nevertheless, the long room maintained its atmosphere of shadowy antiquity and as Gail passed between the glass cases with their comprehensive record of the achievements of the past she grew depressed and troubled in spirit.

A filing cabinet, a desk, and a chair, were at the lower end of the museum. The cabinet, Gail found, contained square folders stuffed with the colonel's notes. Smiling sadly, she took out several of the folders and sitting at the desk began to examine their contents. They were in an appalling state of confusion. Much of the writing was illegible. Old envelopes, scraps of paper, margins of newspaper clippings, leaves from well-thumbed notebooks—anything, in fact, had served the colonel in his moments of inspiration. Gail shook her head at the magnitude of the task before her, and set to work.

Half an hour had passed when Gail quite suddenly had an unpleasant sense of no longer being alone. She had heard no one approach, but she felt that she was watched. A chill ran down her spine and a moment passed before she could force herself to turn around. She was not surprised to find Norman Stark standing a short distance behind her.

"Hello, Miss Hollister," he drawled. "Busy already?"

There was a queer light in his arrogant eyes. Gail's skin tingled.

"I didn't hear you come in," she said coldly. Her hands trembled as they fumbled with the papers before her.

Stark came noiselessly to the desk, picked up one of the papers, and glanced at it carelessly. He dropped it, and perching himself on a corner of the desk bent his eyes on Gail again. The girl shuddered. She felt that he wanted to put his hands upon her. Those heavy supple hands that had brought death to one of his own blood!

"Do you still pretend to believe that you and Mrs. Wessels saw me in the moonlight this morning, Miss Hollister?" he asked, with a grin.

Gail eyed him coolly for a moment. "It was you that we saw, Mr. Stark," she said indifferently. "I recognized you myself as soon as Mrs. Wessels spoke."

Stark lit a cigarette. The grin had left his thick lips. There was something behind the arrogance in his eyes that repelled Gail.

"I suppose you suggested the yarn to Mrs. Wessels," he went on casually.

"Very well, Mr. Stark."

Her coolness irritated him; he eyed her sullenly. "You are making a mistake."

"Mistake?"

"I mean in taking your present attitude. Don't you realize what is involved?"

"Oh, quite!"

"Lies are dangerous tools, young lady."

She nodded. "You will find them so, I fear."

"A charge of murder is pretty serious," he went on.

Gail smiled. "You should have thought of that last night."

This got home. His cheeks flushed blood-red. "You have the gall to accuse me of killing my uncle!" he shouted thickly.

Gail was unmoved by his outburst. "I know what we saw. So does Mrs. Wessels. And so do you!"

Stark stood up, his hands knotted. He stared furiously down at her, as if he had something else to say. But instead of giving utterance to whatever was in his mind he turned on his heel and strode out of the museum. The atmosphere seemed the sweeter for his going.

The encounter had broken the train of Gail's thought and she could not immediately recapture her sense of the notes before her. How consistently the man stuck to his denial! Clearly, Mrs. Wessels' evidence would be insufficient in itself. Her own would be useless, of course. Somehow, she must secure corroborative evidence. But how? The enormity of the task appalled her.

Barely had Gail collected her thoughts again than there came the tread of quick feet behind her. Looking up she saw the young reporter in whose twinkling eyes she had found sympathy when Bartlett was cross-examining her. He greeted her with a friendly smile.

"I'm Ted Perrin of the *Los Angeles Blade*, Miss Hollister," he began, by way of introduction. "I hope I am not bothering you too much."

He perched himself on the corner of the desk, as Stark had done, and regarded Gail with frank admiration in his gray eyes. She did not resent it. He was a pleasant-looking young man, about twenty-five, and Gail thought that he hadn't been a reporter for very long.

"No," she said, with a smile, "you are not bothering me. I suppose you want something for your paper."

"That's about it," he grinned. "But I want to help you, too."

"I need help badly, Mr. Perrin," Gail said seriously.

"I know you do, Miss Hollister. You are in a rotten mess. I wish you'd tell me the truth of it."

"The truth," Gail echoed. "What do you mean?"

Perrin lowered his eyes. "Well," he said, "I've got a hunch you hadn't anything to do with the murder of old Conniston."

"Thank you," Gail murmured. "I wish you'd pass it on to Mr. Bartlett."

"I've tried to," Perrin grinned, "but he won't bite. Why don't you come through with what you know? Tell a straight yarn about this man O'Neil and you'll clear yourself!"

Gail studied him gravely. "You think Kerry O'Neil killed Colonel Conniston, then?"

"Nothing surer. Look at the evidence."

She nodded. "I am doing. Mr. Stark hasn't accounted for his presence here early this morning."

Perrin became very earnest indeed. "I shouldn't stick to that yarn if I were you, Miss Hollister."

"But Mrs. Wessels saw him, too!"

"Yes, she said so."

Gail was silent. The impregnability of this wall of disbelief frightened her. She met it at every turn. "It sounds too thin in face of the other evidence," he went on slowly. "The holdup—the bolted doors and windows—"

"But you just said you don't believe I had anything to do with it!" Gail interposed ironically.

Perrin colored. "To tell the truth I don't know what I believe!" he cried desperately. "Someone let O'Neil into the house and let him out again—that much is certain! From the evidence it looks as if it were you— Oh, damn it!" He broke off savagely. "I don't mean that, either! O'Neil got into the house and you know something about it! What, I don't know. Why don't you tell a straight yarn? I believe you know where he is—he's making a fool of you—using you for his own ends! You are—

you— Oh, Lord!" Perrin ran his hands through his hair.

"Yes, Mr. Perrin?" Gail said.

The reporter drew a long breath. "The trouble is, you are in love with him!"

Gail stared at him speechlessly, but with a singular lack of resentment. In love with Kerry! She had never put it that bluntly even to herself! Was it true? To her astonishment she found herself saying:

"Perhaps I am."

Perrin opened his mouth ludicrously and stared at Gail with a wild look in his eyes. "Oh, Lord!" he groaned, shaking his head from side to side, and he looked as if he meant it, too. Then a flood of color surged into his cheeks and he lost his temper. "Bartlett has got a line on him, already!" he stormed. "Can't you see through him? He's a ne'er-do-well—a cheap adventurer—a slick crook—"

"Mr. Perrin!" Gail was on her feet, dark eyes blazing.

He saw his blunder instantly. "I'm sorry," he mumbled. "I wanted to help you—"

Gail sat down, shaken by the storm of emotion that had swept through her. He had attacked the foundations of her faith in Kerry! She felt herself to be on the verge of hysteria and she had to clench her hands and grit her teeth to keep herself in hand.

Perrin stood up uneasily. A change had come over him. His eyes were evasive in their expression. His manner suggested that having failed in the more desirable expedient he was reluctantly falling back on the only alternative. If Gail noticed this change in his attitude she was too distressed to reflect upon it.

"The inquest is to be held tomorrow afternoon," he remarked, casually.

"Oh," Gail responded, coldly. "Where?"

"Here." Perrin lighted a cigarette with hands that shook. "Bartlett and his men will probably leave after it is over."

Gail's heart gave a leap. "Leave," she echoed. "Where are they going?"

Perrin drew on his cigarette. "Los Angeles," he slowly replied. "They think O'Neil is up there."

"But they are looking for him here!" Gail exclaimed.

"Yes, I know. Bartlett can't afford to take any chances. But— he doesn't think—O'Neil is down here now." Perrin seemed to say this with difficulty.

Gail could not trust herself to speak or to meet Perrin's eyes.

If Bartlett and his men were going away, Kerry's chances of keeping his liberty were excellent!

Perrin was studying the glowing end of his cigarette.

"Stark is going for a day or so, too, I believe," he volunteered, after a pause. "About that reward, I suppose."

"Reward?" Gail cried.

"Yes. Didn't you hear? Stark has offered ten thousand for the return of the intaglios—no questions asked."

Gail stared at him incredulously. "Why, he doesn't—or he isn't supposed to know that they are gone! They haven't got the vault open, yet."

"Oh, they are gone, all right. Anyhow, there's an expert coming down today or tomorrow to open the vault."

Gail was silent. A smile curved her lips. Stark was thorough in his methods, at any rate! Ten thousand dollars reward! And he had the intaglios himself!

Perrin looked at the girl with troubled eyes, nervously drawing on his cigarette. But Gail was too busy with her thoughts to heed him. Reluctantly he turned on his heel and with downcast face walked slowly out of the museum.

"Ten thousand dollars reward!" Gail whispered to herself. "And—they are leaving tomorrow!"

CHAPTER IX
The Riddle of Dimity

Shortly after Gail's encounter with Perrin, Sheriff Green, Bartlett's immediate superior, arrived at the Casa de Ayer, and she was compelled to undergo an examination at his hands every bit as rigorous as the one to which Bartlett had subjected her that morning. Gail was weary of this endless round of question and accusation and by the time they dismissed her she was exhausted. Nevertheless, she stood by what she already had told Bartlett and in face of pronounced hostility on the part of the two officers passionately insisted upon an impartial consideration of Mrs. Wessels' evidence. The latter was the only point in her and Kerry's favor and she clung to it tenaciously.

"Mrs. Wessels saw him—I saw him!" she reiterated. "You can't get over that! You've got to make Stark explain what he was doing in the grounds at three o'clock this morning!"

"We'll attend to Stark, my girl!" the sheriff said grimly. "You might explain a few things yourself, though. What did O'Neil do with the intaglios, for instance?"

Gail looked at him furiously. "I suppose you are after Stark's ten-thousand-dollar reward!"

"We are after O'Neil!" the sheriff said curtly. "We expect to get him, too."

This was all Gail could get out of the man. Her speculations concerning Dimity she kept to herself. The sheriff withdrew shortly afterwards, leaving Bartlett in charge of the case.

That evening, from the patio, Gail watched the sun set in a golden sea and the sky flare and flame like an artist's dream. Darkness came quickly, the stars pricked out one by one, and a golden moon crept above the ridge of the peninsula. As the silver and shadow of the moonlit night replaced the brilliant hues of sunset Gail pondered upon how she might evade Bartlett and his men and get down to the beach unobserved. Not for a moment had she doubted that Kerry would be waiting, but the undertaking filled her with apprehension. She was almost tempted to abandon it. However, Kerry's need of food overrode every other consideration. Food he *must* have!

A little while passed; then she casually crossed the patio and entered the house. The long hall was in semi-darkness. No one was in sight, but the murmur of voices came to her from the library, the door of which was ajar. Nearby was the kitchen. It was in darkness. Evidently, Mrs. Wessels and Dimity had gone up to their rooms. She noiselessly entered the kitchen, closed the door, drew the window shade, and switched on the light.

Quickly she sliced and buttered half a loaf of bread. The ice box yielded cold chicken and boiled ham and she made a great pile of sandwiches, added to it a quarter of an apple pie and a generous slab of Mrs. Wessels' fruit cake. Wrapping her spoil in a newspaper she put out the lights, cautiously opened the window, and set the bundle down on the ledge outside.

Scarcely had she done this than there came the slur of feet in the hall. They were coming towards the kitchen. She was panic-stricken for a moment; a sob broke in her throat. Was this the end? She pulled herself together and with trembling hands softly slid the window down, swept across the floor, and snapped on the lights. She awaited, heart pounding horribly.

The door opened slowly. A gasp of relief forced itself from her parted lips. It was Dimity! She did not know why she should feel relieved that it was no one else, unless it was the certainty that Dimity, like herself, knew more than he had told. He stared at her with suspicion in his brown button eyes.

"Dimity!" Gail whispered. "What do you want?"

Neither of them seemed to notice the absurdity of the question.

"I forgot my pipe," he mumbled.

It lay on the kitchen table. Dimity picked it up and dropped it into a pocket. Averting his eyes from the girl, he started back to the door.

"Dimity!"

He looked at her in sullen silence for a moment. "Yes, Missie?"

"You know something, Dimity. What is it?"

His brown eyes widened, brightened, filled with fear.

"Missie!" he whispered.

"You do, Dimity. You do! What is it?"

He fell back, his hand to his lips. Gail followed him up, step by step. She had the sense of being on the verge of something.

"Do you know who killed Colonel Conniston?"

He gave a little cry and covered his face with his hands.

"You do!" Gail whispered exultantly. She gripped him by the arm. "You must tell me, Dimity!"

His brown eyes, wet with tears, stared into hers. "Tomorrow, Missie! I'll tell you tomorrow!"

And with this, Dimity suddenly wrenched his arm out of her grasp, spun around, and was gone through the kitchen door before she could stop him. Exasperated, Gail jumped after him, but she paused in the doorway and snapped on the lights. Cigarette smoke hung in the hall and the library door was still ajar. If she attempted to stop Dimity, who was proceeding along the hall to the stairs, she would be discovered by whoever was in the library. Discovery meant more interrogation and Gail had had her fill of Bartlett and his questions. He might prevent her from going down to the beach. Moreover, the deputy's antagonism had been so pronounced that she was disinclined to take him into her confidence. (A thousand times better if she had, as Gail presently was to know!)

Gail stood in the darkness of the kitchen door thinking about what Dimity had said. How much did he know?

"Does he really mean to tell me tomorrow?" she whispered to herself.

Oddly enough, she was more depressed than hopeful as a result of the encounter.

Gail passed out into the patio, and shrinking back against the side of the house, peered into the shadows about her and listened intently. There was no one in sight. She heard the murmur of the surf—nothing else. Softly, she crept towards the kitchen window, got the package of food, and listened again. Then she picked her way down the cinder walk, melting into the shadows cast by shrub and vine, and came to the row of cypress trees that skirted the path by the cliff. She stopped again.

Scarcely had she done so, than a man emerged out of the shadow on the opposite side of the patio and stepped into a pool of moonlight. Gail shuddered. It was one of Bartlett's men. He was looking in her direction. Had he seen her? So still did the man stand that he seemed to be carved out of moonlight and shadow. Gail did not dare to move. Her body was drenched with sweat. She did not know what to do. If the man had seen her, and she was found with the package of food in her hand, only one conclusion would be drawn. Yet she dare not attempt to dispose of it.

The man appeared to be listening. Perhaps he had heard something, but had not seen her. If only he would declare himself! The suspense was torture. Ah! he was moving. He was going towards the house!

Gail could have wept with relief. The man passed into the house and she had an intuitive certainty that she was unobserved. Gathering herself together, she flew like the wind down the path and came to the summer house at the head of the cliff trail. Again she stopped and listened and peered at the soft darkness around her. Thump, thump, went her heart. It threatened to burst her breast asunder.

She saw no one; heard nothing, but the wild song of the surf and the indefinite whisperings of the silver night.

Bending low Gail crept to the head of the trail and dropped over the lip of the cliff. There she crouched, her body taut and rigid, every sense on the alert. If she were under observation surely the fact would now be disclosed. For a full minute she waited, but there came no stealthy footstep, no whispering voice. Joyously she rose to her feet and picked her way down the trail. The descent was easy. She reached the silver beach without mishap and fled along it into the shadows cast by the cliffs where they overhung.

The tender beauty of the moonlit beach enchanted Gail. There was magic in the air and it soothed her troubled soul. The tide was far out; the ribbed sand gleamed wet and the sea seemed an infinite crucible of molten metal in which the moon had dipped a silver ladle. For a moment she was a little girl trembling deliciously on the edge of fairyland. But only for a moment; again she started up the silver beach.

Scarcely had Gail gone a dozen steps than she stopped in terror. Against the darkness of the cliff she saw a shadow that moved. It advanced upon her, materialized into the figure of a man. Dropping the package of food, she pressed her hand to her lips to stifle the scream that rose in her throat. The man drew nearer, stood before her, grinning.

"Gail!"

It was Kerry.

CHAPTER X
The Madness of Kerry O'Neil

So intense was her relief that Gail almost flung herself upon him, sobbing. He caught her hands and pressed them until her heart beat with an exquisite gladness. He seemed about to draw her to him. Instead, he held her thus, his dark eyes striking fire in hers.

"I frightened you, Gail. I'm sorry."

"Oh, Kerry! I'm so glad!" she whispered.

He laughed. That ringing laugh of his that always reminded her of a silver bell.

Gail withdrew her hands. "Not so loud!" she cautioned. "Bartlett has brought down half a dozen men. They may be up along the top."

Kerry grinned. "Let 'em come. They won't get me—unless I want them to."

"Want them to!" Gail echoed, in alarm.

"I can't go on this way forever."

"You've had only one day of it," Gail said. "You mustn't think of giving yourself up now, Kerry," she went on earnestly. "The Gills recognized you, and Bartlett thinks—you—did it. But something is bound to turn up before long—tomorrow, perhaps! You will be patient a little longer, won't you, Kerry? I have got oceans of things to tell you."

Kerry knelt by the parcel of food she had dropped. It had come apart, displaying its tempting array of eatables.

"You dear girl!" he cried, and took a huge bite out of one of the chicken sandwiches. "Good!" he munched.

"I knew you'd be starving," Gail cried, hovering over him maternally.

Kerry chuckled. "Not on your life! I had lobster salad for lunch and dinner. There's another left for breakfast."

"Don't be absurd," Gail laughed.

"I'm not," he assured her gravely, when he had taken another bite. "I was down by the Green Crocodile at dawn." He waved his hand towards the tip of the peninsula. "There was nobody around and I found a couple of lobster traps in a pool and there were three lobsters in them. Then I turned up an old kettle on the beach, made a fire, and boiled 'em."

"Alive?" Gail wanted to know.

"Alive," Kerry responded. "Noses in first."

Gail shivered. "You'll dream about them."

Kerry chuckled and helped himself to another sandwich. "I served 'em to myself on an abalone shell garnished with lettuce and celery from the Green Croc gardens." A huge bite. "These sandwiches are darn good, Gail!"

She was laughing at the spectacle of his hunger.

The gay impudence of him! It was this quality that had drawn him to her.

"We've got to talk, Kerry," she told him. "Where can we go? I am afraid someone will hear us if we stay here."

Kerry gathered up the food and taking Gail by the hand led her along the beach to a concavity in the cliff wall. It was not deep enough to be called a cave, but it was arched over and in it was a smooth flat boulder that made a splendid seat for two. They sat and talked and listened to the low tide murmuring its ancient love song to the gleaming sand. When Kerry had taken the edge off his hunger he wrapped the two remaining sandwiches in the newspaper against the needs of the morning and thrust them into a pocket.

"Now," he said, "let's hear it."

And Gail proceeded to tell him what she knew, pitching her voice so low that he had to bring his dark head against the copper-red flame of hers. She told him of what she and Mrs. Wessels had seen in the moonlight, of Dimity and Stark and the latter's ten-thousand-dollar reward. She told him of the bolted doors and windows, of the evidence of the Gills, and of her speculations upon the possibility of there being a secret exit from the Casa de Ayer. Above all, and most emphatically, she told him of the danger of his position, of his inability to accomplish anything by giving himself up, and of her certainty that the guilt of Stark and the innocence of himself presently would be established. Needless to say, she did not tell him how narrowly she had escaped arrest.

"The case appears to hang on my ears," he said, with a grin, when she had finished. Then his face sobered. "It seems to lie between Stark and Dimity, so far, with the odds on Stark." He looked at Gail searchingly. "Sure it was Stark you and Mrs. Wessels saw, Gail? You know how deceptive things look when seen in the moonlight."

"Quite sure, Kerry."

He nodded. "Stark killed Conniston, then. For the intaglios, I suppose. And Dimity must have let him in."

"I don't know about Dimity," Gail said doubtfully. "There may be some secret way of getting into the house. It's just the place for secret doors and secret staircases."

Kerry grinned. "Maybe," he admitted. "I wouldn't count on that, though. Keep your eye on Dimity. I'd bet my last dollar he knows a thing or two. The police seem to have passed him up altogether."

"They are so sure it is you," Gail said soberly. She did not tell him that Dimity had promised to reveal what he knew the next day. It might amount to nothing and she didn't want to raise his hopes without foundation.

"But look at the facts for a minute," he went on. "Dimity was fully dressed when you found the body, and according to you and Mrs. Wessels and Colonel Conniston, he is always listening and watching. Why? Nobody knows. I think I told you that I tumbled over him myself when I rushed out of the library. There's something queer there, take it from me, Gail. Dimity is either miles deep or crazy." O'Neil grew thoughtful. "I wish I could get into the house for an hour or two; I believe I'd turn up something."

Gail was aghast at the notion. "What on earth could you do there?" she cried, and caught him fiercely by the arm; her dark eyes pleaded with him. "I couldn't bear it if they took you!" she whispered, heedless of the implication in her words. "You are not going up there, Kerry. Everything will come out all right. Just be patient a little longer." Then, with an affectation of lightness: "It's your turn, now."

O'Neil stared at her with a blaze of light in his dark eyes and Gail found herself trembling at his side. Then his mood changed as by an effort of will. He fell silent and a flood of color mantled his lean face. For a moment, he stared seaward. Gail saw that his clenched hands were white at the knuckles.

"I don't know how to begin, Gail," he began, penitently. "I've made an awful fool of myself. I don't know how you can believe in me as you do. It was just the kind of idiotic thing I *would* do, of course, and it seemed absolutely right to me last night— I was just getting my own back and all that—but now, with you sitting here— Oh, darn it all! here goes.

"Years ago my dad and old Conniston were all over the world together. That's how Conniston got his collection—most of it, anyhow. But Dad wasn't much of a man to collect. People, the way they lived, what they were thinking about, and all that sort of thing, interested him more. He was all sympathy, feeling, generosity, emotion. I never met a man who cared less for material possessions, money and what it will bring, than he did. In a sense, that's why I'm in this mess—not that I blame Dad for it, of course. There was money in the family, then; but Dad was always in the South Seas, or India, or Tibet, or South America, or Europe, and he left his affairs to the lawyers.

"After he married my mother things were different. She was a woman of firm character and that was the end of Dad's traveling around. Well, he'd seen a good deal of the world and he was very fond of Mother, so he settled down in New York. I was born a year or so later.

"Dad and Conniston grew apart as men often do, but they didn't lose their affection for each other. Though I imagine Conniston was a little impatient with Dad for giving in to Mother as he did; and Dad may have felt a little shamefaced about it, too. They corresponded occasionally, but they never saw each other again. I think my mother regarded Conniston as a sort of natural enemy of the home life she wanted. Anyhow, she discouraged the friendship. Conniston bought this house here, but he was always going off somewhere. In fact, he made quite a reputation as an explorer.

"Two years ago my parents went to Europe. They returned on the *Atlantis*. You know what happened to the *Atlantis*, Gail. She went down off the Newfoundland banks and my folks were drowned."

There was silence for a minute. Gail's hand crept into Kerry's. In the shadows, they were like two bronze figures cast against the impressive statuary of the cliffs. Then the night seemed to draw them to its breast, to soothe them with its white magic. Kerry went on again.

"I found Dad's affairs in an awful mess when I took hold of them. There was hardly any money left. His lawyers had bungled things badly. I've an idea there was crooked work somewhere. It didn't matter much to me just then. I had graduated as a mining engineer and I had done pretty well, considering what an impetuous ass I'd always been and all the traveling around I had done. But six months ago I did another fool thing. I bought a silver mine in Mexico. The mine is all right, but when I'd paid for it I found I hadn't any money left to develop it. And that brings me to the Conniston intaglios.

"As I said, Dad never really cared for collecting old stuff; but Conniston was crazy about it. Especially about these intaglio gems. It seems that he got most of them while Dad was with him and Dad, I understand, helped him, financially and otherwise. Just what the arrangement was I don't know— there was no legal formality about it; my father was the last man in the world for that sort of thing; he'd trust the devil himself if he asked him to. But it seems that he had a half interest in the intaglios. They were worth about two hundred thousand, then.

"When Dad married and settled down Conniston was perfectly honest about the gems. He wanted to sell them and pay Dad his share, but Dad wouldn't hear of it. He didn't need the money and he knew how Conniston adored the gems. So their sale was put off indefinitely. Conniston was delighted with the arrangement, of course. Commercially, it was sound enough. The gems were increasing in value every year. Well, I had almost forgotten about them when I found I needed money for my mine—needed it badly. I hated to hurt Conniston by forcing a sale of the gems, but it was that or lose every dollar I had in the world.

"When my parents were drowned Conniston telegraphed and wrote his sympathy and I believe he felt their death deeply. But he didn't say anything about the intaglios and I was too full of trouble and worry to do anything myself. I intended to see Conniston about them later on, of course; but I didn't need the money then and I kept putting it off. You'll call that my father's irresponsibility, I suppose." Kerry grinned sheepishly. "I didn't think Conniston was trying to gyp me out of my share of the stones and I don't think so now. I supposed he had had 'em so long and Dad had been so indifferent about them that he expected me to make the first move.

"Well, I let things slip until a month ago when I realized how badly I needed money for the mine. I wrote Conniston telling him I was coming to see him. But I went straight to Los Angeles first and got rid of that stuff to the museum and"— Kerry looked up with a grin and Gail found herself coloring— "and met you, and let another month slip by. The other day I thought I'd better get busy. Yesterday, I came down here— without letting you know I was coming; you didn't tell me you were coming, either—and proceeded to make a fool of myself all over again.

"I seem to have the knack of getting in wrong, Gail. Some folks are that way. Coming down on the stage I worked up a grudge against old Conniston for not offering to sell the stones two years ago. If I had done so then there might have been some excuse for it. But there wasn't now—I had been as careless about it as he had. Anyhow, by the time I reached the Casa de Ayer I had a fair-sized grudge against him and I met him with a chip on my shoulder. I demanded—*demanded*, mark you—my share of the value of the intaglios.

"That was where I made my fool play. If I had asked him for a settlement I probably would have got it. But I *demanded* it. And, as you may know, Colonel Conniston wasn't the man to listen to the demands of anyone—especially those of a man half his age. He went up in the air at once. Perhaps he had a sort of guilty feeling at having kept the intaglios as long as he had. If so, my 'impudence,' as he called it, gave him an excuse to justify himself. I was hopping mad, too, by this, and we went at it hotter and hotter for half an hour.

"I have an idea that I called him an old rascal and I think I must have given him the impression that I thought he was holding out on me. He began to rave. At first, he had said that he expected a good offer for the gems from Conrad Gill, the diamond broker, that very evening, but now he finished up by telling me that I'd never see a dollar of the money, that I had no legal hold upon him, that I was an 'insolent pup,' and that I'd better get out of the house before he threw me out. I don't think he really meant it, even then, but I took him at his word."

"He didn't, Kerry!" Gail cried breathlessly. "He meant to do what was just!"

Kerry nodded. "I think so, too, now. Well, I rushed out of the room, tumbled over Dimity, and got to the front door just as Mrs. Wessels was opening it to admit the Gills. I hurried down the drive, supposing that one of them was Conrad Gill, and came to the highway. Then I stopped and began to think. Down in Mexico I'd got into the habit of carrying a pistol and I found I had the thing in my pocket. It put the idea into my head. I must have been clean crazy even to think of it. And yet, believe me or not, Gail, it seemed sane and reasonable enough to me then.

"You see, I'd got it into my head that Conniston meant to gyp me out of my share—as he said, I had no legal hold upon him—and I felt sure that if the Gills got away with the stones that would be the last of them, so far as I was concerned. Well, I wasn't going to give up without a fight and I didn't much care whether I had the law with me or not. A man gets that way sometimes when he's seen as much as I have.

"But before I made this fool play I wanted to be sure that these men bought the intaglios. I had a pretty fair idea of the lay of the house and I sneaked back down the drive and round to the library window. There was an opening between the curtains and I got a good view of the room. I saw the Gills and

Conniston. The intaglios were on the table. And old Gill had his check book in his hand. That was enough. I was sure they were sold and I didn't wait any longer. And they weren't sold, after all!

"You know what happened, Gail. I suppose you'll say it was the rottenest, the most idiotic thing you ever heard of—even if I did unload the gun first. When I saw you in that car—" He broke off suddenly, covered his face with his hands. "I knew then what an ass I had been and I ran—like a spanked puppy. And there you are. I don't suppose you'll understand—if there is anything to understand."

There was silence again.

Gail was smiling a little. Kerry had told his tale with a fine dramatic sense that had made the apparently inexplicable absurdly clear and understandable to her. And he had said he didn't suppose she would understand! Her eyes danced. There wasn't an ounce of subtlety in him. Every word he had uttered had been a flame that illumined the foursquare halls of his character; everything he had done had been in keeping with that bundle of impulses which she knew as Kerry O'Neil. The reckless irrationality of the man! How she loved him for it! Suddenly, she found his fine dark eyes upon her. There was in them that which made her heart leap. She began to tremble, to feel herself in terror of him.

"Gail!" he whispered, huskily.

"Yes, Kerry?"

"I can't help it, girl—I've got to tell you! I can't help it!"

She waited, tensely. His eyes drew her as magnets draw.

"I'm an odd cuss, Gail. I never amounted to much—don't suppose I ever shall. I've been keeping it back for weeks—wanted to get this other thing straightened out first. And now I'm wanted—by the police—for murder—" He broke off with a sob; his face twisted with an inarticulate agony that wrenched the girl's heart. "I'm a lowdown cuss talking to you like this now. I ought to be shot! But— Oh, Lord! I can't help it, Gail—I love you!"

He caught her fiercely by the shoulders and swung her around.

"You are not laughing at me, Gail!" he whispered, huskily. "I couldn't stand it if you were! Lord!" he groaned again. "I shouldn't be saying this—I don't know what I'm saying—I can't help it! Forgive me, Gail!"

But he did not let her go. The strength of his hands held her fast and Gail was content that it should be so. Her fear of him was gone. She knew herself to be the master of the situation. He was hers now and for all time. Happiness thrilled her as a burst of song. She wanted to press his head to her breast, to run her hands through his hair.

"Help it!" she echoed, with a smile. "I don't want you to, Kerry."

His hands tightened on her shoulders; he held her at arm's length. "Golly!" he whispered, with awe in his voice. "Golly! Do you mean it, honey? Do you mean it?"

He was like a little boy who has unexpectedly found his way into the fairy palace of his dreams. Gail was laughing and sobbing at once.

"You silly dear!" she cried. "Why shouldn't I mean it?"

"Gail!"

He took her into his arms then and held her tenderly. They did not speak for a long while. A world of dim lights and soft shadows encompassed them and their hearts were flooded with an exquisite melody.

"I am going to get out of this mess quick," he told her presently. "Then we'll shake the intaglios out of Stark, sell the mine, and I'll show you the old world from stem to stern. Leave it to your Uncle Kerry!"

He spoke with a superb confidence, and Gail, whose faith was boundless, knew that it would be so.

She gently disengaged herself from his arms.

"I must go, Kerry," she whispered. "They may be looking for me."

"Let 'em look," he grinned. "I've just found you, girl—I can't let you go!"

"But you must, dear!" she insisted firmly. "I'll come tomorrow night and bring you more food."

Kerry grew thoughtful. "Better hadn't—now I come to think of it," he said. "I don't want you brought into it, Gail. Aiding and abetting, you know."

Gail smiled. She knew better than to tell him that she couldn't get into it any deeper than she was already.

"There won't be any danger," she went on. "The inquest is to be held in the afternoon and Bartlett and his men are going up to Los Angeles after it is over. They think you are up there. Stark is going, too."

The effect of this announcement upon Kerry was startling. He stood up, his lean face aglow, and drove his fist into the palm of his other hand.

"Great!" he exclaimed. "Just what I wanted!"

"What do you mean?"

"Bartlett and his men and Stark are going north, you say. That will leave only Mrs. Wessels and Dimity and you. What luck! I've got a hunch there's something in that library that Bartlett has missed. I'm coming up to have a look round—"

Gail sprang to her feet, aghast. "You are not! Are you crazy—"

"What's wrong? Why not?"

"Someone may come! Bartlett may change his mind! A hundred things may happen! You are not coming up, Kerry!"

"Yes, I am," he said coolly.

Gail looked at him in silence. His face expressed a quality of determination she had never seen in it before and she knew that anything she might say would be useless. A presentiment of danger oppressed her. He saw the unhappiness in her eyes and taking her hand pressed it gently.

"I'm sorry, Gail, but I've got to come. Being down here is getting on my nerves—I've got to have action. Even if it means bumping into friend Bartlett. But don't worry—I won't do that!"

"Kerry—"

"It's no use, Gail. I'm coming. I'll be there about ten o'clock. Open the library window, then go to bed. I don't want you mixed up in it."

Gail shivered a little. The beauty of the night seemed to screen a threat.

"All right, Kerry. If you've made up your mind."

He accompanied her to the foot of the trail, kissed her tenderly, and let her go.

"Good-night, Gail."

"Good-night, Kerry."

He stood there, the moonlight full upon his tall figure, until he could no longer see her.

CHAPTER XI
The Shadow on the Drive

The inquest was held in the library of the Casa de Ayer the following afternoon. A lawyer had come down from the office of the district attorney and Gail was again subjected to a grueling cross-examination that all but broke her heart. How she maintained the sturdy front she had presented to Bartlett and the sheriff she never quite knew. Perhaps it was the flame Kerry O'Neil had kindled within her that sustained her. But maintain it she did. Mrs. Wessels stood by her magnificently.

Nothing developed in the way of new evidence. Stark, of course, coolly denied having been near the place at the hour of the murder; and when the Gills and Bartlett had given their evidence, and long before the jury had gone out, it became pitilessly clear to Gail how completely Mrs. Wessels' statement had been discounted. The jury at last filed out to its deliberations, deeply conscious of the gravity of its office.

Gail hadn't the slightest doubt as to what the verdict would be, but the suspense of waiting for it harrowed her afresh. It came fifteen minutes later.

"We, the jury, find that Philip Conniston died of valvular lesion of the heart and that, in our opinion, his death was hastened by strangulation, apparently at the hands of Kerry O'Neil."

The grave tones of the foreman as he pronounced the verdict were like a knife thrust in Gail's heart. She could feel Stark's eyes upon her, cold, ironical, triumphant. Mrs. Wessels led her from the room weeping.

They had tea together in the kitchen. Dimity did not join them. Gail had seen little of him all day. There had been no opportunity to question him. Indeed, he had seemed to avoid her.

It was a silent meal. The verdict of the jury had distressed Mrs. Wessels almost as much as it had Gail. She was a staunch and generous soul capable of those fine loyalties to which some women give themselves so unsparingly and she had espoused Gail's cause without knowing just what it was. Gail had hardly resisted the temptation to confide in her. When the meal was over Gail escaped to the sanctuary of her room.

It was now after six. Night was coming on. Sky and sea were

a riot of color; the hills to the north were thinly veiled in a
pale mauve glow. Presently, the shadows began to deepen and
on the western rim there remained of the sun's golden light
only a dull red glow which Gail, in her present mood, found
threatening, sullen, and sinister.

Her thoughts were of Kerry and his impending appearance
at the Casa de Ayer. His insane determination to examine the
library had filled her with terror that had grown upon her as
the day lengthened until now she was certain that nothing
but disaster could come of it. The coroner, his jury, and the
newspapermen had gone. But in the drive below were a high-
powered police car, the Gills' limousine, and Stark's sleek gray
roadster. Perrin had said they were leaving the Casa de Ayer
after the inquest. Why didn't they go? Gail kept asking herself
fretfully.

(As a matter of fact, the Gills and Bartlett had dined with
Stark—much to Mrs. Wessels' disgust—and they were lingering
over a bottle of old Conniston's port.)

From the fact that it was only seven o'clock and that Kerry
was not to arrive until ten Gail drew little comfort. Her nerves
were on edge; she could not sit still in her chair; her limbs
were trembling.

She began to imagine eventualities that had not occurred to
her before. Perhaps Perrin had been mistaken! Or possibly
Bartlett and Stark had changed their minds. An even more
alarming possibility presented itself to her. Might not Perrin,
at the instigation of Bartlett, have lied to her in the hope that
she might lead them to Kerry? Then she reflected that this
could not be so unless they at least made a pretense of leaving
the estate.

So acute did her distress presently become that she got up
and going downstairs passed into the patio. The moon had not
yet risen and the patio was in shadow. A cool breeze blew in
from the ocean. It freshened her and lightened her depression.
She dropped onto a rustic bench beneath a wistaria vine.

A little while passed.

Suddenly, Gail heard a soft footfall in the shadows in front
of her. Every sense on the alert, she listened attentively, peering
into the darkness ahead. A figure materialized out of the
shadows, paused, came towards her. It was Dimity.

"Dimity!" she whispered.

He did not speak, but he stopped in front of her and she got
the impression that he was going to.

"What is it, Dimity? You've got something to tell me?"

He nodded. "Yes, Missie. But not here—people around. In the summer house—later on. You know it!"

Gail was quivering with excitement. "Tell me now—here! You must, Dimity! Do you know—who did it?"

She had contemplated the possibility that he knew a hundred times during the last two days—but she had not really believed that he did. Now she was certain. It meant—everything!

He gestured angrily. "Mebbe! No, I won't tell you here! 'Tain't safe. The summer house— Ssh!"

He broke off suddenly, finger to his lips; his eyes darted toward the door which gave entrance to the house from the patio. Gail stiffened in her chair. She, too, had got the impression that someone was standing there, listening. Dimity looked at her sharply.

"Ten o'clock!" he whispered. "They'll be gone, then!"

Quickly, he turned, and with an agility surprising in one of his years dived into the shadows from whence he had come. Gail let him go. She was staring intently towards the door. Was there someone there—listening? Who could it be? She got up and softly made her way across the patio, paused at the terrace, went on to the door, paused again, and listened. There was no one there. She passed into the hall. The murmur of voices came from the library, the door of which was closed: the scent of cigarette smoke faintly assailed her nostrils; but she saw no one. Mrs. Wessels was in the kitchen, washing dishes.

Nevertheless, she could not rid herself of the impression that they had been watched and she stood quite still, listening intently and peering along the shadowy hall. Who could it have been? Decker? Perhaps. But why should he disappear so quickly? Was he with the others in the library? Had he overheard Dimity? Well, it didn't matter if he had. Then Gail reflected that she had received nothing more definite than an impression. Perhaps, after all, their senses, abnormally keen due to the strain they were under, had deceived them.

She had no time to speculate further upon this point for just then she heard the scrape of chairs being pushed back in the library. Her heart began to race. Were they really going, at last? On her toes she fled down the hall, rounded the newel post, and swept up the staircase to the door of her room. She did not enter, but stood there in the shadows, peering down into the hall. The front door she could see clearly.

Bartlett, Stark, and the Gills emerged from the library and leisurely made their way towards the front door. They were chatting about the case and much of their conversation reached

Gail as she impatiently waited for them to manifest their intentions. She heard her name and Kerry's mentioned once or twice, and there were several references to "Los Angeles." A remark about the vault came to her imperfectly, but she sensed its substance. An expert had been sent for, he had been expected that morning, but he hadn't turned up. The remark was to the effect that he would arrive the next day.

Bartlett would have one of his men here to meet him, Gail reflected. The thought bothered her.

An antique hall stand stood in an alcove near the front door. Mr. Gill went to it, took down overcoat and hat and donned them. Conrad, his son, followed his example; so did Bartlett and Stark. Chatting animatedly, they passed out into the night.

Gail ran to the window of her room. She saw the Gills get into their limousine, heard the engine roar into life. It swept around the lawn and purred down the tree-bordered drive. Bartlett followed in the police car and Stark came behind him in the gray roadster. Not until the headlights of the three cars had vanished over the rise in the highway did Gail realize that they had indeed gone. A sob of relief broke from her lips. She looked at her wristwatch. It was just eight o'clock. The moon was rising above the ridge of the peninsula.

She would see Kerry in two hours. Thought of his coming at once thrilled and terrified her. She was eager for the sound of his voice, for the touch of his hand, but she was haunted by a presentiment of danger. Then she shook herself vigorously. What was there to be afraid of? Bartlett and his men and Stark had gone; Mrs. Wessels—the dear soul!—had announced her intention of retiring early; and Dimity—

Ah, Dimity! The thread of her thought snapped. She was to meet him at the summer house at ten. He had intimated that he knew who had killed Colonel Conniston. She recalled the joy with which she had received the intimation down in the patio a few minutes ago. But now, after even this short interval, she wasn't so sure. Dimity's mind was unbalanced: what could he have discovered, unless—? Her suspicions of him crowded back into her mind. This might be an attempt to throw dust into her eyes—engineered by Stark, perhaps. She did not know what to think. If only it were ten o'clock.

Ten! Again her thought snapped. Kerry was to be at the library window, which she would presently open, at that hour. He would come by way of the cliff trail which led up to the summer house. Dimity would see him! How the little man would react Gail hadn't the remotest idea; but the situation, should it come about, might contain all the elements of disaster.

She must meet Kerry on the beach and if he still insisted on coming up to the Casa de Ayer bring him by way of another trail which she had found that morning. And while he was in the library she would keep Dimity in the summer house. Her plan seemed sound. It did not occur to her to open the window, then go to bed, as Kerry had so largely commanded her.

Gail had been sitting by the window for an hour or so when, quite suddenly, she thought she heard a faint sound, an indistinguishable sound, in the landing outside, or in the hall below. She went to the door and peered out into the shadowy landing and down into the hall. The sound was not repeated and she attributed it to the breeze outside or to the surge of the tide on the beach. A light, she noticed, shone beneath the door of Mrs. Wessels' room. Evidently, the housekeeper was about to retire.

A little later—towards half past nine it was—Gail went downstairs, it being her intention to descend to the beach at once and intercept Kerry before he climbed the trail. Purposing to leave the house by way of the window in the library, she entered the latter room. A red glow in the grate pulsed against the dark interior. Conniston's body had been removed. Gail shivered a little as she glanced around. There was a coldness, a stillness, a sinister something about the room, that chilled her blood. She went to the draperies that concealed the window and drew them back.

Her hand was upon the bolt which had played so tremendous a part in the affair of the early morning before, when she stopped suddenly. Her body grew tense and the color ebbed from her cheeks. There was a pool of moonlight upon the drive and athwart it lay the shadow of a man: a tall lean man whose body was invisible against a mass of shrubbery close by.

Gail went sick for a moment; then she drew a long breath that steadied her. She did not move. She did not dare to. The room was in darkness, but a movement of the curtains might attract the attention of the man outside. She must wait; she must think. Her intuitions were unusually keen and she felt sure that the man whose shadow she saw was neither Kerry nor Dimity. Could it be Decker? The shadow suggested his lean figure, but Decker was on his way to Los Angeles—supposed to be. Had Bartlett dropped him and sent him back with instructions to keep his eyes open and himself out of sight? Or, reverting to her fears of an hour or two before, was this departure a pretense and had Bartlett and his men come back secretly? If they had, it must be in the hope that she might lead them to Kerry!

Just then the shadow moved slowly on. It vanished. She hadn't been seen!

Fighting down the panic that threatened to overwhelm her, Gail thought rapidly. It was nine-thirty now. Kerry might be on his way up to the house. He would run into the arms of whoever was out there. She must prevent it. How? If she stole out to meet him and she was seen she would be followed. But she must risk it. There was nothing else she could do. If she was followed, at least Kerry would have a better chance of getting away than if he stumbled into them unawares.

Gail drew back the bolt and let the curtain fall. Then she quietly hurried into the hall and along it to the patio door, which she unbolted. The center of the patio was white with moonlight, but towards the sides were deep shadows and picking her way through these Gail came to the path which skirted the cliff. She stopped beneath a cypress tree and listened. Silence. Turning, she fled down the path and drew near to the summer house. Dimity was not yet there. She crept to the head of the trail, stopped, and listened again.

And just then she heard the crack of a stick and the rustle of grass in the orchard beyond the cypress trees at her left. Decker—if it were he—had seen her, was after her! Gail was panic-stricken. Should she stay where she was or go back or go on? The rustling grew louder. She could distinguish the tread of feet. Better go on. With a sob in her throat she swept down the cliff trail, reached the beach, flew along it, dived into the shadows flung by the overhang of the cliff.

Keeping within the shadows cast by the cliff Gail plunged wildly down the beach, sobbing hysterically, stumbling over drifted sand and smooth round boulders. Her breath came heavily, tearing agonizingly at her throat. If only she could see Kerry! She must find him! He must have his chance to get away! She kept on, her feet dragging in the loose sand.

Suddenly, a figure loomed up in the shadows in front of her. It was a man. He came towards her. It was Kerry.

"Gail!" he whispered. His arms closed about her.

For a moment she clung to him, trembling. She could not speak. The thud of her heart against his alarmed him.

"What's wrong, Gail?"

"Decker!" she gasped. "He came back! He's after me. You must get away—he'll see you! Quick, Kerry!"

Instead, he drew her into the mouth of a shallow cave in the cliff wall.

"Now—tell me!" he whispered.

She did so, in a hasty word or two, and implored him to go.

"Let him come!"

"Are you crazy?" Gail stormed. "If he finds you here—"

She broke off suddenly; her hand tightened on Kerry's arm. There had come a soft footfall on the sand. They stood rigid, staring at each other. Gail was white to the lips. Kerry's lean body tensed; there was a sort of panther-like grace about him.

"Stick up your hands, O'Neil! And come out of there!" It was Decker.

Silence again.

Neither of them moved. They could not see the man outside. Probably he could not see them, but he knew they were there. The cave was small. If he began to shoot a bullet would find one of them!

"Come out, O'Neil, or I'll rip you open!" Decker roared. "You, too, Hollister! Sharp about it!"

Gail was in despair. Was this to be the end of her strivings on Kerry's behalf? She looked at him piteously. His mouth was drawn into a thin hard line, but there was a ghost of a grin in his dear eyes. He nodded reassuringly and raising his hands above his head indicated that she should do likewise.

"Coming, Decker," he drawled.

His coolness amazed Gail.

He stepped out of the cave, hands aloft. Gail followed him. Decker detached himself from the cliff wall and stood before them, automatic leveled at Kerry. His small eyes glinted maliciously.

"Well, O'Neil, I've got you!"

"So it seems," Kerry agreed. "What are you going to do with me?"

Decker laughed unpleasantly. His hand went to a pocket and Gail heard the clink of metal. The gun wavered a little. It happened suddenly, then. Gail gave a little scream. Kerry had taken a short step forward and appeared to stumble over a stone at his feet. But instead of falling his body twisted lithely aside, his palm came down in a terrific sweep, and he struck the weapon from Decker's hand unexploded.

CHAPTER XII
The Inverted Numerals

For a moment—no longer—the two men were held apart by the abruptness of this equalization of their fighting resources. And then their bodies collided with a thud, interlocked; and losing their footing on the treacherous sand they went down in a whirling tangle of arms and legs.

Gail saw nothing clearly. A mist seemed to float before her eyes. She was like one in a nightmare who watches a combat which he can neither stop nor take flight from; she was at once remote and perilously near.

Nevertheless, she sensed acutely the intensity of the struggle. So closely were the two men interlocked as they writhed on the sand that their eight limbs seemed to be the members of a single body. She had an impression of snarling hate on Decker's part, of a cold and grim fury on Kerry's. The thud of human flesh, grunts of pain, an oath or two, the heavy breathing of racked bodies, came to her as from a distance. The thing was savage, abysmal; they seemed to have slipped back into the beginnings of time. The sweet tranquility of the night was like a fairy's garment rent and torn.

It stopped as suddenly as it had begun. Gail saw one of the men stagger to his feet and stare down at his prostrate opponent. The issues at stake crowded back into her mind and she shut her eyes, afraid to look.

But when she opened them again she saw to her relief that the victor was Kerry. Decker lay still. Kerry was on his knees beside Decker, stuffing a handkerchief into his mouth and fastening it in place with another one. The handcuffs which Decker had intended for Kerry the latter now clamped on his wrists. His legs Kerry secured with a belt Decker had worn around his waist. A leap of fury in the man's eyes indicated his return to consciousness.

Kerry stood up again and looked at Gail. His lips and nose were bloody, but he was grinning exultantly and Gail grinned back at him. Kerry was hers and she was proud of him! But she must get him away before anyone else arrived on the scene.

Kerry, however, had other plans in his head. "Come on, Gail!" he said curtly. Seizing her by the hand he began to hurry her along the beach towards the trail.

"You are not going up there?" she gasped.

"I certainly am! I'll never have a better chance. Come on!"

Gail's eyes blazed. "You reckless fool!" she cried scathingly. "I came down here to warn you and you tell me you are going up there—right into their arms!"

Kerry was astonished. "Decker is safe enough," he protested. "You didn't see anyone else. Why shouldn't I go?"

Her flash of temper died down.

"You dear fool, Kerry!" she cried softly. "How shall I ever keep you! Don't you understand? If Decker came back mightn't Bartlett and Stark have come back, too? Mightn't their leaving be nothing but a trick to get me to lead them to you? I believe it is!" she added, with a backward glance at the writhing figure of Decker.

Kerry began to grin again. "Maybe," he admitted.

"Do you want them to take you?"

"I don't believe I do—not before I've had a look around, anyhow."

"Yet you say you are going where they are?"

"I want to see if you are right."

She frowned impatiently. "You don't think I am, then?"

His grin became a chuckle. "I shouldn't be surprised if you were, Gail."

Her eyes widened with distress and he became serious instantly, taking her hand in his.

"It amounts to this, Gail," he said, earnestly. "I can't hide on the peninsula much longer. I doubt if I could get away right now—Bartlett will have his men strung across it, whether he thinks I am in Los Angeles or not. He can't afford to take any chances—I am a desperate character! They've been combing the ridge all day—nearly had me a couple of times this afternoon. It's only a matter of hours before they rout me out, and I want to have a look around that house first. I can't get it out of my head that I'll turn up something of value. Bartlett may get me, but there's an even chance that he won't. I'm going to risk it, anyhow. If he does get me, it'll be only a few hours sooner, anyhow. You see what I mean? I've simply got to go, dear."

There was sense in what he said, as Gail realized. But the thought of his being taken now, even though capture ultimately was inevitable, terrified her. As for his idea that he might find evidence which had escaped Bartlett—she didn't think much of it. But she saw that he had made up his mind. Nothing she might say, would move him.

Gail thought for a moment longer. "Will you promise not to give yourself up, and not to let Bartlett take you, unless you can't help it?" she begged.

"Yes, Gail."

She looked back at Decker who was still torturing the sand with his writhing. "Come on, then."

They started down the beach at a trot, keeping well within the shadows cast by the cliff. Kerry was for turning up the trail by which Gail had descended the cliff, but she kept on.

"Not that way. There's another trail below the patio. It's much steeper, but it will give us a better chance of keeping out of their sight."

"If they are there," Kerry chuckled. "Lead on, Cap."

They came to the other trail a minute or so later. It was more difficult of ascent than the first, as Gail had said, and they were obliged to labor up it with the utmost of caution. Gail was in front. When she reached the top of the cliff she bent double, passed swiftly over a patch of moonlight on the edge of the cliff, and plunged into the shadow of a great cypress at a corner of the patio. Kerry joined her.

The Casa de Ayer was as darkly portentous as when Gail had left it. A glimmer of light shone from the hall, but the rear rooms were in darkness. Moonlight fell on it weirdly and Gail was possessed by the fantastic notion that an invisible shadow lay upon and around the house, a shadow that forbade them entrance, and that it was the shadow of the man who had built it and the shadow of the man who had died within its walls.

Then she heard Kerry whispering: "There's no one here. Bartlett hasn't come back. Let's go!"

Gail cautiously led him across the patio, taking advantage of every scrap of shadow that offered them cover with a dexterity that brought a low chuckle from Kerry and would have won the admiration of an Indian trapper. They crept into the house.

It seemed like entering a tomb to Gail; and when she found herself in the library her sensations were those of one who stands in the presence of the dead. She closed the door and made sure that the curtains covered every inch of the window; then she switched on the light. The somber interior leaped out at them. Gail shivered. Kerry glanced appreciatively around him.

"Hurry with what you are going to do!" Gail whispered

anxiously. "And don't speak so loud! Mrs. Wessels may hear you."

Following one possessed of a "hunch" is a nervous proceeding at best. Gail hadn't the remotest idea what Kerry was going to do now that he was here. Indeed, for a minute or so, it appeared as if Kerry himself hadn't. He stood in the center of the floor, peering about him and frowning at the shadows beyond the range of the lamp. Gail's nerves were on edge. She could not keep still. A feeling of catastrophe took hold of her. She wished Kerry were anywhere but here.

"Oh, do hurry!" she pleaded.

"Don't get excited, old dear."

He went to the table and sat down behind it. So far as Gail could remember the articles upon it were not altered in any particular. Pen and ink, writing pad, the Venetian mirror, and the lens were still there, as they had been when she found Conniston's body forty odd hours before. The two chairs were still drawn up in front of the table, also.

Kerry studied the top of the table, taking care to keep his hands off the polished surface. Then, covering his fingers with a handkerchief, he opened its two drawers. They were stacked with bundles of letters, documents, and notes in the colonel's wretched handwriting, confined by broad elastic bands. Kerry took several packages out of one of the drawers, spread them on the desk, and began to go through them thoroughly. The neatness with which they were arranged suggested Bartlett's methodical hands and Kerry was careful to return each bundle to the drawer exactly as he had found it. He worked swiftly, but the papers were many and nearly twenty minutes elapsed before he got through the first drawer. He finished the second some fifteen minutes later and stood up, frowning.

"Nothing there," he muttered.

"Did you expect there would be?" Gail demanded, fretfully. "Hasn't Bartlett been through them already?"

"There might have been," was the cheerful response. "Don't worry, Gail. There's no one here."

Kerry picked up the Venetian hand mirror, looked at it critically, and put it down again. Then he went to the vault which was some six or eight feet away from the backs of the two chairs drawn up in front of the table, switched on the droplight, and stared at the door earnestly for a moment. From the vault he turned to the fireplace and dropping on his knees poked among its dying embers.

What he expected to find there Gail hadn't the remotest idea and in spite of her fears she smiled as she watched him perform the solemnities of the detective of fiction. But Kerry was too deeply absorbed in his investigations to observe their effect on Gail. Perhaps they were not as unproductive as they seemed and, perhaps, like the detective of fiction, he was concealing whatever discoveries he had made until the psychological moment for their disclosure should arrive. He now commenced a tour of the room and examined minutely each article of furniture in its turn.

By the time another ten minutes had passed Gail was frantic with anxiety. The smallest sound sent a shiver of terror through her and continually she listened for the tread of footsteps in the hall. Kerry's nonchalance contributed to her misery. She felt that she must scream if he did not quickly go.

As a relief to her feelings she began to wander around the room. Thus it happened that presently she stopped by the table. Scarcely aware of what she was doing she picked up the Venetian mirror, stared at it in a puzzled way and started to put it down again. But before she had completed the act she caught the reflection in the mirror and her hand was arrested. Then she stood the mirror on its end, handle up. The corner of the writing pad was reflected in the glass. Her expression enlivened; a look of absorption crept into her eyes.

"Kerry!" she whispered. "Come here—quick!"

He ran to her side.

"Look into the glass!"

He did so.

"What do you see?"

"Figures," he muttered. "Reflected from the blotter. 32—71—49—18, I think they are." He looked at Gail, frowning a little. "It's an awful scrawl. Somebody wrote 'em down quick and blotted 'em quick—see how thick and smeared the strokes are. That isn't the colonel's seven—he put a curl in his horizontal stroke."

Gail had a queer light in her eyes. "What do you think they mean, Kerry?" she whispered, tensely.

For a moment he did not get her meaning; then his dark eyes blazed suddenly.

"Lord!" he whistled. "The numerals of a combination—the vault!"

"If only it should be!" Gail breathed. "We'd have a real clue! Try it, Kerry!"

Kerry bent back the corner of the blotter and neatly tore it off.

"Little bright eyes!" he chuckled. "I came up here to hunt clues and you beat me to it!"

"You shouldn't have torn the blotter!" Gail expostulated. "Bartlett—"

"The devil with Bartlett!" said Kerry O'Neil.

He ran to the vault, spun the dial. If these figures were the combination, as they devoutly hoped, there was no indication as to whether the first turn of the dial should be made to the "right" or to the "left." Kerry turned to the left, carefully setting the 32 to the indicator; then to the right, 71; to the left, 49; to the right, 18.

Would it open? Gail held her breath as Kerry's fingers closed on the handle. It held! There was silence for a moment.

"Try starting from the right instead of the left," Gail said, in a small voice.

Kerry twirled the dial again. His hand was trembling as he turned to the right and stopped at 32; then to the left, 71; to the right, 49; to the left, 18—

Gail endured an agony of suspense as Kerry gripped and swung upon the handle. "Kerry!" she cried. It had turned.

He gave a little shout of triumph and opened the door. They entered the vault.

There were many shelves and drawers, several files, a few account books, and great bundles of documents that probably appertained to the Conniston collection. Gail drew out two shallow trays. They were lined with white satin and they were empty. She looked at Kerry significantly.

"Gone," he said.

Gail nodded. "Of course."

They lingered for a minute or two in the vault, pulling out a drawer here and there—none of them were fitted with locks. Then they went back into the library. Kerry looked at the triangle of blotter in his hand.

"Not so much of a clue after all," he said moodily. "The figures are too scrawly to be recognizable as the handwriting of any particular person. I make the same kind of a '7' myself. Still, it may help...."

Gail wasn't listening to him. Her face had whitened to the lips. She caught him fiercely by the arm.

"Kerry!" she whispered. "There's someone coming!"

They fastened their eyes upon the door. Footfalls, soft and secretive, came from the hall behind it. Gail whirled upon Kerry, pushed him towards the window.

"Go—quick!" she whispered. "The window—it's open!"

He looked at her beseechingly. "I can't leave you—I can't—like this—"

Gail dug her fingers cruelly into his arm. "You must! You promised—you'll make it all the worse for me!"

He hesitated for a moment, his eyes entreating her to let him stay. Then he turned and dived between the curtains. Somehow, Gail got the vault door shut; she hadn't time to turn the handle. The footsteps paused outside the library door. Gail pulled herself together and waited. She could hear the watch on her wrist ticking with incredible loudness. The window curtains grew still again.

The door opened. A man entered. It was Norman Stark.

CHAPTER XIII
Underground

He stopped abruptly when he saw Gail. She stood by the table, one hand resting lightly on it. Her head was tilted a little to one side and her eyes were cool and inquiring in their expression. The light from the lamp brought out all the latent fire in her hair; a faint glow suffused her cheeks.

"It's a trap, after all," she was thinking, bitterly. "Perrin lied to me."

But the trap had been clumsily sprung and the bird had flown—unless Bartlett had netted it outside. He hadn't—she was sure. Kerry had *promised* and he was clever enough to outwit a dozen policemen.

"I must keep him here until Kerry has got away!" she reflected desperately.

The curtains behind which he had disappeared tugged at her eyes like magnets, but she kept her gaze upon Stark. There were suspicion and perplexity in his face. His eyes darted around the room, met hers again. And then she saw that he carried a pistol.

"Are you looking for game, Mr. Stark?" she smiled, in a friendly way.

His heavy face reddened. "I thought I heard someone moving around," he muttered.

"Probably you did. I've been here for some time."

His eyes narrowed. "Are you alone? I thought I heard voices."

Gail laughed. "Voices! Can't you see for yourself?" Then, taking a chance: "Perhaps you heard me talking with Dimity. Won't you put your pistol away?"

Stark dropped the weapon into a pocket. The suspicion lingered in his eyes, however. Kerry must be descending the cliff by this, Gail thought.

"What are you doing here?" he demanded.

"Looking for clues."

Stark grunted sardonically. "Find any?"

"I didn't expect to—you were so careful," Gail drawled.

A tigerish expression leaped into his eyes. "You are still pretending to believe that rot!"

Gail changed the subject. "Perrin told me you were going north."

He calmed down at this. "That was my intention, but I turned back."

"Did you? I wonder why."

Stark laughed unpleasantly. The sound rasped on Gail's raw nerves. He moved towards her with that swift catlike gait by which she had identified him as the man she had seen in the moonlight. The suspicion had left his eyes; their expression terrified her.

"I wanted to see you, Gail Hollister."

She fell back, trembling. His eyes burned and his hands reached out towards her. The strength oozed from her limbs; she could not move. He seemed a mountain of a man bent on destroying her. His hand touched her arm. Ugh! Those hands! That still figure she had found on the floor!

"Mr. Stark!"

"You little peach, you!" he whispered fatuously.

Gail screamed. Not, however, at the touch of Stark's hands upon her arm, but at the sudden appearance of Kerry from behind the curtains. He had not gone, after all! His lean face was white with fury and as Stark whirled upon him, fumbling at his pistol pocket he hurled himself upon the man.

Stark reeled back. He recovered himself in a flash and the pistol leaped into his hand. Before he could use it Kerry struck him savagely on the mouth. Stark dropped the pistol, bellowed with pain, and spat out a broken tooth. He rushed at Kerry who stepped lightly aside. Kerry's fist, cunningly directed, shot out like a ram. It caught Stark on the point of the jaw as Kerry had intended it should. The man toppled back into the grate and lay still.

Gail had backed to the wall near the door. Kerry sprang towards her.

"That beast, Gail! He *touched* you!"

She drew her hand across her eyes. Now that Kerry was here it seemed like an evil dream. He caught her hands and held them tightly and they looked at each other in one of those tender silences that are too precious for speech. Gail quickly realized his danger and broke the spell.

"Oh, do go, Kerry!" she cried. "Someone else may come—"

Gail did not finish. Her eyes, dilated with terror, were staring over Kerry's shoulder.

"Pretty neat, O'Neil. Now put up your hands and keep 'em up!"

It was Bartlett.

He had stepped into the room from behind the window

curtains as Kerry had done a minute or two before. In his hand was a pistol which he leveled at Kerry and his cold eyes flickered a little as they rested on the young man.

"Put 'em up, O'Neil!" he said again.

Kerry obeyed reluctantly. His dark eyes coolly, calculatingly met the deputy's. He did not speak.

"Come towards the center of the room where I can see you.... That's far enough. Stay where you are, Miss Hollister!"

Gail was sick at heart with this disastrous turn of events and she was only too glad to hide her misery in the shadows near the wall. There was silence for a moment and Bartlett surveyed his captive with interest.

"Well, O'Neil, you've made us a lot of trouble. You might as well have given yourself up at first."

"Think of the fun I'd have missed," Kerry drawled.

"Think of the fun you are going to have," Bartlett responded dryly. His words were prophetic. "That was a nasty one you handed Stark."

The latter was showing signs of returning to consciousness.

"It was," Kerry admitted. "There's plenty more where it came from, too."

Gail had got herself in hand again and was thinking rapidly. She had the faculty of grasping all the possibilities of the situation at a glance and she saw a chance whereby Kerry might get away if only she acted quickly enough and Kerry had the wit to follow her.

Stark had left the door ajar. Gail stood well within the shadows beyond the circle of light cast by the lamp and so near the door that without moving she had been able to take the key out of the lock unobserved. Immediately behind her was the light switch. Bartlett stood ten feet or so in front of Kerry. Near Kerry was a chair.

Her plan was to divert Bartlett's attention from Kerry for an instant, and in that instant switch out the light, fling open the door, and hurl herself into the hall. If Kerry was quick-witted enough to topple the chair in front of Bartlett who would be confused by the darkness and the suddenness of it all, and rush after her into the hall, whereupon she would endeavor to lock the library door while Bartlett was tumbling over the chair, her plan might succeed. It all depended on Kerry. There was something about the nonchalant pose of his body that suggested watchful waiting; Gail thought he would seize the first opportunity that presented itself.

"What were you doing here?" Bartlett demanded of Kerry.

"Looking for clues," Kerry responded airily.

"Find any?" Bartlett asked, as Stark had asked Gail five minutes or so before.

"We did, Mr. Bartlett!" Gail said promptly.

The deputy looked at her ironically. "Did you, now?"

"Yes," Gail prattled on. "We found that the Conniston intaglios really are gone!"

"Wasn't that clever of you!" Bartlett mocked.

Gail was watching him like a cat. She saw Kerry's shoulders stiffen a little.

"I thought so, too," she agreed brightly. "Look: we opened the vault!"

Bartlett's head jerked sideways. He saw that the handle of the vault slanted and he involuntarily took a step toward it. His automatic, Gail saw, no longer covered Kerry. Her hand flashed to the switch. The lights snapped out.

"Kerry!" Gail screamed into the flooding darkness. "The chair—trip him—the door!"

She flung the door wide open and, prompted by an instinctive sense of danger, dropped to her knees just as Bartlett's pistol loosed a stream of lead and fire in her direction. With charming inconsistency, it simply hadn't occurred to Gail that Bartlett might put his gun to the use for which it was intended.

But there was not time to be terrified. The thud of a falling chair punctuated the crack, crack, of Bartlett's pistol. There came another thud and an oath; then a stream of oaths. Kerry's body jackrabbited past Gail and she hurled herself back into the hall, swinging the door to behind her. The crack of its closing shook the house. She thrust the key into the lock and turned it just as Bartlett hurled himself upon the door and tugged savagely at the handle. He bellowed at them furiously, and a shot tore through one of the panels and sang past Kerry's head.

"This way—quick!" Gail panted.

Kerry squeezed her hand and they raced to the front door. It was locked and bolted. There was no key in the lock.

"The patio door!" Gail sobbed.

They flew back down the hall. The patio door was open as they had left it, but as Gail thrust her head outside heavy footsteps beat on the terrace and a stout figure rolled out of the gloom. It was Peters, the village policeman. No escape that way! Gail had half expected this, hence her reason for trying the front door first. She drew back, slammed the door to, and bolted it. A weighty body collided with the door; a mighty fist pounded upon it.

"Open up there!" a voice roared.

Gail shrank back, in despair. "I'm sorry, Kerry," she whispered piteously.

He put his arm around her, more disturbed by her distress than by his own plight.

"Never mind, dear!" he said huskily. "You tried darned hard, the Lord knows!" Then his irrepressible sense of humor reasserted itself and he grinned. "You certainly put it over Bartlett, all right!" His face sobered again. "I suppose it *had* to come."

But Gail was inconsolable. Her failure enraged and terrified her. She saw what impended in its darkest colors. Kerry would be arrested, the authorities would look upon the case as closed; the trial would then commence and proceed to its inevitable conclusion. She grew sick with horror at the thought of it.

Voices rang out in the patio. One of them was Bartlett's. The pounding on the door, which had not ceased since Gail had bolted it, went on with fresh vigor. Someone began to hammer on the library door. Stark! was Gail's thought.

"Open up, you fools!" Bartlett roared.

"Might as well get it over with," Kerry growled. He moved towards the door.

Off the hall, near the patio door, was an alcove which Gail had noticed that morning, though she had not inspected it closely at the time. In drawing back from the patio door they had stepped into it. As Kerry started forward, Gail's hand, groping wildly behind her, encountered the handle of another door. She clung to it with the desperation of despair. Hope came to her. The cellars of the Casa de Ayer! She had forgotten them.

"Kerry—wait!" she drew him back into the alcove. "The cellars—there must be a way out!"

He looked at the door doubtfully. "I'd better get it over with, honey. It's coming, anyhow. It'll only make it all the worse!"

Gail turned on him in a fury. "You promised! Are you going back on your word!"

O'Neil muttered beneath his breath and jerked at the door handle. The door was locked, but there was a key in the lock. He turned it and opened the door. A yawning darkness was revealed.

"I'll go down alone," he said. "You've been through enough for one night."

"Don't be an idiot!" Gail said tersely.

Before he could stop her, she had pushed him aside and started down the invisible stairs. He stared after her in bewilderment. She had completely run away with the situation. The positive role he had always filled so gracefully had been taken away from him and he had been given the negative one to do the best he could with. He followed her down, shaken a little.

The pounding on the patio door filled the house with thunder.

Gail had missed the switch at the head of the stairs, but Kerry struck a match and the tiny flame gleamed on the globe of a droplight. Gail snapped it on and the cellar was dimly revealed as a large square apartment with a wood floor. Through the shadows against an outer wall they saw a door. Gail rushed upon it and shook it vigorously.

"It's locked!" she cried with a sob.

"There's a window!" Kerry shouted.

There were two of them, in fact; but they found them unassailably barred. They were caught as neatly as any rat that ever walked into a trap!

Gail felt as if she would collapse. Sheer nerve had carried her this far, but she almost had come to the end of her tether. Kerry had lost his grin, something he rarely parted with for very long, and his face was white and wretched. The action of the last half hour had been so intense that until just now he had not properly realized how seriously Gail had involved herself on his behalf.

"I've got you into an awful mess!" he groaned, running his hands through his hair. "And we haven't accomplished a thing! I should have stayed down on the beach! Why is it I always stew things up so?"

Gail was touched at his misery.

"You couldn't help it, Kerry," she told him gently. This wasn't strictly true, as both of them very well knew.

"You are a dear girl!" he mumbled huskily.

Just then heavy feet trod on the floor above. Bartlett and his men must have got in through a window, Gail thought. She stared around the cellar in despair.

"Look!" she whispered. "Another door! Over there!" Gail swept across the floor, Kerry close behind her.

It was near that corner of the cellar farthest from where they had been standing. The shadows were deep there and a large packing-case partly concealed the door. The latter was unlocked and they entered. Kerry's head struck a droplight. He turned it on and they found themselves in a small, square, windowless apartment with a sound oak floor. The ceiling was cobwebby and the atmosphere was musty. There were several wooden lockers and many shelves upon which stood tall bottles furred with dust.

"Old Conniston's private stock," Kerry commented.

He took a step forward, tripped, and would have fallen headlong if Gail had not caught him by the arm. Glancing down at the floor, they saw the ring of a trapdoor. It was over this that Kerry had tripped. A groove had been neatly cut out of the board beneath it, but the ring had been left upright by the one who had last used the trap.

"A trapdoor!" Kerry muttered.

So well had the trap been fitted into the floor that they had to look closely to find the line of demarcation. If the ring had not been left up, they wouldn't have known the trap was there.

Gail looked at Kerry in silence. Her eyes were startled and questioning in their expression; then, as Kerry bent swiftly and lifted the trap, they filled with a dancing excitement, a sort of ecstasy, and a glowing consciousness of prophecy fulfilled.

She found herself staring down at a ladder that dropped into a fissure in the rock upon which the Casa de Ayer was built. The stench of rotting kelp rose on the salty breath of the ocean and with it came the musketry of the incoming tide.

CHAPTER XIV
Green Lights

Gail saw her own thought reflected in Kerry's excited eyes. "This is the way the man that killed Conniston got in and out of the house!" he cried.

"Stark!"

"If it was Stark."

"Of course it was, Kerry! He came through the grounds, climbed down the summer house trail—that's the quickest way to the beach—and came up through here! He went back the same way." Gail was on fire with the implication she found in their discovery. "Don't you see? Bartlett will have to find a new theory. Dimity is out of it—anyone might have done it! Oh, Kerry, what luck!"

Kerry nodded slowly. "Probably Stark knows of the trap. But so will Dimity. Don't be too sure Dimity is out of it, Gail. He knows a thing or two, I'm positive."

"You seem to have forgotten that Mrs. Wessels and I saw Stark on the grounds!" Gail reminded him impatiently. She refused to admit even to herself that the unfavorable conditions under which she and Mrs. Wessels had seen Stark were reason enough for Kerry's opinion that they might be mistaken.

The murmur of voices in the room above terminated this pointless argument. Gail stared down into the black pit at her feet, shuddering.

"It looks terrible, Kerry. You are not afraid to try it?"

Kerry chuckled, himself again. "Leave it to me, dear." Then his face sobered. "It means leaving you alone," he muttered in troubled tones. "Bartlett will be raging—"

"Let him rage. You promised, Kerry, and you are going!" She pointed to the trap. "This is new evidence. Bartlett has got to consider it. Don't worry about me. I can take care of myself."

His hands fell on her shoulders. He looked at her silently for a moment; then he drew her into his arms. The contact of his body with hers renewed her courage, quieted her nerves. She was like a candle newly lighted at the flame of some inexhaustible torch.

"You are great, Gail!" he mumbled, brokenly. "I'm not worth it!"

Kerry pressed her hands until she could have cried out with

the pain of it. Then he set his foot on the ladder and went down into the darkness. His face flashed up at her before it vanished from sight and she had to press her hands to her lips to stifle the cry that rose to them. She thought of the cavern as some prehistoric monster that had swallowed him up.

He had no matches, the cavern was in pitchy darkness, he knew nothing of the way through it. In terror Gail knelt by the trap and listened. Momentarily she expected to hear a cry and the thud of a fallen body. She heard neither. The small noises of his descent came to her faintly. A match flickered, went out.

"Kerry!" she called.

"All right!" His response came to her clearly. A minute passed.

"Kerry!" she called again.

"All right!" Less distinctly this time.

The noises of his descent grew fainter ... she lost them altogether.

"Kerry!" she called for the third time, as loud as she dared.

If he made reply, she did not hear it.

Voices at the head of the cellar stairs roused Gail to action. Every second she could delay Bartlett and his men would count in Kerry's favor. She sprang up, closed the door, and looked around the cellar for some means of barricading it. Her eyes fell on one of the lockers which Kerry had concluded contained part of Conniston's private stock.

She found it heavier than she had expected, however, and at first she could not move it. But the tramp of feet on the cellar steps spurred her on to fresh endeavor and she tugged at the locker again until her arms threatened to spring out of their sockets. It moved; sluggishly it crawled across the floor. The men were running about in the larger cellar, now, rattling the outer door, shaking the three windows. Every second she expected the grind of the locker on the floor to betray her. Another yard ... another foot.... It was done! Now she let down the trap and turned out the light. There was nothing else she could do. Blindly she groped her way to one of the other lockers and collapsed upon it, physically and spiritually exhausted.

Her body hung limply; she felt weak and ill; a fog of depression rolled over her spirits. The atmosphere of the cellar stifled her. It was like a hand upon her throat.

Suddenly, one of the men in the outer cellar shouted; feet thundered across the floor; a line of light sprang along the bottom of the door and the door was shaken violently.

"Open up!" Bartlett roared. "Or we'll smash it in!"

Gail did not move.

Someone put his shoulder to the door. It creaked and groaned, but the locker did not stir. A body was hurled against it. The locker moved a little and a slit of light showed in the tiny opening that had been made. Again the door was assaulted; and again and again. Each time the locker gave a little until, at last, the opening was wide enough to permit the entrance of a man.

Bartlett was the first inside. The eye of his torch fled around the musty interior, lighted on Gail's head, circled the cellar again. Then it bore down upon Gail, a malignant eye, demanding an accounting.

"Where is O'Neil?" the deputy roared.

Gail shut her eyes against the blinding glare of the torch, pressed her lips thinly together, and said nothing. She was thinking: "Every second will count. They have lights and Stark will be familiar with the cavern. On the other hand, Kerry has five minutes' start and he should be more at home on the beach than they." Yes, he had a chance—if he hadn't broken his leg or his neck. And she prayed with all the intensity of her soul that he had not.

Bartlett seized her savagely by the arm. "You hear me! Where is O'Neil?"

She did not answer. His fingers dug into her flesh like talons of steel.

Stark had just entered, torch in hand. He was swollen of lip and sullen of eye and he glared at Gail balefully. Peters and another man were behind him. Both of them carried torches and the light of Peters' torch circled around the ring in the trapdoor. His shout brought them crowding around him. As he lifted the trap Stark gave a cry of amazement.

"I never saw this before!" he shouted thickly.

So he intended to pretend ignorance of the trapdoor! was Gail's quick thought. But he would, of course.

Bartlett cast the beam of his torch into the black depths at his feet and recklessly dropped down the ladder. Stark and Peters followed close behind him.

Gail dragged herself to the trap and stared down into the cavern below, shivering a little. Stark had vanished behind a bend in the rock wall; but the other two were still in sight and by the light of their torches Gail got a sort of photographic impression of broad shallow steps roughly hewn out of the gray sandstone rock on the right side of the split. They swiftly followed Bartlett around the bend and Gail became aware of the fact that she was alone again.

Just then she remembered her appointment with Dimity in the summer house!

The events of the last hour had been so swift and furious in their passage that she had completely forgotten it. She glanced at her wristwatch. It was midnight. And Dimity had told her to be there at ten! The shooting would have brought him back to the house, running, she reflected. Probably he was upstairs now.

Dimity had intimated that he meant to tell her who had killed Colonel Conniston. But Gail was in a pessimistic mood and as she passed wearily up the cellar steps she had little hope of getting anything of value out of him. Dimity's mind was unbalanced and it was too much to expect that his conclusions would be anything but a reflection of his mental disorder and, consequently, worthless. However, if he did know anything she was going to have it out of him.

In the hall Gail ran into Mrs. Wessels in hair curlers and dressing gown.

"Lor' bless you, Miss 'Ollister!" the housekeeper exclaimed in relief. "Where 'ave you been! Wot is it, dearie? You look that poorly! And it's not to be wondered at, neither! Wot with all this shooting and shouting and men traipsing into a body's bedroom!"

Gail smiled wanly. "I'll be all right presently. Have you seen Dimity?"

Mrs. Wessels stiffened. "That I 'aven't!" she exclaimed indignantly. "And I 'aven't seen this man O'Neil or got 'im 'id in my bedroom as Bartlett let on 'e thought I 'ad, neither!" Mrs. Wessels spread her hands eloquently, almost pathetically. "I ask you, Miss 'Ollister, if it's decent to ask a respectable woman like me if she's 'iding a man in 'er bedroom? ... If poor Wessels 'ad been alive Bartlett would've been 'ash by this, let me tell you!"

"I am sure he would, and deservedly, too," Gail agreed feelingly. "But I didn't mean it that way. Is Dimity in the house?"

Mrs. Wessels was instantly mollified. "I 'aven't seen 'im, dearie. Funny, isn't it? He must 'ave 'eard the shooting and all the racket they was making. I looked in his room, but 'e wasn't there. A funny oddity, Dimity, Miss 'Ollister!"

Gail nodded and Mrs. Wessels gazed at her with kindly invitation in her eyes. Gail longed to throw herself upon the housekeeper's capacious bosom and pour out the tale of her woe. Perhaps she would, later on; but first she must find Dimity. Was he still in the summer house? She had better see.

Gail passed out into the patio, conscious of Mrs. Wessels' eyes following her disappointedly.

She hurried across the patio and came to the path that skirted the top of the cliff. Looking down upon the beach she saw human forms racing along the moonlit sand, and recognized Bartlett, Peters, and Stark. They were stabbing at shadow and crevice with the beams of their torches. Of Kerry she saw nothing whatever and a sigh of relief rose to her lips. He had got out of the cavern safely, at any rate.

Her relief should have risen above every other emotion. But oddly enough it didn't. She was again conscious of that demoralizing sense of disaster which had been with her throughout this tremendous night.

It was suddenly intensified by the sight of Decker stumbling across the patio towards her, his hands still manacled in front of him. The moonlight was full upon the man and Gail stood where she was for an instant, transfixed by the dark malevolence, the insensate rage in his face. Then, with a terror she could not define leaping through her veins, she fled down the path to the summer house.

Just then, far out at sea, a green light flamed. For perhaps three seconds it burned; then it went out to reappear an instant later for another three seconds. Again it flashed out and again it reappeared for approximately the same short length of time.

As she flew down the path, Gail saw the signal—if signal it was. But she was too overcome by her emotions to reflect upon it. Besides, Dimity was in the summer house waiting for her. She could see him sitting on one of the benches, his queer head flung back as if he were counting the stars.

Gail stepped onto the threshold of the summer house, but she drew back as if an invisible hand barred her entrance. Then she went in, her eyes dilated with fear.

"Dimity!" she whispered. "Dimity!"

He did not speak.

"Dimity!" she cried, in anguished tones. "Dimity! Dimity! Dimity!"

Still he did not speak.

Gail put her hand on his; it was as cold as her own. She bent nearer, looked into his face; and then, with a scream, she fell back, white to the lips. Something seemed to snap within her as the cord of a stringed instrument snaps when it is too tightly strung. Red lights blazed up before her eyes. No! they were green lights and they flashed to her messages which she could not understand.

Suddenly, everything around her went black and she pitched forward on to her face.

CHAPTER XV
Gray Tweed

When Gail awoke the next morning the curtains were drawn back from the window and her room was brilliant with sunlight. For a moment she had to close her eyes again, so intense was the white light that played upon them.

She reopened them with a sense of spiritual exhaustion. Into the space of a single hour she had compressed the emotional experiences of a lifetime and she felt as if her return to consciousness were less an awakening than an escape from a place of shadows, weird and terrible, of grotesque and leering faces, into a world that was sane and clean and real. She was exhausted, but her brain was clear and she found herself calmly examining that sequence of events which had terminated with the finding of Dimity in the summer house.

They had brought her back to the Casa de Ayer and carried her up to her room. She had a dim recollection of faces bending over her and of much spirited argument. One of the faces had stood between her and the others, as a wrathful guardian angel might stand. Dear loyal Mrs. Wessels! She had almost seen a flaming sword in her hand! After that there had been hours of nightmare and burning fever and Mrs. Wessels ministering to her continually. Towards dawn she had slept. And now she was awake again.

Her first thought was of Kerry. Had he managed to elude his pursuers? Her impression was that he had. And as she considered the pros and cons of the situation, recalling that the faces Mrs. Wessels had fended off from her had been red with anger, her impression became certainty. But where had Kerry got to? The peninsula was limited in extent. How long could he evade Bartlett and his men?

She began to think of Dimity. The little man's cold white face, his staring eyes, his queer gnome-like head flung back— just as she had seen him in the moonlight—moved across her vision so vividly real that she had to clench her hands and bite her lip to keep from screaming.

It meant, of course, that Dimity had had nothing to do with the death of his master and that Stark alone had conceived and carried out the crime. It meant, also, that Dimity somehow had discovered that Stark was guilty, that it was Stark who had overheard them in the patio, not Decker, as she had supposed, and that Stark had killed Dimity to still his tongue. He had entered and left the house by way of the trap and relocked the vault to create in the minds of the police the impression that the affair was an "inside job." The trap had been accidentally discovered and he had promptly denied all knowledge of it.

"The beast!" Gail cried passionately. Then, gently: "Poor Dimity!"

The door opened just then, putting an end to Gail's meditations, and Mrs. Wessels entered, troubled of face, and laden with a tray from which arose the aroma of coffee.

"'Ow are you feeling, dearie?" she inquired tenderly, over the top of the tray.

Gail wasn't sure just how she felt, but she contrived a smile of sorts. It brought an answering beam to Mrs. Wessels' honest face.

"Oh, better! Lots better!" she cried, a little unsteadily. "I wouldn't have been but for you, though!"

"It wasn't nothing at all, Miss 'Ollister."

The housekeeper set the tray down upon a chair near the bed and took her reward in the form of a warm kiss planted on Gail's forehead.

"It's a pity to wake you at all, after the 'orrible night you've 'ad!" she went on, indignantly. "I 'ad my time to keep that man Bartlett away from you after they brought you in from the summer-'ouse, I can tell you! 'E got a piece of my mind, 'e did. But I can't 'old 'im off any longer. He says 'e's coming up if you are not downstairs in ten minutes. 'Shame!' I said to 'im. 'An' the young lady not out of 'er nightdress! Traipsing in and out of women's bedrooms without so much as a "by your leave" or anything!' But 'e says he's coming so you better get up. This is a real nice grapefruit, Miss 'Ollister, and 'ere's a bit of 'ot toast and a poached egg done soft."

Gail accepted the tray. "You are too good to me, Mrs. Wessels," she whispered. "Tell Bartlett—I'll be done—in ten minutes."

Gail took a spoonful of the sugared grapefruit. She wanted to ask Mrs. Wessels about Kerry ... and about Dimity, but she was afraid to. She was afraid of the truth. There was something behind Mrs. Wessels' tender solicitude that was going to hurt her. Was there no limit to one's capacity for pain?

"Did Kerry O'Neil get away?" she found herself asking.

Mrs. Wessels folded her arms.

"Yes, Miss 'Ollister ... 'e got away."

Gail's heart warmed a little. There was something else, though. She could feel it. The housekeeper seemed to be waiting. Gail nibbled at a piece of the toast.

"Dimity is dead, Mrs. Wessels," she faltered.

"Yes, Miss 'Ollister ... 'e's dead."

Gail was silent for a moment.

"Do you know ... anything about it?"

"Yes.... His 'ead was smashed in with a wrench or an iron bar or something, Bartlett said. Oh, Miss 'Ollister, it was 'orrible! I can't tell you!" Mrs. Wessels' face crimsoned. "If I could get my 'ands on the man that did for 'im!" she cried with a vigor of expression that was a revelation in character to Gail.

"Does Bartlett know who did it?" Gail whispered.

Mrs. Wessels looked down at her folded arms. "He said 'e does, Miss 'Ollister."

"Who did he say—Stark?"

"No, 'e didn't say it was Mr. Stark, Miss 'Ollister."

Gail felt a sudden tightening at her throat. "Who—then?"

Mrs. Wessels put her arm about the girl's shoulders. "Now, don't ask me that, dearie!"

"Tell me!" Gail cried fiercely.

Mrs. Wessels' round face was quivering. "If you will 'ave it, then. Bartlett said it was this Kerry O'Neil. Now don't take on about it, there's a brave girl!"

The housekeeper's arm tightened around Gail and she sat on the bed beside her. But Gail was not "taking on." She was taking it quietly: just a sudden clenching of her hands and a blazing of light in her eyes.

"It wasn't Kerry, Mrs. Wessels," she said calmly. "He couldn't have done it. You've got to believe in him—as I do!" Her voice rose passionately. "I couldn't bear it if you thought he had! You've got to stand by me—I've no one else—" Gail was weeping now.

Mrs. Wessels stroked her hair. "I'm not going back on you, dearie! Don't you say that to me! 'Ave a good cry—it'll do you a world of good. I don't think Mr. O'Neil did it. 'Is 'Ighness, Norman Stark, hasn't explained 'imself yet. It upset me so, Dimity going that way ... that's all. Dimity was queer, but a good sort for all of 'is watching and listening. I'm bothered about 'is urn. We'll 'ave to do something with it. 'E 'asn't a soul."

"We'll have to take care of it," Gail found herself saying mechanically.

She passed the tray back to Mrs. Wessels.

"It's lovely, but I can't eat a thing. Later on, perhaps. Tell Bartlett I'm coming."

As Gail hurried into her clothes she came to a decision. Nothing had been gained by withholding from Bartlett such of the facts of the case as he had not already discovered. Kerry would have been infinitely better off had he given himself up at first, as he had wanted to. Gail arrived at this conclusion, reproaching herself bitterly for advising him otherwise; but Dimity's death had demonstrated its truth, for now Kerry was in worse case than ever. She had determined to tell Bartlett everything: of the history of the Conniston intaglios, of Kerry's interest in them, of his reception by Conniston, of their quarrel, of the motive behind the holdup, and of Dimity's "watching and listening." Just what effect her belated frankness would have on Bartlett she did not know, but Kerry was too deeply involved to suffer by it.

Bartlett was in the library impatiently awaiting her. He sat at the table. Behind him stood Decker, sullen of face. He had got rid of the handcuffs, but his wrists were badly swollen. Stark nonchalantly held his old position by the window. The coolness of the man staggered Gail. He dared to stand there, insolently appraising her! With deep satisfaction she noticed that his mouth was swollen and that he had lost two of his front teeth.

"Sit down," Bartlett said curtly. He indicated one of the two chairs on the other side of the table. Gail obeyed, and clasped her hands.

"Miss Hollister," Bartlett went on, "there is just one thing that will keep you out of jail."

He paused so that his pronouncement might sink in. Gail was not greatly disturbed by it. She had gone through so much that the threat, real as it might be, had not the power to move her deeply. She was curious as to his meaning, however.

"What is that?" she inquired.

"I want the Conniston intaglios. You know where they are."

Gail smiled wearily. "I don't know anything about the Conniston intaglios."

Bartlett's fist crashed down upon the table. "You do! Where are they?"

Gail meditated. Evidently Bartlett had his eye on Stark's ten-thousand-dollar reward. But she suspected that it would take more than the recovery of the intaglios to keep her out of jail, if the evidence against her warranted her arrest. She considered Bartlett narrowly for a moment and was taken by the thought that his faith in his theories had been shaken. This was as it should be, of course. The discovery of the trapdoor must have struck at the root of it.

"I don't know anything about the intaglios," she repeated calmly. "But if you like I'll tell you what I do know. And I'll answer any questions you care to ask me."

"Too bad you didn't do that the other morning!" Bartlett rapped out. "It might have helped you then—it won't now. But go ahead, if it'll relieve your mind."

His indifference was largely assumed, Gail believed. He was really intensely interested in what she had to say. So was Stark. He was leaning forward with a look of anticipation in his gray-green eyes.

Gail began with her friendship for Kerry, proceeded to the holdup and the shock it had been to her, and went on to her arrival at the Casa de Ayer. She described in detail her interview with Conniston, the strangeness of his manner when she mentioned the intaglios, the glimpse she had got of Stark in the moonlight, and the finding of Conniston's body. Then she related how Kerry had come in through the library window and cut the cord which bound the legs of the dead man, and why she had deemed it advisable that he should keep in the background.

By now she had got into the swing of her narrative and with a fine sense of the dramatic she described Kerry's interest in the intaglios, their history, his interview with Conniston, and his return to the estate, where he had passed the night. This brought her to the holdup again, to the motive behind it, and to the character of Kerry O'Neil. With a brilliant stroke or two she depicted that extraordinary young man and prayed that she had secured the effect of reality.

There remained the matter of Dimity. Gail now told of the old man's "listening and watching," of their encounter in the patio, and of his insistence that she meet him at the summer house. She mentioned her belief that they had been overheard and that she attributed Dimity's death to this fact. Stark she did not mention.

When Gail had done there was silence for a moment. Bartlett lit a cigar with maddening slowness.

"Quite a yarn, so far as it goes!" he drawled. "You don't expect me to believe it, do you?"

Gail took it coolly. "No," she said steadily. "I supposed you wouldn't."

Bartlett drew on his cigar. "If you'd told me this before," he said harshly, "we might have got O'Neil and saved Dimity."

Gail whitened. "What do you mean by that?" she whispered. She knew very well what he meant.

"I mean that Dimity got onto something and that O'Neil cracked him over the head to shut his mouth. We'll get him, of course. I've got ten men on the peninsula looking for him. And there's a posse out from the village. If the posse gets him, and there's a rope handy, the Lord help O'Neil! Come through with the intaglios, my girl!"

"Do you mean to say you are going to stand for that sort of thing!" she cried, in a frenzy of terror and fury. "You know what a mob is capable of, yet you sit there—doing nothing! What a cold-blooded beast you are!"

She spun round and rushed towards the window. Stark barred the way.

"Not so fast, young lady!" he jeered. He put his hand on her arm.

Gail sprang back as if she had been stung and Stark's face darkened at the expression that leaped into her eyes.

"Don't you touch me!" she cried passionately.

"Oh, sit down!" Bartlett shouted. "I've got enough men out there to stop that sort of foolery. Sit down and tell me what you've done with the intaglios."

Gail faced him again. "I don't know anything about them! Ask Norman Stark! He can tell you! Ask him about Colonel Conniston and old Dimity!"

Stark's heavy face crimsoned. "By God, girl! Have you the gall to accuse me of that, too!"

Gail whirled upon him again. "Yes, I have! You overheard us in the patio! You came back here—"

"Silence there!" Bartlett thundered. "Stark, shut up! Hollister, sit down! Sit down, I tell you!"

Gail faced him defiantly. She was bewitchingly lovely in her anger. Then she sank down into the chair.

"Stark did not kill either Conniston or Dimity!" Bartlett said curtly. "That is clear to me if it isn't to you. He is more interested in the intaglios than anyone else, that cock and bull yarn of O'Neil's to the contrary. Conniston died without a will. Stark is his sole heir."

"There you have his motive!" Gail cut in wildly.

"Keep quiet!" Bartlett roared. "Dimity was a possibility, I'll admit—but he's dead, and that lets him out. Mrs. Wessels couldn't have pulled the thing off. That leaves you and O'Neil. The evidence is against you and there's enough of it to hang

O'Neil—"

"There isn't!" Gail cried. "Your theories are without
foundation!" (She wished this were true!) "You say Stark didn't
kill Conniston. How do you know he didn't? Has he been able
to prove that he was in Los Angeles when Conniston was
killed? Have you forgotten that Mrs. Wessels and I saw him in
the moonlight? You say he did not kill Dimity. How do you
know he didn't? You and Stark came back last night because
you thought I might lead you to Kerry, but you were not
together all the time. How do you know he didn't follow Dimity
to the summer house?

"You narrow your suspects down to Kerry and me. Have you
forgotten that trapdoor we found last night? Stark—or anyone
else—might have entered and left by way of it a dozen times,
for all you know! Evidence!" Gail cried witheringly. "You are
so sure that Kerry O'Neil is the man you want that you are
blind to everything else!"

Astonished at her own eloquence, Gail delivered herself of
this final shaft and eyed the deputy, flushed and defiant. Her
summary of the defects in the evidence against Kerry and
herself had been shrewd and intelligent; but she was too wise
to believe that these defects were as significant as she had
pretended. Bartlett, she perceived, was unshaken in his belief
that Kerry was guilty; but he was troubled by the growing
complexity of the case.

"Not bad," he drawled presently. "You've forgotten one thing,
though."

"What?"

"How do you account for having the combination of the vault
in your possession? You or O'Neil opened the vault last night."

Gail nodded. "Kerry thought he might find something you
had missed and he insisted on coming up. He was right. We
found the combination."

Bartlett grunted ironically. "Found it, eh! You'll have to do
better than that!"

Gail shrugged impatiently and pointed to the writing pad,
one corner of which Kerry had torn off.

"Someone scribbled down the combination and blotted it on
the corner of the pad," she explained. "I caught the reflection
in this mirror." Gail picked up the Venetian mirror which still
lay on the table and demonstrated how this had come about.
"We tried the combination on the vault door. It opened. Stark
came in, then."

"Where is the corner of the blotter?"

"Kerry tore it off. He still has it."

"He would have, of course." This dryly.

There came an interruption just then. Unnoticed by Gail, Mrs. Wessels had hovered in the doorway throughout this spirited argument. Now she advanced into the room, hands on her hips.

"Wot's all this about a will, Mr. Bartlett?" she demanded aggressively. "I 'eard you say a minute ago—"

"There is no will!" Bartlett rapped out. "Conniston died intestate. Stark is his heir."

"Indeed!" Mrs. Wessels exploded. "Let me tell you there is a will. Or there *was!*" she added significantly.

"How do you know?"

"The colonel told me 'imself! And what's more I saw it lying on that very table!"

Mrs. Wessels said this with a fine sense of effect. Stark took a quick step forward; then he stopped abruptly. Gail felt her pulses quicken.

"Did you read the will?" Bartlett queried.

"Did I—*wot!*" Mrs. Wessels exclaimed indignantly. "The colonel said 'e was providing for Dimity and me. ''Andsomely,' too, 'e said, like the gentleman he was. That was enough for me!"

"Did you witness the will?"

"No."

"Did Dimity?"

"I don't know."

"Do you know to whom Conniston left the bulk of his estate?"

"I didn't ask 'im!" Mrs. Wessels said pointedly.

Bartlett pondered for a moment, frowning. "Queer!" he muttered. Then he looked up at Stark's glowering face. "Know anything about it?"

"Certainly not! Never heard of it!" Stark growled. "The woman is crazy!"

"I am not in the 'abit of telling stories!" Mrs. Wessels declared wrathfully.

"I phoned Prescott, Conniston's lawyer," Bartlett commented thoughtfully. "He said there was no will, so far as he knew. If there is one, it's a holograph, I suppose."

"Yes—if there is one!" Stark sneered.

"There must be—or have been," Gail observed deliberately. "Colonel Conniston wouldn't have spoken of it to Mrs. Wessels unless there was. Perhaps," she hazarded shrewdly, "its contents will explain its disappearance—when we find it."

Bartlett frowned at her and Stark muttered angrily beneath his breath. Further hostilities were prevented by the intervention of Decker. During the last minute or two he had been prowling around the vault. Now he came quickly forward.

"Take a look at this, will yuh, chief!" His nasal voice was shrill with excitement.

He laid something on the blotter in front of Bartlett. Gail saw what appeared to be a tiny fragment of gray tweed cloth such as might have been pulled out of a frayed coat sleeve. Stark came over and Mrs. Wessels edged nearer.

"Where did you find this?" Bartlett demanded.

"Stuck on the edge of the vault door." Decker proudly indicated the place. "There's grease on the cloth—that's what made it stick to the steel."

Bartlett picked up the lens which still lay on the table and examined the fragment through it; then he looked up.

"Someone who wore an old gray tweed coat shut the door and caught his sleeve in it. Mrs. Wessels—"

But the housekeeper was already hurrying out of the room, troubled of face, and shaking her head. Bartlett did not call her back. His expression was no longer cold and assured, but deeply perplexed. He seemed to be groping about in a mental way as a man gropes in a darkened room.

Gail had grasped the situation in a flash.

"The owner of the gray tweed coat with the frayed sleeve, Mr. Bartlett—is he the man you want?"

"Maybe."

"If his name should be O'Neil, the answer would be 'yes,' I suppose?" Gail ventured ironically. "And if it should be—"

"Stark!" the latter supplied venomously.

"Yes, Stark," Gail went on coolly. "The answer would be 'no'?"

Bartlett did not reply.

"It might be Conniston's," he muttered to himself, after a moment.

A minute or so later Mrs. Wessels reentered the room carrying a coat on her arm. The coat was of gray tweed and its sleeves were badly frayed and spotted with grease. Gail stared at it, wrinkling her brow.

And then, as she recognized the coat, a cry of astonishment broke from her lips.

Bartlett took the coat and compared the fragment with one of the sleeves. Both were the same in color and fabric.

"Whose is it?" he said curtly.

Mrs. Wessels' fat face was quivering; there were tears on her cheeks.

"Out with it!" Bartlett roared. "Whose coat is it?"

Mrs. Wessels drew a deep breath. "Dimity's," she whispered. "'E was wearing it the night the colonel was—killed."

CHAPTER XVI
Driftwood

"Dimity!"

Gail found herself whispering the little man's name as she climbed the staircase. The thing was too incredible for belief. There was something uncanny about it. And yet, the fact remained that Dimity had closed the vault door within the last day or two. And if he had closed it, was it not in reason to assume that he also might have opened it? His death had seemed to clear him of all *guilty* knowledge of the affair; but this tiny fragment of cloth from a frayed coat sleeve threatened to involve him deeper than ever. Gail's former suspicions trooped back into her mind. Had Stark and Dimity been in it together, after all? But if they had, why had Stark killed him? And why had Dimity insisted that she meet him at the summer house? And why—

Gail pressed her hands to her head. Her brain seemed to be bursting with its weight of theory and counter-theory. The affair had resolved itself into a giant paradox at which her intelligence beat unavailingly. She entered her room and shut the door. It was good to be alone.

The window was open and the curtains trembled in the cool morning breeze. Stepping onto the balcony she sat down on the low wall that enclosed it. The visibility was crystal clear and she could see down to the end of the peninsula.

Gail began to think of Dimity again. Would the discovery of this fragment of gray tweed shake Bartlett's belief that Kerry had killed Conniston and Dimity? Could he consistently hold to his first theory and suspect Dimity at the same time? Gail did not see how he could until she recalled that she herself had entertained the possibility of Stark and Dimity being in the affair together. Might not Bartlett widen his theory to the extent of assuming that Dimity was an accomplice of Kerry's, and that the latter had killed him because of expediency or greed?

Weary of fruitless speculation, Gail let her eyes rove over the slope. They encountered a group of men who appeared to be methodically combing the sage brush just above the road, a mile or so below the house. Bartlett's men, she thought, with a shiver. He would have others, too, no doubt. She watched them until they vanished behind a rise in the slope.

A little farther on and nearer the top of the slope she saw another group of men, similarly engaged, but less methodical in their operations. This would be the posse of which Bartlett had spoken. She had a terrifying vision of Judge Lynch enthroned, but it passed quickly. Bartlett was hardly the man to stand for that sort of thing.

Gail was about to reenter her room when a small screwed-up package of paper lying on the floor of the balcony within the shadow of the wall attracted her attention. Picking it up, she was astonished to find herself looking at a crumpled envelope with Kerry O'Neil's name and Los Angeles hotel address typed on it. The envelope was weighted. She opened it and a small key and a triangle of blotting paper fell out. A bit of paper, neatly folded, was also enclosed. There was writing on it. She opened it with trembling fingers and read:

"Don't worry. I'll look after myself.
Love to you—and Bartlett.

K."

Gail pressed the note to her lips and laughed and wept with joy. Kerry had crept back in the small hours of the morning and tossed it up on to the balcony! He had risked his liberty to assure her that he was safe! What a reckless, lovable mortal he was! The key, she supposed, belonged to the handcuffs Decker had had to have filed off his wrists. Gail looked at the scrap of blotter thoughtfully.

"I suppose I had better give it to Bartlett," she muttered. "He may be able to identify the handwriting."

She went downstairs. Bartlett was just leaving the house, accompanied by Decker. To the latter Gail gravely presented the key. The scrap of blotter she handed to Bartlett. He studied it for a moment, in silence, then he looked at Gail sharply.

"Where did you get this?"

Gail told him, saying nothing of the note.

His face darkened. He seemed about to speak. Instead, he thrust the scrap of blotter into a vest pocket, and started for the door.

"Mr. Bartlett."

"Well?"

"Are you still of the opinion that Kerry O'Neil killed Colonel Conniston and Dimity?"

"Why shouldn't I be?"

And with this Bartlett passed on.

Stark had disappeared and Mrs. Wessels was bustling about in her kitchen. Gail looked dismally around her, depressed in spirits. She had undertaken to prove Kerry's innocence by establishing Stark's guilt, but apparently he was still as deeply involved as ever. She did not know where to begin or which way to turn; whether to seek outside advice or to rely upon herself alone. A horrible sense of futility crept upon her and she faced the day and its burden of inactivity and suspense with dread, completely at a loss to know what to do with herself. Catalogue work, in her present mood, would be unendurable.

And then she thought of the secret passage by means of which Kerry had escaped from the Casa de Ayer the night before. Her spirits rose. She would explore it and see where it led to.

"I'll need a light," she reflected.

Bartlett's overcoat hung on the hallstand near the door. An electric torch protruded from one of the pockets. Her eyes danced as they fell upon it.

"How nice of him!" she whispered.

A quick glance around, and Gail had deftly possessed herself of the torch, tingling delightfully with a sense of guilt and daring. She ran softly to the cellar door and paused for an instant, listening. Then she fled down the steps, preceded by the light from the torch, and passed into the smaller cellar. The trap was open.

As she bent over it, flooding the cavern with light, the dank breath of kelp and salty sea and the remote musketry of the surf brigades rose to meet her. Not a gleam of sunlight was visible. The entrance of the cavern must be some little distance away, she reflected.

Examining the upper reaches of the place by the light of the torch, Gail saw that the steps were hewn out of the north wall which sloped steeply to the slanting bottom of the cavern, some thirty feet below. The south wall dropped with a marked incurve so that the bottom of the cavern was considerably wider than the top. The opening below the trap was oblong; perhaps some twelve feet in length and eight in width. From where she stood Gail could not tell whether the cavern extended straight beneath the patio to the beach or not. She suspected that it didn't.

The character of the place caught her imagination and she realized how strongly its possibilities as a secret exit must have appealed to the romantic instincts of the old-world aristocrat who had built his home on top of it.

Not without trepidation, Gail cautiously let herself down the ladder into the mouth of the pit. She found the top step with her feet and her hand encountered a line of rusty cable which was pegged to the gray sandstone wall. The cable seemed fairly solid and using it to steady herself, she carefully began to descend the rough-hewn steps, swinging the light beam ahead of her.

Gail had gone but a short distance when the wall swung sharply to the right and she found herself in a large vaulted chamber that reechoed thunderously with the musketry of the tide. She peered around her breathlessly, overcome by the weirdness of the place, and led on by the exploring beam of the torch to fresh exclamations of wonder.

Continuing, she found the descent easier, and she quickly reached the sloping bottom which was covered with sand and pebble and small boulders. As she picked her way down the treacherous floor she thought of Kerry escaping along it at midnight with nothing but matchlight to guide him, and she prayed that his gift for extricating himself from impossible situations had not deserted him.

The chamber ended in a narrow passage, the straight gray walls of which rose some forty feet above her. Gail had followed the passage a short distance when it turned abruptly to the left and she saw an oblong of brilliant sunlight ahead of her. The walls grew damper. Garlands of dried kelp brought in by the summer high tides crackled beneath her feet. Sand fleas burrowed before the flare of the torch and the boom of the surf grew louder. A minute later she passed out onto the beach.

The mouth of the cavern was a mere slit in the face of the rock, indicative of anything but the remarkable natural chamber behind. It was a hundred yards or so north of the patio. Gail had never been on this part of the beach before, her several excursions to the shore all being below the house, and she looked around her with fresh interest.

She was in a small cove rather completely cut off from the beach on each side of it by protecting arms of rock which jutted out into the ocean. These arms of rock, some fifteen feet in height, were not unscalable; nevertheless, they presented a definite barrier to anyone who might wish to reach the cove.

The cliff was over a hundred feet in height at this point and dangerously concave near the top, the base having crumbled away due to the action of the elements, so much so, indeed,

that the bottom of the cliff and a narrow strip of the beach
adjoining it could not be seen from the top. Near the center of
the cove and against the base of the cliff was a flat outcropping
of rock, and upon this rock was a huge pile of driftwood.

Gail approached the pile curiously. She had come within a
yard of it when she tripped and would have fallen had she not
quickly recovered herself. Looking down, she saw a four-gallon
oil can almost completely buried in the sand. It was over this
that she had stumbled. She took hold of the handle and to her
surprise found that the can was full—of coal oil.

Her curiosity deepened and she looked at the driftwood
thoughtfully. It had been piled recently and judging from the
can of coal oil a fire was intended. But why should anyone go
to the trouble of preparing for a fire on this isolated part of
the beach? Gail didn't know and she wanted to rather badly.
There was something about this pile of driftwood that teased
and eluded her, that touched but did not awaken a latent chord
in her memory.

And then a voice hailed her.

"Well, what do you make of it?"

Gail whirled on her heel.

Perrin, the reporter, stood behind her.

CHAPTER XVII
The Man Hunt

Gail had not spoken with Perrin since they had talked together in the museum two days before, and she had not seen him since the inquest. He had led her to believe—presumably at Bartlett's instigation—that the latter, his men, and Stark were leaving the Casa de Ayer the previous night. And while Kerry, having recklessly stepped into the trap, had tempestuously stepped out of it again, her feelings towards Perrin were anything but amicable and she felt that she ought to treat him with the contempt she thought he richly deserved. But Gail had grown wary of late. Perrin might be persuaded to help her; she had better not be too severe with him.

"I don't know," she said, eyeing him coolly. "Where did you come from?"

He nodded towards the spur of rock on the south side of the cove. "I was going back over there. I came through the cave. Queer place, isn't it? Like an old-world castle. It'll make good dope for the *Blade*."

Gail's eyes sparkled. "Well," she said, "if it makes good copy—that's the important thing, I suppose."

Perrin reddened. "Rub it in!" he mumbled. "I don't blame you. Bartlett had a hunch O'Neil might turn up if he thought the coast was clear and he picked me for the job. He thought you'd have more—confidence in me than you would have in anyone else."

"Quite a compliment to you," Gail murmured.

Perrin shuffled miserably. "It was a rotten thing to do, in a way. But—we all thought O'Neil guilty. We still think so—especially after last night."

Gail changed the subject. "I wonder who piled that driftwood there. It seems such an odd place for a fire."

Perrin nodded, vastly relieved at the turn in the conversation.

"That's what I thought. It's quite a climb over the rocks, whichever way you go. The wood is bone dry and there's a can of coal oil. Whoever built it must want a devil of a big blaze. It would make a great signal on a dark night."

"Signal," Gail echoed. "A signal."

The word found sympathetic response in her memory, but the association of ideas she wanted eluded her.

Perrin leaped at the possibilities of the idea.

"That's it!" he cried, excitedly. "It's just the place for a signal fire! The driftwood can't be seen from the top of the cliff and I don't suppose people come around here much during the day, or ever at night. Look at that ledge, and notice the incurve of the cliff. The ledge would raise the fire above the beach, the in-curve would reflect the blaze back on itself! It would be seen for miles out to sea!"

Gail looked at him silently for a moment. Or rather, she set her eyes upon his honest face: she was looking back into the fastnesses of her own mind. Perrin seemed to sense that she was striving to recall something and he waited expectantly for her to speak. Quite suddenly, Gail had what she was seeking. Green lights! Merely green lights. What could they have to do with the affair at the Casa de Ayer?

"Someone was signaling last night!" she cried breathlessly. "At least, I think—no! I'm *sure!* I saw three green flashes, one after another."

"What time?"

"Just before I found—Dimity!"

"Midnight," Perrin muttered. He looked doubtfully at the heap of driftwood. "I wonder if they were signaling to whoever built this—it hasn't been fired yet."

"Perhaps a fire meant 'safety'; no fire, 'danger,'" Gail suggested.

Perrin slapped his thigh. "Bootleggers!" he shouted. "I'll bet my hat! They saw Bartlett and his men nosing around and they were scared off."

"But they wouldn't run liquor in here," Gail objected.

"No, but they might signal from here that it was safe to run it in somewhere else! Down towards the point, perhaps."

Gail nodded, her interest gone. She could not understand why she had thought that the driftwood or the green lights might be connected with the affair at the Casa de Ayer. Perrin tempered his enthusiasm to her changed mood.

"A lot of stuff has come in around here lately," he went on. "Right under the noses of the revenue men, too. Maybe I'll get a write-up out of it."

He paused, aware of her lack of interest, and glanced towards the south arm of the cove.

"I was going back that way. Do you want to return through the cave?"

"It doesn't matter. I'll come with you."

They walked to the spur of rock in silence. Gail was thinking and Perrin helped her over the barrier without comment. When they were down on the other side Gail turned on him suddenly.

"I suppose," she said, "you believe that Kerry O'Neil killed Dimity?"

"Bartlett thinks so."

"Don't you ever think for yourself?"

Perrin reddened. "What else do you expect?" he demanded petulantly. "If O'Neil killed Conniston, and Dimity knew this, O'Neil had the strongest of motives for finishing him, too. Lord! I wish you hadn't asked me!" Perrin groaned miserably. "I've got to look at the facts as they are. You would, too, if you weren't in love with him. Can't you see O'Neil is using you? It won't help him, either. They'll get him—bound to! And he'll hang on the evidence!"

Gail was undisturbed by this outburst.

"How do you account for that fragment of Dimity's coat sleeve which Decker found on the vault door?"

Perrin shook his head. "I can't—unless he and O'Neil were in it together, and O'Neil killed Dimity because he didn't trust him."

"But if Kerry killed Dimity he must have done so *before* he came up to the house with me," Gail went on. "He couldn't have done it afterwards—Bartlett and Stark and Peters were too close behind him."

"I know."

"Then he must have killed Dimity while I was with him," Gail said deliberately. She paused; her eyes, wide and deep, questioned Perrin gravely. "That would make me an accessory to the crime, wouldn't it?"

Perrin whitened a little. "I've been thinking about that, too," he mumbled.

"And you believe—"

"I do not!" he shouted furiously. "I don't give a damn what Bartlett says! You couldn't have been in on it!"

Gail smiled triumphantly. "Then Kerry O'Neil couldn't have, either! And if he didn't kill Dimity he didn't kill Colonel Conniston!"

Perrin shook his head. "No," he said doggedly. "O'Neil is guilty. I'm sure of it. There's something wrong somewhere, though. The pieces don't fit."

He thought for a minute as they proceeded along the beach. "Tell you what I'll do. I've got a hunch there's something behind these killings that Bartlett hasn't got onto. What it is, I don't know. Maybe Stark is the man we want, after all, instead of

O'Neil. Mind, I don't think he is—but I'll watch him for a day or two and I'll try to get on to your viewpoint. Will you do something for me?"

"What?" Gail asked quickly.

"I am going to stick down here for my paper until the case breaks. If you know anything, or get onto anything, give me the first shot at it."

"I will indeed!" Gail cried. She was delighted at her small success.

They returned to the Casa de Ayer by way of the summer house trail, discussing the case with an air of detachment which lent itself to a better understanding of their respective points of view. Perrin had a flexible mind and Gail had high hopes of completely winning him over.

Mrs. Wessels met them in the patio. She responded to Gail's anxious inquiry as to whether Kerry had been taken with a decisive shake of her head.

"Not as I've 'eard, Miss 'Ollister. But there's a gentleman waiting to see you in the sun room. And a fine gentleman 'e is."

"Who is it?" Gail asked.

"'E wouldn't say."

Curious as to who it should be, Gail first returned the torch to Bartlett's overcoat pocket; she then proceeded to the sun room. On the threshold of the room she stopped with a cry of delight and surprise. Then she rushed towards the slightly built elderly man with the neat brown beard and the jovial intelligent eyes, who was coming towards her.

"Dr. McEwan!" she cried, enraptured.

"My dear Gail!"

The director of the Westcoast Museum took the girl's hands in his. His brown eyes were smiling, but they were troubled and questioning, too. For a moment Gail was too overcome to speak and when she found her voice it was husky with emotion.

"You don't know how glad I am to see you!" she cried.

Dr. McEwan smiled whimsically; then his kindly face sobered a little.

"I have come to look after you, my dear. By all accounts you need someone. What have you been doing with yourself?"

Gail laughed unsteadily. "Have you seen Mr. Bartlett?"

"Yes. I met him as I drove in. I happen to know Bartlett. He's a clever chap, in his way. Poor Conniston! I've read the newspapers, of course, but I want you to tell me all about it, just as it happened. Every word of it, remember!"

Gail shut the door of the sun room and they sat down together by the broad expanse of window overlooking the sun-bright ocean. For the second time that morning Gail told her story, omitting nothing, not even her love for Kerry. That, of course, was the mainspring of everything she had done. Dr. McEwan listened to her without comment. He was one of those sympathetic listeners who win confidences by the golden quality of their silences.

"You seem to have got yourself into a pretty mess, my dear," he smiled, when she had finished.

"I couldn't have done anything else, Dr. McEwan."

His eyes twinkled for a moment. "Well, you might have done nothing at all." He sobered again. "This man O'Neil, Gail. You don't know much about him—neither do I. He's had rather a spectacular career. Are you sure—are you quite sure your feelings for him—"

Gail cut him short. "Don't—please! There'll never be anyone else! I've known it from the first! I couldn't have done what I have if it weren't true!"

There was such a wealth of feeling in her voice that he looked at her in surprise.

Her eyes widened with distress. "You are not going to tell me you think as Bartlett and Perrin and the others do!" she pleaded. "I don't think I could stand it—if you did—"

He patted her on the shoulder. "Now, now, Gail. You must brace up. I'm not going to believe anything about anybody until I've looked around for myself. Dear, dear! I never expected to turn detective, but one never knows! Sometimes the lay mind gets a different angle of a case. You must face the facts, though—whatever they are. You don't like Stark?"

"He's a beast!"

McEwan nodded. "Well, perhaps he is. Are you and Mrs. Wessels sure it was Stark you saw in the moonlight?"

"Quite! You may ask Mrs. Wessels."

"Very well. I shall start with the assumption that Stark was here the night Colonel Conniston was killed."

"If he was here, he killed Conniston; and if he killed Conniston he killed Dimity!" Gail cried.

"Not so fast, my dear. We must prove one thing at a time."

Dr. McEwan stood up.

"I shouldn't be surprised if everything turns out happily," he said, with a twinkle. "Bartlett gave me permission to nose around—he really wants to solve the thing, you know. I think I shall begin in the library—that is where it happened.

"No, don't come with me," he went on, as Gail rose to her feet. "I want to go about it in my own way. I'll have a chat with Mrs. Wessels and Stark. And I'll take a look at that cave and that pile of driftwood. There's Dimity, too. All of you have the advantage of me there. Still, one can never tell. Brace up, my dear—and don't worry."

Dr. McEwan strolled out of the room, fingering his neat brown beard.

Gail felt as if her burden of responsibility had been cut in half. There was something so splendidly dependable about Dr. McEwan, so fine and good and true. His reputation as an archeologist was worldwide; he had that quality of imagination which illumines the sciences with the torchlight of art. Gail expected much of her director, Dr. McEwan.

The afternoon passed, night came on, and Kerry O'Neil had not been taken. Throughout the day, all over the peninsula, there had been unceasing activity on the part of Bartlett and his men. At the house, cars roared up and down the drive. Bartlett frowned and Decker scowled. An atmosphere of uncertainty settled upon the Casa de Ayer, haunted its dark-timbered rooms, variously affected those who entered and left its portals.

Dr. McEwan pursued his investigations unobtrusively and without comment ...

All night Bartlett's men searched the peninsula, stabbing the depths of gully and cavern with the slanting beams of their torches, but when morning came O'Neil still was at liberty.

It was incredible to Gail. The peninsula was limited in extent; Bartlett had thrown a cordon of men across it to prevent Kerry's escape to the north; more men had combed every inch of it; and beyond the point and on each side of the peninsula the ocean presented an impassable barrier. Where, then, had Kerry managed to hide himself?

At first Gail had been overjoyed at Bartlett's discomfiture, but as the second day wore on her delight was tempered with uncertainty, then with apprehension; and finally, there still being no word of Kerry, she found herself in terror. She imagined him lying at the bottom of some hidden gully with a broken leg. Or perhaps he had fallen over the cliffs, been killed, and his body been carried out by the tide. Dr. McEwan thought differently, however.

"No, no," he said, when Gail had expressed her fears to him. "That young man of yours has too much imagination to let himself fall over a cliff in the dark. He'll turn up before long. Bartlett is convinced he is still on the peninsula."

"But they've looked everywhere!" Gail objected.

McEwan smiled. "Trust your Kerry, my dear, and don't worry. He's probably right under Bartlett's nose."

And with this Gail had to be content.

Dr. McEwan, indeed, was the only undisturbed member of that considerably augmented household. (Bartlett, Decker, Stark, and McEwan had all taken up quarters there—much to Mrs. Wessels' disgust. The Gills had gone back to Los Angeles, but were to return for the inquest for Dimity's death the next day.)

Bartlett maintained his cold, humorless front, but behind it was anxiety and seething fury. The morning papers had panned him severely for his conduct of the case and he had whipped his men up to a frenzy of effort. Gail kept out of his way as much as possible, for she realized that he might take it into his head to arrest her at any moment.

Stark was sullen and restive and inclined to resent McEwan's presence. The latter, however, professed to be unconscious of the attitude of his host. He pursued his investigations calmly and skillfully questioned whom he chose.

Suspicion, unrest, tense expectancy gathered in the Casa de Ayer like thunderheads in a summer sky. Keen-eyed reporters prowled around the place, bared the innermost recesses of cupboard and closet, questioned all and sundry. The house was in turmoil.

Still no word of Kerry. It was rumored that Bartlett had sent for bloodhounds. Gail was frantic when she heard it. The rumor was denied, however.

Perrin, the reporter, was away most of the day. After dinner he returned and Gail ran into him in the patio. His face was flushed with excitement.

"What is it?" she whispered.

"Where can we go? Is McEwan around? I've got on to something!"

Gail hurried him into the sun parlor and there they found Dr. McEwan sitting by one of the windows looking out across a sunset sea of mauve and gold, of cerise and blue, and flaming orange. He looked up with a smile as they entered. Gail had introduced Perrin to him the day before. They were familiar with each other's purpose.

"Hello, there," he said.

Gail shut the door, pushed Perrin into a chair, and dropped

into another herself.

"Mr. Perrin has got something to tell us!" she announced breathlessly.

The young man grinned. "I don't know that it amounts to much, after all, sir."

"Let us hear it, Perrin."

"Miss Hollister seemed to think that Stark knows more about the death of Conniston than he had admitted to," Perrin began. "I didn't think so, myself, but I thought I'd make one or two inquiries down at the village. Now Stark has a gray sport roadster—one of those high-powered Druids—and I figured that if he was down here the night Colonel Conniston was killed he came in his Druid. You don't see many of them on the road and it occurred to me that if Stark had driven through the village that night—or morning—some late bird might have noticed the car.

"I went to the garage first—there were half a dozen men hanging around the office. They were talking cars, of course—you'd think there wasn't anything else to talk about these days—and I dropped in a word or two about the Druid models. That got them going on Druids. Then I switched to the Conniston murder.

"Nothing came out for a while. In fact, I didn't expect anything at all—it was just a shot in the dark. But shortly one of the boys said that a man by the name of Bill Dale saw a Druid sport roadster roar through the village the other night—or morning. I could hardly believe my ears at first. Then I inquired about Bill Dale and finally located him in the barber shop.

"Dale is a sullen, boozy cuss and I couldn't get him to talk for a while. At last he loosened up and told me that he had been out looking for a drink—around one A.M., I guess, the morning Conniston was killed. He got his drink—two or three, perhaps—stuck around the booze shanty for a couple of hours or so, and came out onto the main street. And then and there he saw the Druid scorch past. It was about three, now. I gave him a couple of dollars and he loosened up again and told me some more.

"A man by the name of Burke lives in the village. He owns an ancient Ford which he parks on the street near the hotel day and night when he's not using it. Burke's Ford has a ripped top that flaps in a funny way—it's the village joke—everybody knows it. Now Burke was playing poker in Sullivan's pool room all of the night Colonel Conniston was killed and he and the men he was with swear he didn't leave the table between nine P.M. and four A.M. But Dale went out for his drink about one A.M. and he swears he saw Burke's Ford rattle off down the street in this direction. Remember, this happened two hours *before* he saw the Druid.

"I looked up Burke next. He doesn't amount to much, either—same type as Dale. But he claimed that his Ford was used by someone that night—or morning. He's a crank on his gas cost. The day before, he'd been on a fishing trip and when he got home he had taken a note of his gas consumption and his mileage. The next morning he found that his speedometer registered five miles more than it had the night before. It is just five miles from here to the village and back." Perrin looked at Dr. McEwan with a grin. "That's all, sir."

There was silence for a moment. Gail was trembling with excitement, but she waited for McEwan to speak. Perrin, notwithstanding the casual manner of his recital, had an air of achievement.

"And a good deal, too, I should say," McEwan commented. "You have done pretty well, young man."

Gail could restrain herself no longer. "*Now* are you convinced that Mrs. Wessels and I saw Stark in the moonlight?" she cried triumphantly.

"I am!" Perrin burst forth.

McEwan chuckled. "We mustn't forget that there are other Druid cars on the road and that one of them may have been driven out in this direction about the time Conniston was killed. The road is closed further on, I understand, but the driver of the car may have got onto it by mistake."

"I never thought of that!" Perrin exclaimed.

"However," McEwan went on, with a twinkle, "I rather think it was Stark's car that the man Dale saw."

"You have found something yourself!" Gail joyously accused him.

Dr. McEwan took a large envelope from an inner pocket and drew out of it a sheet of carbon paper of the letterhead size. He held the carbon up to the light and Gail saw that it had been used but once, and upon a typewriter.

"I found this in the drawer of Colonel Conniston's library table along with other writing materials. Bartlett seems to have missed it. There is a small portable typewriter in a case on the floor near the table. Conniston's handwriting was almost illegible and he seems to have used a typewriter for all of his correspondence, keeping a carbon copy for his files.

"The letter which appears on this carbon was written to

Norman Stark on the 20th of August—Conniston died around midnight of the 23rd, or very early in the morning of the 24th. The impression is intact—probably it was the last letter Conniston wrote. I read it from the carbon paper and it interested me intensely. I looked for the copy on the file, but I could not find it, though copies of other letters to Stark were there. Here is a copy I made myself from the impression."

McEwan took a sheet of notepaper from the envelope and handed it to Gail. Perrin glanced over her shoulder. They read:

NEPHEW:
I have definitely made up my mind in this matter. If you wish to come down on the 23rd or the 24th and go into it again, as you suggest, you may do so. But I warn you that nothing you may say will have the slightest effect upon the decision I have come to.
                          PHILIP CONNISTON.

Perrin whistled. "Short and sweet, eh! Get the force of that 'Nephew'!"

McEwan nodded. "They were not on very good terms, I understand."

"What was the trouble?"

"Stark's morals, I believe. Conniston was rigid on that point."

"Do you suppose it refers to Conniston's will?" Gail asked thoughtfully.

McEwan meditated, stroking his beard. "I think it does. Judging from the wording of this letter there was other correspondence about the matter, whatever it is. But none of it is on file."

"The will is gone," Gail said quickly. "So are the intaglios. Is there any doubt in your mind now that Stark took them and that he killed Colonel Conniston and Dimity?"

McEwan replaced the carbon and the copy in the envelope and returned it to his pocket. He looked at Gail whimsically!

"I understand your feelings for O'Neil, my dear, but I wish you would try and take a more objective view of the case. We now have damaging evidence against Stark, Dimity, and O'Neil. For instance, if Dimity is innocent, how did that fraying of his coat sleeve get caught in the vault door? To me none of these men are guilty, for the simple reason that any one of them may be guilty. We can theorize endlessly, of course. But what we want is proof."

"A case of take your choice," Perrin muttered.

"Precisely. I wish O'Neil would give himself up."

"Kerry didn't do it," Gail said simply. "And Stark did. I can feel it."

"I hope O'Neil didn't, too, my dear; but don't depend on intuition too much. I think we had better keep what we have discovered to ourselves for a day or two. Bartlett believes that Stark is innocent. I don't want him to change his attitude towards Stark—just yet."

"How about that rattletrap Ford Dale saw heading this way?" Perrin demanded suddenly. "Do you suppose there is anything to it?"

McEwan grew thoughtful. "I don't know," he said. "There are so many loose ends sticking out of the case that one is at a loss to know which are connected and which are not. That pile of driftwood and those green lights that Gail saw, for instance. Better make a few more inquiries down at the village, Perrin."

They talked a little while longer; then Doctor McEwan returned to his investigations and Gail went up to her room. There was still no word of Kerry O'Neil.

CHAPTER XVIII
Suppressed Evidence

The search for Kerry O'Neil went on through the night.

Gail got little sleep. She imagined him in a dozen fearful situations: alive but maimed; broken and dead; perishing for lack of food; carried out to sea. Hope would come to her sometimes and she would steal out of bed to the window and peer into the white night, praying that he had been found as earnestly as she had previously prayed that he might not be. But always the activity on the peninsula continued unabated; car headlights slashed white lanes through the night, torchlights stabbed at shadow and gully and cavern. If anything had happened to him she felt that she would die.

Dawn found Gail sitting by the window. Her eyes were tired and anxious; the color had gone from her cheeks; she was weary in body and spirit. The sun touched her hair and a faint glow relieved the pallor of her face. Presently, she heard Mrs. Wessels moving around below, whereupon she passed into the bathroom and filled and got into the tub. The cold water refreshed her; she dressed quickly and went downstairs. Mrs. Wessels was in her kitchen. She greeted Gail tearfully and tenderly.

"They 'aven't got 'im yet, Miss 'Ollister," she went on. "But don't you be aworriting about 'im, now, 'E'll be all right. Turn up like a bad penny, 'e will."

Gail was on the verge of tears herself and she could only nod her head despondently. Mrs. Wessels perceived her distress and pointing to a bronze vessel which stood on the kitchen table near the butter dish, turned to matters less intimate, if equally uncheerful.

"There it is, Miss 'Ollister," she said soberly. "Dimity's urn that's got 'is dead wife's ashes in it. I found it in 'is room last night. Wot's going to become of it is more than I know."

Gail hastily retrieved the urn from the breakfast miscellany and examined it with respect. The vessel was of bronze, in shape like a bulging vase; it had two curved handles and a solid base of the same metal. There was no inscription on it. The urn was effectively turned and Gail judged that it had cost Dimity a good deal. What a queer whim to indulge! And how he must have cherished the memory of his dead wife! Her eyes grew dim at the thought. She put the urn down on a chair.

"Hasn't Dimity anyone at all?"

"Not a living soul!" Mrs. Wessels declared solemnly.

Gail thought; then her face lighted up. "They are usually kept in mausoleums," she said. "But sometimes people carry them around with them; and sometimes they seal them up in niches in rocks and cliffs where their loved ones would like them to be. I know just such a place. I am sure Dimity would like it, too. Perhaps I ought—I wonder if Stark—"

"I shouldn't ask 'im! It isn't 'is corpse!" Mrs. Wessels said stoutly. "I wish you would put it away, too. 'Aving it around makes me think of poor Wessels in 'is corfin."

"I believe I will," Gail whispered, more to herself than to the other.

"You'll need a bit of breakfast first, dearie," the housekeeper observed. "It'll take a stummick for that job.... Wessels never would go to a burial without 'is dinner.... 'Ere's a bit of 'am and a egg. Real nice, too."

And so, after lunch, it being low tide then, Gail found herself approaching Cathedral Rock. She carried the urn wrapped in a clean sheet that made her think of a shroud. An abalone shell which she had picked up on the beach was the only interment tool she had. She had left the house openly, but no one had attempted to stop her. O'Neil was still at liberty and Bartlett and his men were too intent on finding him to pay attention to anyone else. Dr. McEwan had disappeared immediately after breakfast.

As she neared the great rock its atmosphere found response in her being again. There was a quality of stability and permanence about it that soothed her troubled spirit and gave her a sense of peace she had not known for several days. As she stood in front of the rock and looked up at the altar-like effect of its facade, thinking of what she had come to do, it seemed more impressive than ever.

She climbed the tiny steps and curled up on the sun-warmed platform, by the side of the font-like pool sunk into it. A tiny crab scuttled into the dark niche behind. The font was roughly three feet long, eighteen inches wide, and two feet deep. A residue of sand lay at the bottom and it was filled to the brim with seawater as clear as crystal.

Gail proceeded to bail out the font with the abalone shell. It was a lengthy undertaking and she wished she had brought a pan of some sort from the house. At last she reached the sand deposit which proved to be a foot or so in thickness and she pressed the shrouded urn down into it until it was almost entirely covered with sand. Then, using the shell, she scooped up more sand and rock and pebble and completely filled in the font, not, however, without appreciating the significance of what she was doing.

"I'll get Kerry to cement it in someday," she told herself.

She did not think of the corrosive effect of salt water on metal. She did not think of the legal aspect of what she had done. Merely had she a sense of the moral rightness of it: Dimity would wish the ashes of his wife to be at rest and she had made it possible for them to be.

For a little while longer Gail sat on the sun-warmed ledge; then she made her way around the rock, passed from beneath its impressive shadow, and with no definite objective in view continued along the beach towards the point. She had not gone below Cathedral Rock before and she regarded the unfamiliar contour of the cliff with lively interest. The solitude, the harsh beauty of rocky spur and promontory, and the lash of the surf stimulated her. Curiously enough, she began to feel as if she were approaching some sort of a climax.

Presently, there came a bend in the shoreline and the grounds of the Casa de Ayer vanished from sight. The cliffs, rent and caverned here and there, stretched before her as precipitously as ever. On the top of the cliff, just beyond the bend, she saw a thickly wooded grove of well-grown cypress trees. The grove was between the edge of the cliff and the unused dirt road which ran along the top. Near it, a steep trail wound down the cliff to the beach below.

At this point the beach consisted of a flat outcropping of rock, some hundred and fifty yards long. Gail climbed on to this outcropping of rock and had gone about half way across it when she came upon a narrow sloping depression, not unlike the approach to a city subway, which appeared to run down into the bowels of the cliff.

Her curiosity was instantly aroused and Gail had permitted it to lead her down the depression a dozen yards or so when she found herself facing a sort of tunnel blocked by a stout wooden door. There was a small barred opening in the door and through it came the boom of huge volumes of water cannonading in subterranean caverns and the stench of kelp rotting in foul and sunless regions. The door fascinated Gail. Oddly enough, she felt that it concerned her intimately and she longed to see what lay behind it as intensely as Bluebeard's wife must have desired to know the secret of the room in which hung her seven predecessors.

A brass plate with an inscription of some sort engraved upon it was secured to the door. The poor light had prevented her from seeing it at first glance. Above her head hung a tangled mass of ice plant; she moved it aside. A shaft of sunlight fell across the plate and she read:

Here Died
Don Silvestre Calderón
Gentleman of Spain
1780-1846

Gail smiled sadly. This, then, was the pit in which the body of the man who had built the Casa de Ayer had been found. It was said that he had died of a broken heart.

"Gentleman of Spain!" Gail whispered.

What an epitaph! She had heard that Colonel Conniston had had the door put there and had set the plate upon it.

The door was fastened with padlock, hasp, and staple. Involuntarily, Gail's hand went to the padlock and she shook it. To her surprise it came away in her hand and she saw that corrosion had rotted the steel. The hasp and the staple were sound. Evidently, all three had been replaced by Colonel Conniston or Dimity from time to time; the hasp and staple more recently than the padlock, however.

Gail hesitated fearfully for a moment; then she pressed upon the door. It swung inward and she fell back before a blast of air as foul as a chemist's nightmare. She advanced again, put her head inside the tunnel, took a step or two forward, stopped, and peered blindly ahead.

Light crept in at some remote point, saving the cavern from utter darkness; but her eyes were not yet accustomed to it and she could see nothing. Nevertheless, her impressions of the place were alarmingly vivid. The floor of the tunnel sloped steeply; it trembled as if a mighty ram were belaboring it from below. She was deafened by the thunder of the imprisoned waters which rose in terrifying volumes of sound, pillars and clouds of sound that seemed to encompass her with a physical touch, then fell abruptly into awful valleys of silence. Terror struck at her heart. She imagined herself standing on the verge of a bottomless chasm that would presently engulf her. The hiss and bite and snarl of the tortured waters reminded her of wild beasts in a cage. The stench sickened her.

She wanted to get away from the place, but her eyes were becoming accustomed to the dim light and she was determined to have a glimpse of it first. A tiny creature slid over her foot and she jerked up her leg with a scream. Gail would have fled then had not the cavern begun to shape itself out of the dimness. And then the foul horror of what she saw held her to the spot as if it were endowed with an insidious magnetic power.

Some three feet in front of her the tunnel opened into a vaulted chamber as large as a fair-sized room. She had a vision of black rock agleam with the sinister luminosity of pitch, of oily snarling water, of rotting kelp aswarm with flies.

And then she saw a vast shape moving out of the gloom towards her. It was gleaming black and rounded like the body of a bear, but it had neither arms nor legs nor head. The upper portion of its roundness was alive and agleam and aquiver in a horrible way. Her blood congealed in terror as she stared at it. She tried to scream, but her lips and throat were parched. The strength ran out of her limbs as water from a leaky vessel and she would have fallen had not the wall of the tunnel bolstered up her swaying body. With a prayer on her lips, she closed her eyes and waited.

A full minute passed. Nothing happened. Her terror began to lose its sharp edge; some of her strength returned. She found courage to open her eyes and peer into the gloom before her. It still was there, that gleaming monster, limbless, headless, as it had been a minute or two ago; it still moved; the top of it still was alive and aquiver. But it had come no nearer. Then she gave a cry and a little shrill laugh.

It was merely a round rock, smooth and black and gleaming, that she saw. It was balanced on a sort of natural pivot and it oscillated as a pendulum does, with the rise and fall of the tide. On the top of it countless tiny crabs darted back and forth like bits of dark quicksilver. Her imagination had done the rest! Nevertheless, the place was a pit of death and the stink of it was the stink of death. She could imagine a man confined in it for the space of a night and a day going out of his mind.

Gail backed out of the tunnel and drew the door to behind her. With trembling hands she slipped the hasp over the staple and hung the broken padlock on the latter. She exhaled the odor of the cavern from her lungs, inhaled deeply several times, and started up the depression. Then she stopped abruptly.

Two men were standing at the top of the depression, looking

seaward. Gail supposed they had come along the beach behind her—she had not noticed them ahead—and stopped to talk. She was in the shadow and below them, so they did not see her. There was no reason why she should have stopped, so far as she knew; her pause had been involuntary. She was about to proceed when she got a view of their faces.

Gail was not timid by nature, but there was in their expressions a quality of character that made her halt. The smaller of the two was a little rattish man with a narrow face and a crooked mouth. The other was altogether different in type, and it was he upon whom Gail focused her attention.

He had a big, heavy body and a hard, though not unhandsome face, whitish in complexion, and indicative of neither pity nor kindliness. Its hardness was the hardness of cruelty, not of strength of character. Nevertheless, there was a certain sinister elegance about him, a hint of breeding grown rank. He was of that type about which some women can never quite make up their minds, which most men stigmatize as bully and braggart and coward.

Gail frowned in perplexity. She was conscious of sensations she could not define. Something urged her to creep nearer. She did so, noiselessly, holding her breath. A queer tingling excitement thrilled her. Their voices came to her clearly. Suddenly, her body grew rigid. The big man was speaking.

"We shan't be able to bring the stuff in around here, now," he said, in a voice thick with passion. "You'll have to see Swanson to-morrow. Each day costs us another five hundred." He swore venomously.

The little man snickered. "Be dam' glad we don't have to tell what we know!" he cackled. "If that fly cop knew we seen that guy bat the old man over the head we'd be in the soup for fair! What's the name of the lad they are chasin'?"

"O'Neil, I think. I hope they string him up by the neck!"

"Me, too!"

The big man moved on. "Let's get out of this, Daniels. We can't do anything hanging around here!"

The other followed him.

Gail stood erect. Her face was dead white; her eyes were blazing. She could hardly credit the evidence of her senses. These two men knew who had killed Dimity! They had seen it done! And they were going off … about their own affairs! They were not going to speak! They hoped Kerry would be strung "up by the neck!"

For only a moment longer did fury blind her to the counsels

of reason. She grew calm and crouching at the top of the depression stared after the two men thoughtfully.

They knew who had killed Dimity. That much was certain. But they would not admit the fact unless they were compelled to. Gail had no doubt on this point. Their own interests—they were rum runners, she supposed—demanded that they keep silent. But if she informed the police and had the two men charged with knowledge of the crime they would simply deny everything. If she approached them herself they might harm her; they might even do away with her—that little rat of a man looked capable of anything! In any event, nothing would be accomplished.

Gail saw that they were going towards the trail which ascended the cliff near the cypress grove. No doubt they had a car on the road above. She must get its number; otherwise she would have no means of tracing them.

Near the foot of the trail a spur of rock jutted out from the side of the cliff. She must get to this spur of rock and hide behind it while they were ascending the trail. If she waited until they were out of sight the car might be gone before she could get to the top. She must run the risk of them seeing her.

Gathering herself together, Gail fled across the outcropping of rock towards the spur. She had covered about two thirds of the distance when the little man stopped and half turned around. Gail halted, believing herself caught. But the little man merely glanced seaward; he quickly resumed the steep ascent. A moment later Gail was in the shadow of the spur, flushed and breathless, and with a savage joy in her heart.

The two men reached the top and disappeared over the edge of the cliff. Gail ran from behind the spur and started up the trail. It was steep, had been used but little of late, and here and there was actually dangerous. But Gail was intent on getting to the top before the men drove off and she negotiated the more difficult bits with daring unconcern. Reaching the top, she bent low and peered over the edge. The men were getting into a powerful touring car which was parked on the dirt road a hundred yards or so from where she was. At that distance she could not distinguish the license number.

Close by, was the cypress grove. The men were sitting in the car now, staring off down the road. Bending low, Gail flew across the sandy cliff towards the grove and reached it without being seen. The trees extended as far as the dirt road and she swiftly made her way through them, stopping, a moment or so later, on the edge of the bluff. The touring car was just starting off in the direction of the Green Crocodile, but she could see the numbers on the license plate quite clearly.

Gail repeated them to herself over and over until they rang in her ears like a well-loved refrain. She would never forget them.

The touring car vanished in a cloud of dust.

But Gail quickly lost her sense of triumph. She had got the number of the car and by means of it the two men could be easily traced. But what then? She had no means of forcing them to admit what they knew. Her word against theirs would be valueless. Her achievement, promising as it had seemed, really amounted to nothing. Dr. McEwan might be able to help her, but she did not see how he could.

Gail turned back into the cypress grove and made her way through it towards the cliff, coming out upon the edge of the latter a short distance south of the trail. She stood there, on the verge of tears, with the sun-brilliant ocean at her feet. It was a dead world that she saw for hope had risen in her breast and died again.

Suddenly, a voice hailed her.

"Hello, old dear! Wouldn't they take you with 'em?"

CHAPTER XIX
Conspiracy

The voice was ironical in tone. It came from her left. Gail whirled around and saw a girl sitting on a flat boulder in the shadow of one of the largest of the cypresses, a dozen yards or so away. She was smoking a cigarette and regarding Gail with a look of amusement and curiosity in her worldly-wise eyes. Gail returned her frank inspection with interest, annoyed at finding herself under observation.

The girl was a sophisticated-looking creature, extremely pretty in a hard, artificial sort of way. Her hair was bobbed and blond and elaborately marcelled. She wore flesh-colored silk stockings and a bizarrely patterned sport suit which became her well. Her eyebrows were a thin, dark line and her cheeks and lips suggested artificiality rather than art. But her eyes were natural. The only natural feature of her face, indeed. They were blue and brilliant and bold, but they were honest and by their honesty Gail judged her.

"You must have been watching," Gail said calmly.

Cigarette's amusement deepened. "I was," she admitted, frankly. "Couldn't help it, could I? Me up here and you sleuthing them two down there. You'd have done the same yourself, wouldn't you?"

Gail felt that there was more than mere idle curiosity behind the other's interest.

"Perhaps. It doesn't matter. I thought I was alone."

The bold eyes narrowed a trifle. "You look kind of peaked, honey. Better sit down."

The boulder was long and narrow like a bench. Cigarette moved over invitingly. Gail hesitated for a moment; then she sat down. The girl opened her vanity case, an elaborate affair of crocodile skin, disclosing, among other things, a packet of cigarettes.

"Smoke," she said hospitably.

"Thanks, I don't," Gail murmured.

"Too bad. You oughter. 'Smoke Kangaroos and be nonchalant,' as the ad says."

There was silence. Gail waited. She had a queer feeling of expectancy. The silence continued. Cigarette seemed at a loss—probably for the first time in her life.

"I suppose they call you Red," she drawled, at last.

Gail smiled. "Not as a rule."

"They oughter, with that mop. Anyways, I'm going to."

Gail relaxed. "Yes, do. No one ever has." She looked at Cigarette's corn-colored bob. "I suppose you are—"

"Blondy!" the other grinned. "We know each other, now." She flipped her cigarette over the cliff. "Say, Red, you are Gail Hollister, aren't you?"

Gail looked at her sharply. "How do you know?"

Blondy twisted a ring on her finger. Its single brilliant stone was not too obviously spurious.

"I read the papers—and seeing you around here."

"Oh!" Gail had forgotten that she had become a front-page celebrity in picture as well as in prose. "What about it?" she asked curtly.

The bold eyes were inscrutable. "You've had a pretty tough time of it, haven't you?"

"Perhaps."

Blondy looked out to sea. "The odds," she went on slowly, "seem to be against this feller O'Neil the cops are chasin'."

Gail's cheeks began to flame. "Mr. O'Neil had nothing to do with it!" she declared emphatically. "Stark killed Conniston and Dimity! We have got new evidence—" She stopped abruptly, angry with herself for defending Kerry to this girl. Who was she? What right had she to question her?

Blondy sensed the rising storm. "Now, don't you get het up, dearie! You've got to stand by your man! Besides, I'm not saying he done it!"

"You believe he did—like the rest of them!" Gail cried passionately.

"Well, you know what the papers say. You see, I don't know your man—you do! It makes all the dif. Anyhow, you got to stand by him, whether he done it or not. Why don't you tell me about it—about him. It helps to get a thing off your chest."

There was sympathy in Blondy's tone. Gail softened and looked at her steadily for a moment.

"There is something behind your interest," she said candidly. "What is it?"

Blondy waved an airy hand. "Maybe there is, Red. Never mind now. Go ahead!"

Gail pondered. There was something likeable about this uncultivated girl. Perhaps it was her honesty, her complete lack of dissimulation; she did not know. But whatever it was, she was inclined to follow the suggestion, for she longed to unburden herself to one of her own sex—to get it "off her chest," as Blondy put it. She felt that Blondy might understand in a sense that Perrin and Dr. McEwan could not. And how she longed for someone who could believe in Kerry as intensely as she did herself!

So Gail told her new friend what there was to tell, every tiny irrelevant incident of it, with the exception of what she had overheard on the beach twenty minutes before. That only did she keep to herself. The telling was effectively done, with a proper emphasis on the high lights of the affair, such as her love for Kerry and her faith in him, and the mystery of Dimity and the villainy of Stark.

"That's all," Gail said, when she had done.

Blondy looked at her wistfully. "Lord! I wish somebody loved me as you do that Kerry O'Neil of yours!" Then her face hardened rather terribly. "No, I don't! I hate men! They are a pack of wolves, the lot of 'em!"

Gail had her own opinion as to this and expressed it. "Some of them, yes," she admitted cautiously. "Stark, for instance. But—you haven't seen Kerry O'Neil."

Blondy laughed shortly. "I'd like to." Her face softened again. "Maybe you are right. Do you know, Red, I've got a hunch this Kerry O'Neil of yours is straight."

"Have you!" Gail whispered ecstatically. "Have you! I've been longing to hear someone say that! Do you mean it, Blondy?"

"I guess so. I like the way you tell it. But—this bird Stark, now. Are you sure he's the one you want?"

"Certainly! Who else could it be?"

"Oh, I guess you are right. Stark was there, of course; but I just wondered if he done the dirty work. It looks kind of funny finding that piece of Dimity's coat sleeve on the vault door. Still, Dimity couldn't have killed himself."

"I think it was put there," Gail said, giving expression to her latest theory.

Blondy nodded. "Maybe. There's nothing new about a frame-up. I wish you'd tell me the rest of it, Red."

Gail stared at her. "What do you mean?"

"Why did you trail these two men up the cliff?"

Gail frowned. She had not intended to say anything about what she had overheard to anyone until she had seen Dr. McEwan. But as she looked into Blondy's worldly-wise eyes she felt that the girl was on her side and that she wanted to help her.

"Why are you asking me these questions?" she demanded

suddenly.

Blondy looked at her steadily. "I've got a hunch I can help you."

"Help me to prove Stark guilty!" Gail was incredulous.

"Maybe. I don't know. You'll have to tell me the rest of it, first."

Gail fell silent.

"Don't if you'd rather not."

"I will tell you!" Gail cried, suddenly making up her mind. "I never saw those two men until half an hour ago. They were talking—I heard what they said—they saw Dimity killed!" Gail repeated what she had overheard, her voice rising hysterically. "They saw who did it and they haven't told the police—they don't intend to! They don't care if Kerry hangs! You were right—men *are* wolves! I've got to make them tell what they saw, Blondy, and I don't know how to do it!"

Gail began to weep. Blondy put her arm around the trembling shoulders and drew the girl to herself. Blondy's face changed oddly. It seemed to harden and tighten behind its mask of artificiality; her lips drew down into a thin red line.

"So Nick saw who done it!" she muttered.

Gail stopped crying; she flung up her head, her eyes wide.

"'Nick,' you said! Nick who? Do you know them?"

Blondy nodded. "Pretty well—both of 'em. Joe Daniels, the little one, and—Nick Kessler, the big one. They hang around the Croc a lot."

Gail stared at her in wonder. "The Croc?" she echoed.

"Uh-uh! The Green Crocodile." Blondy jerked her head towards the end of the point. "I'm there, too."

"You mean you live there?"

Blondy smiled crookedly. "Yes, in a way. I come up here once in a while to get away from it. Men! Ugh! I hate 'em. I'm an entertainer, Red."

"An entertainer!" Gail was confused by the term.

"Yes. I dance with the men that haven't got partners. There's good money in it and it isn't as fierce as it sounds by a long shot. These jobs are what you make 'em, you know. As good or as bad as you want 'em to be. Not that I'm any lily-white angel! Not me!" Blondy added vigorously.

"I see," Gail said uncertainly.

"Now these two birds you are after," Blondy went on calmly. "You'll never shake it out of 'em. They are rumrunners—bad eggs, both of 'em. Nick Kessler would hang his own grandmother if it paid him! I know him! He's bad! *Bad!*"

Gail was struck by an odd note in Blondy's tone. "You seem to! Who are you, anyway?" she asked sharply.

Blondy laughed. "Me! I'm Mrs. Nick Kessler."

Gail sprang to her feet, white with anger. "You—his wife! You've got me to tell you everything you wanted to know! And now you are going to warn him!"

Completely losing control of herself, she advanced upon Blondy with clenched hands and spots of scarlet on her white cheeks.

"Aw, sit down!" Blondy cried wearily. "What's a husband between friends! This is California—I got my decree a month ago. Sit down, Red!"

Gail found her temper almost as quickly as she had lost it.

"I'm sorry," she cried contritely. "I don't know what I'm saying."

Blondy nodded understandingly. "S'all right, old dear. I get that way myself, at times. Nerves, and the hectic life, I guess. Kessler made my life a hell—never mind why I married him— I'm through with him. And I want to help you." She lit a cigarette. "Kessler is bad," she repeated. "Threats won't scare him. We must get at him some other way."

"Daniels?" Gail suggested.

"Daniels don't count. Kessler is your man. But he'll stick at nothing. Nothing!" she added significantly. "Remember that! He'd have done for Conniston himself if he could have got his hand on them stones. They must be worth a pile of money," she added reflectively.

Gail shivered. "Do you happen to know just what they were doing down on the beach the other night?"

"Nick has been in bootleg for some time. He and Daniels and a man named Swanson. They've been running it in around here under the noses of the revenue men. A good deal of it goes to the Green Croc. Those green lights you saw would be on Swanson's power boat, I guess, and the pile of driftwood was intended for a signal fire to tell him to come in somewhere else. Down towards the point, maybe. That Kerry of yours and those cops put a crimp in their plans. I guess they were giving their old stomping grounds the once over just now. Naturally, Nick is sore. I'm no sniff hound myself, but I'd like to do him in the eye just for old time's sake."

And with this pious reflection Blondy resumed her cigarette.

Gail tried to think her way through the problem that confronted her. But she found herself in a sort of mental cul-de-sac from which there was no escape, save by the way she had come. And that meant retreat. And retreat meant throwing away the most promising clue they had yet found and starting afresh. Her brain seemed dead to inspiration and tears of anger welled up in her eyes.

Blondy had been thinking with the cool deliberation of her type, drawing on her cigarette, looking seaward, the clear artificiality of her face unmarred by line or wrinkle. Suddenly, her expression enlivened, her eyes began to dance. She gave Gail a long, searching look.

"Say, Red! How far will you go for this Kerry O'Neil of yours?"

"The limit," Gail said simply.

"Hm! I wonder!" Blondy drew skeptically on her cigarette.

Gail flushed. "I will, I tell you!"

"Uh-huh! Well, listen. I've got an idea. You've got the looks to put it over, but—it'll take nerve. I'm wondering if you've got the," Blondy paused, and delicately sought a word, "the innards."

"Of course I have! What is it, Blondy?" Gail was flushed with eagerness.

"Hm! We'll see. Kessler is crazy about girls. New girls. Swell girls. Good-looking girls. Maybe that's why he married me. But his special is redheaded girls—like you. Well, Nick likes his booze—too darn much for a man in his line. He hangs around the Green Croc a good deal. He drinks there and when he's drunk he talks—he talks too much. Now, here's what I'm getting at. They want another entertainer at the Croc—one of the girls left last week. If I speak to Joe Beasley he'll give you the job—if you'll take it. If you do, I'll steer Nick on to you— not that he'll need much steering! He'll drink and it will be up to you to make him say what you want him to say. I'll show you where to take him to and I'll stick around out of sight, but near enough to overhear what he says. I can work that part of it, if you've got the nerve to tackle Nick. When you want me, I'll be your witness. How about it, Red?"

Gail listened to this extraordinary proposal in consternation. Was the girl actually suggesting that she enter a questionable roadhouse as an entertainer—a term apparently as elastic as one chose to make it? Did she think that she, Gail Hollister, would use such charms as were hers to entice evidence out of a beast in his cups? For the moment she quite forgot what was at stake.

"In a place like that!" she exclaimed, in horror. "I couldn't! Oh, I couldn't!"

Blondy contemptuously flipped away the stub of her cigarette. "Scared, eh!" she drawled. "I thought so."

If Blondy had used a whip on Gail the effect would not have been more startling. She sprang to her feet, white to the lips. For a moment so intense was her feeling that she could not speak.

"Don't you dare say that to me!" she cried passionately. "I didn't think what I was saying. Of course I'll do it! I'll do anything that will give Kerry a chance!"

Blondy waved her hand. "I thought you would, old dear. I know just how you feel. Sit down and we'll talk it over."

Gail subsided; her cheeks were scarlet with confusion. "You must think me an awful baby!" she cried unhappily. "I hardly know what I'm saying. I'll do anything—anything at all! But will it work out as you think?"

"Don't see why it shouldn't—if you play up to Nick."

"I will! What about Daniels?"

"Daniels is a rat. He'll say anything Nick says. If you get it out of Nick, the police will get it out of Daniels. I know them birds!"

"Are you sure you can get me on? Won't it hurt you—afterwards?"

"Jim Beasley will do it for me—if I ask him. It won't hurt me—I'm leaving him next month."

"What shall I have to do?" Gail asked breathlessly. The scheme had fired her imagination.

"Oh, nothing much. These jobs are what you make 'em, as I just said. Look pretty, use your eyes a bit, and dance with the men when they ask you. It isn't nearly as tough as it sounds. They'll ask you to drink, but you don't need to if you don't want. When Nick shows up keep away from the others and let him drink all he'll take. Then he'll begin to tell you things. I know Nick. Leave the rest to me."

Blondy opened her vanity case and took out the cigarettes. "Did you never smoke, Red?"

Gail recalled one or two furtive experiments. "I have tried it," she admitted.

"Better practice up, then. A hot cig is mighty handy when a man gets fresh."

Gail laughed nervously and took the cigarettes and matches. Blondy eyed her critically as she proceeded to light up.

"You'll do," was her comment. "But I'll have to doll you up a bit. More rouge on your cheeks and higher up—lips redder—hair confined—no, we'll leave it free. Gee, kid!" she exclaimed enthusiastically. "You'll be a reg'lar redheaded devil! Nick'll go crazy about you!"

Gail blushed at this unstinted praise. "It's awfully good of you, Blondy!" she said earnestly. "I'll never forget you for it."

"Oh, piffle! I want to get back at Nick. Just remember you are going to put it over. You can, if you will. It'll take brains, but you've got 'em, Red. This is Friday. How about starting in tonight? Nick won't be on hand till tomorrow—big doings Saturday nights—but the extra day will give you a chance to get your hand in."

"Tonight—yes!" Gail acquiesced. "I want to get a few of my things first, though. Where shall I meet you?"

"Right here." Blondy looked at her wristwatch. "It's three now. Be here at five. I have a coop parked back in the grove. I'll run up to the Croc now and speak to Joe about you; then I'll come back and drive you down. Don't worry about an evening gown. I've got a green silk rag that'll make you look like a million dollars. Shall I run you back to the house?"

"Better not," Gail said. "Bartlett might stop us."

They talked for a minute or two longer. Then Gail followed Blondy through the trees to a clearing in the center of the cypress grove in which her tiny "coop" was parked. A trail of sorts led out through the trees into the dirt road. The little car coughed and barked as Blondy gave it the gas.

"Five o'clock, old dear!" she called back, waving her hand. "Don't forget to practice up on them cigarettes."

The coupe shot out into the road and presently vanished in the direction of the Green Crocodile as Kessler's car had an hour or so before.

CHAPTER XX
The Green Crocodile

The dust settled down in the road again and Gail found herself alone. Rather enormously alone for Blondy left behind her a void that filled slowly. In her hand was the packet of cigarettes which she had forgotten to return. She eyed it resentfully, seeing in it a symbol of the distasteful course of action to which she had committed herself.

But as she stood there thinking about the role she had undertaken to play her attitude towards it changed. She began to see it as something daring and colorful, as requiring all her wit and courage, as an exciting means to a very definite end, an end so desirable, so rich in its promise, that her heart sang with joy. Gail smiled to herself. Again she wondered if she were indeed the Gail Hollister who had come down from the Westcoast Museum five days before.

As Gail made her way down the trail and along the beach her thoughts were of Kerry and the ease with which he had evaded Bartlett and his men. How he had managed to do it was still as incomprehensible to her as ever, but she no longer feared for his safety. Her contact with Blondy's exuberant personality had steadied her nerve. She was certain that everything would be well.

Mrs. Wessels was waiting for Gail at the top of the summer house trail. She seemed vastly relieved at sight of her.

"Is there any word of Mr. O'Neil?" Gail asked.

"There isn't, Miss 'Ollister. Bartlett 'as been looking for you, though. 'Opping mad, 'e is, too. 'E says you oughtn't never to 'ave left the house."

"Why not?"

Mrs. Wessels was surprised at the question. "Dimity's inquest, of course," she said. "They are 'olding it at six o'clock. Bartlett says you've got to be there."

Gail stopped abruptly. "The inquest!" She had completely forgotten about it.

They would want her, of course, and she was to meet Blondy at five. If she went on into the house she might not be allowed to leave it until after the inquest! She thought of turning back; then she saw one of Bartlett's men in the patio. His attitude was meant to suggest that he was unaware of her presence;

nevertheless, she felt sure that he was watching her. She must go on into the house and trust to her wits to get her out of it again unobserved.

"What is it, dearie?" Mrs. Wessels inquired solicitously.

"Nothing. Is Dr. McEwan here?"

"I 'aven't seen 'im all afternoon."

They entered by way of the patio door. Gail slipped up to her room unnoticed.

She had realized that her stay at the Green Crocodile might extend over several nights. She gathered together a nightdress and toilet articles and wrapped them in a sheet of brown paper which she found in the clothes closet, tying the parcel with a piece of string. A reassuring glance in the mirror and she was ready. Quietly she opened the door and listened. No sound. Creeping to the top of the stairs she listened again, then cautiously descended them. There was no one in the hall. Mrs. Wessels moved in her kitchen. The murmur of voices came to her from behind the library door.

Her plan was to cut across the patio, fly down the cliff path, and descend to the beach by the summer house trail. Once there, she would be reasonably safe. To reach the beach unseen was her problem.

There was no one in the patio. She flew across it like the wind, gained the cliff path, and stopped. No one pursued her. She heard no command to return. Her spirits rose and she fled down the path, neared the summer house, and turned to the head of the cliff trail. And there her high hopes fell into ruin. A man sprang from behind the summer house. A hand of steel closed on her wrist.

"Not so fast, Hollister! Not so fast!"

It was Decker.

Gail shrank back from him. "How dare you!" she cried indignantly. "Take your hand off my wrist!"

Decker snickered. "Not just yet, my girl. We'll go back to the house, first!"

"Let me go!" Gail stormed. "You've got no right to stop me! Let me go!" She tried to wrench herself free.

Decker's grip tightened cruelly; his eyes brightened with malice.

"Keep still!" he snarled. "Or I'll put the bracelets on you! Come on!"

To resist would only make matters worse; Gail knew that he would like nothing better than an excuse to carry out his threat. In despair, she permitted him to lead her submissively back to the house. As he followed her upstairs she had to shut her eyes to keep the tears from streaming down her cheeks.

Decker stopped before her door and took the key out of the lock; then he pushed her into the room. "Stay there until you are wanted!" he growled. Slamming the door, he locked it.

Gail dragged herself to the bed and with a choking cry dropped helplessly upon it. The parcel slipped from beneath her arm and she covered her face with her hands.

For a little while she remained thus, her shoulders trembling. Then she raised her head and glanced at her watch. It was just four-thirty. She had promised to meet Blondy at five. Her despair turned to fury which focused itself upon Decker and she had to bite her lip and clench her hands to keep herself from giving hysterical expression to it.

She got up and tried the door, beat upon it with her fists. Then she began to pace the room with quick, nervous steps. The watch on her wrist showed a quarter of five. She stopped by the window. It was open and she passed out onto the balcony and stared down into the grounds. There were several cars parked in front of the house, but no one occupied any of them. Nor did she see anyone in the grounds. She grew calmer and began to think.

Just then a powerful roadster driven by a young man shot out of the tree-hemmed drive, swept around the lawn, and skidded to a standstill in front of the house. Leaving the engine purring, the young man sprang out, carrying a dispatch case, and hurried up to the front door. Gail supposed that he was a messenger of some sort. She heard him wield the knocker.

"He's left the engine running," Gail muttered to herself.

Suddenly, a thought struck her. She was instantly on fire with it; her eyes blazed. Whirling around, she rushed back into the room, snatched up the brown paper parcel and flew out onto the balcony again. There was still no one in sight.

Below the balcony was the sloping, red-tiled roof of the conservatory. An immense bougainvillea vine embraced the roof, its profusion of magenta blooms reaching up to the low balcony wall. Another swift glance around the grounds; then Gail dropped over the wall and slid down the sloping roof, clutching desperately at the wiry branches of the vine. The blooms rose like butterflies on the wing.

She gained the edge of the roof soiled but safe and let her feet hang over the eaves. A terrifying drop of some fifteen feet into a bed of scarlet geraniums lay below her. Gail did not hesitate. Dropping the parcel, she gritted her teeth, swung over the edge, and let go.

The soft earth broke the force of her fall and Gail rose unhurt among the shattered plants. Glancing breathlessly around, she picked up her parcel and started towards the purring car a dozen yards or so away. Half the distance had she covered when a man emerged from the driveway on the other side of the lawn. It was the man who had watched her from the patio a little while before. He seemed to divine her purpose, for he started across the lawn, shouting.

In a flash, Gail made up her mind. Flying across the intervening distance she tossed the parcel into the seat of the roadster and sprang in after it. Her feet found the clutch and the gas throttle; the roadster roared around the circular drive, and swift as a comet sped to the entrance of the lower drive which led direct to the highway.

The man on the lawn had stopped. He was shouting and waving his hand. Gail smiled triumphantly and settled low in the seat behind the wheel; and then, as a pistol cracked and a bullet bit the dust at the side of the car, her smile lost its quality of triumph. A second bullet whined over her head; a third ricocheted from the steel frame of the windshield.

Gail swung the car into the highway on two wheels, escaping destruction by inches, and straightened it out. Her face was white, but her hands were firm on the wheel and she was still smiling.

Ahead, the road was clear as far as she could see—some three miles or so. Her foot depressed the throttle again and she looked at the fluttering indicator of the speedometer with a thrill of exultation. Fifty, it registered. Then fifty-five—fifty-eight! The wind made a Viking's song in her ears. Her hair stood out from her head like a hammer of gold.

The dirt road was fair and the car was winged; a demon of speed rioted in her blood. Nevertheless, she did not permit her ecstasy to blind her to the issues at stake. Bartlett's man probably had started in pursuit already. There was only one road: the one she was on. How could she evade capture? Every second counted. She thought quick and hard. And then a way occurred to her. There was no other, so far as she knew.

To drive up to the Green Crocodile in the commandeered car was out of the question. She must get rid of it—hide it somewhere—quickly. Some two miles ahead was a bend and a rise in the road. On the other side was the cypress grove in which she had promised to meet Blondy. A car would have started in pursuit already, she felt sure. If she could back the roadster into the clearing in which Blondy had parked her coupe, before the pursuing car topped the rise, her chances of escaping were fairly good. The cypress grove, as a possible hiding place, would not occur to the deputies until she was safely within the questionable confines of the Green Crocodile, They would never think of looking for her there.

Her faith in Blondy was implicit. It simply did not occur to Gail to doubt the sincerity of her new friend. To the seriousness of what she was doing, its illegal aspect, she gave no thought whatever.

A pistol cracked somewhere behind her. Gail gripped the wheel a little more firmly and cast a quick glance over her shoulder. A car was some two miles behind. On the brown dirt road it looked like a huge black beetle. The beetle swelled a little and Gail knew that it was gaining.

Purring as with a sense of achievement the roadster, under Gail's deft pilotage, took the rise in the road and topped the crest at a diminished speed. A quarter of a mile ahead were the cypress trees, and coming from the opposite direction was Blondy's coupe. Gail's heart began to hammer against her ribs, but she kept her hand steady on the wheel. She had perhaps two minutes in which to accomplish her strategy.

Completely hidden from those in the car behind, the roadster swept down the rise like an arrow of silver, and streaked past the cypress grove. Gail flung on the brakes. The car rocked from side to side of the road and came to a shuddering standstill, enveloped in billowing clouds of dust.

As she tugged at the gear shift, Gail had a vision of Blondy's tense face in the coupe ahead. Reversing, she shot the roadster back into and along the trail which led to the clearing.... Again the roadster stopped, enshrouded by the fretted shadows flung by the conifers.

Gail waited, gripping the wheel so tightly that her knuckles gleamed white. The seconds were little hammers of time that beat on the anvil of her heart. Would Blondy have the presence of mind not to betray her by any manifestation of dismay or astonishment? She sat rigid in the seat, the breath hissing between her clenched teeth.

There came the roar of a powerful engine behind her. It beat on her eardrums like artillery fire. A streak of black whizzed past. It had gone!

Gail fell back against the leather upholstery, shuddering at the narrowness of her escape. She heard the staccato bark of Blondy's coupe and the little machine rattled into the clearing.

Pulling herself together she glanced at the watch on her wrist. It was just five o'clock. The last fifteen minutes had seemed as many hours. Blondy stopped her coupe and put her head out of the window.

"Well," she said, with a grin, "you beat 'em to it. What were you making?"

Gail picked up her parcel and got out of the car. "S-sixty!" she gasped, halfway between tears and laughter.

"Pretty good on that road, I'll say! What's the bright idea?"

Gail explained in a hurried word or two. Blondy grasped the situation in a flash.

"Jump in!" she exclaimed. "The sooner we get to the Croc the better. They'll come back quick."

Gail put her foot on the running board. Then she looked up at the sophisticated face above her.

"You are taking a big risk, Blondy," she said, unsteadily. "You oughtn't to. If Bartlett should hear of it—"

"Slush!" Blondy said eloquently. "Who cares if he does! I'm tickled to death to get a poke at Nick! Jump in!"

Gail obeyed, near to tears now, and fell into silence. Blondy backed the coupe out into the road, swung it around, and turned it in the direction of the Green Crocodile. Then she shot the little car ahead at a speed that seemed to threaten its extinction and theirs.

"I'll never forget what you are doing, Blondy," Gail said huskily, between bumps.

Blondy squeezed her hand. "Piffle! I seen Jim Beasley about you. He said to bring you along. He's a good egg, Jim is, but hard-boiled. He'll give you the job all right, but don't tell him you haven't had experience in the game. Talk to him as if you had a million dollars on your back. I'll show you the layout when we get there. You can get away with it, all right. That red hair of yours will carry you anywheres. And don't be afraid of Nick. Stick a cig in his eye if he gets fresh. The bunch will stand by you. Nobody loves Nick around there."

But Gail's narrow escape had unnerved her, she was beginning to lose confidence in herself, and she accepted these instructions in silence. Was she capable of filling this role she had undertaken to play? Had she within her that quality of dissimulation essential to success? To Blondy, the role of siren— how she hated the word!—would come as naturally as tea and toast. But to Gail Hollister, authority on matters of antiquity, the venture was at best an exploration into the unknown regions of her own personality. There was another thing, too.

Was Blondy's inspiration as practical as she seemed to think? Gail was too upset in her mind to actually detect any weaknesses in it; nevertheless, she sensed their existence, and because she could not grasp and examine them, feared them the more.

Then she drew herself up sharp, shocked at the trend of her thought. If she continued in this frame of mind she would fail as surely as the sun would rise tomorrow! Something like the courage of desperation came to her. She wasn't going to fail. She was going to "put it over," as Blondy had said!

Some ten minutes later the little coupe rattled into the cypress-shadowed courtyard of the Green Crocodile at the end of the point.

Gail looked at the notorious roadhouse curiously. She saw a large two-story wooden building painted a deep bottle-green, octagon in shape, with large glass-enclosed verandas and small windows with green shades discreetly drawn. The house commanded a magnificent sweep of peninsula and ocean from every side. It stood in the center of several acres of ground which were enclosed by a high board fence, also painted green. Above the house sprawled a huge electric sign shaped like a crocodile, the lights of which were green. An ingeniously devised reflector was so placed as to deflect much of the light of the sign from the grounds below.

The gardens were laid out in shrubbery, fairly well kept. Here and there were nooks and arbors discreetly embowered with vine and creeper. Equally discreet was the disposal of the lights set here and there in the grounds. The place had a raffish air; it seemed to wink at one with its tongue in its cheek, so to speak, like a discreetly inebriated elderly gentleman who is more at home in the concealing shadows of night than in the brilliant light of day.

A side door led them into a bizarrely furnished office. The floor was covered with a Persian rug. Several oil paintings of exciting incidents in horse races hung on the walls. Near a window stood a colossal antique desk; behind it sprawled a man. He held a cigarette between his lean, yellow, hairless fingers; the heels of his patent leather shoes were set on the edge of the desk.

"'Lo, Jim," Blondy said casually. "Meet my friend, Red Burns."

Gail started at this unexpected nom de plume. It had not occurred to her that she must go under any name but her own while she was at the Green Crocodile. Recovering herself, she smiled inwardly at Blondy's inventive genius.

The man behind the desk deposited his feet on the floor. He seemed to be running his eyes up and down Blondy, as if he were estimating the potentialities of that sophisticated person. Thinking herself unobserved, Gail stole a look at the man. She saw a curious figure.

His face was wrinkled like the skin of a last year's apple, whether by dissipation or premature old age Gail could not tell. His eyes, frosty blue in color, were shrewd and penetrating in expression. His figure was slight and stooped, but supple and wiry and it was clad in a brown tweed suit of generous pattern. Gail judged that he had an acid tongue and that his years were anywhere between forty and sixty.

"Burns, eh?" the man shrilled, seeming to glance at Blondy's hair. "Pretty good! Where'd you grab off that name?"

He stuck a thin claw of a hand out at Gail, apparently, still keeping his eyes on Blondy, however. She stared at it for an instant; then, covered with confusion, shook it limply. The man was cross-eyed! He had been sizing her up all the time, not Blondy!

She recalled Blondy's instructions to talk to the man "as if you had a million dollars on your back," and she looked down at him boldly.

"What's wrong with my name?" she drawled with a downward twist of one corner of her mouth. "Don't you like it?"

Gail was aware of the tempered warmth in Blondy's smile. Her confidence returned; then a gust of courage, fierce and exultant, ran hot through her veins. She was going to put it over!

Beasley cackled again. "Like it!" he wheezed. "Sure, I like it. Why shouldn't I? Smoke?" He extended a silver cigarette case and matches.

Gail nodded, casually took one of the cigarettes, and slowly, deliberately, lit it, staring boldly down at Beasley the while.

"Well, do you want me, or not?" She breathed cigarette smoke through her nostrils.

Beasley, via Blondy, gave her that up and down look again. "Can you dance?"

"Can she!" said Blondy.

"Can I!" drawled Gail. "Got a victrola handy?"

"Oh, never mind now. I'll spot you quick enough if you can't!" Again that cackling laugh. "Like men?"

"Eat 'em alive!" Gail said.

Once more that glow of warmth in Blondy's eyes.

"Ever worked in a roadhouse before?"

"Like to know where I ain't worked in this line."

"Tough as they make 'em!" muttered Beasley. "Don't look it, either. How old are you, Red?"

"Never mind. I'm no spring chicken."

"I guess not," Beasley agreed. "That cigarette case," he went on, meaningly, "is mine."

Gail grinned impudently. "Sorry!" she said cheerfully. Taking the cigarette case out of the pocket of her sweater into which she had slipped it, she handed it back to him. "I guess I thought it was mine, Jim. I am that way sometimes. It's my complex. When do I start?"

"Start!" Beasley cackled. "Who said you'd ever start?"

Gail shrugged indifferently. "I got to know now. Got a line on something else."

Beasley gave her a long, hard look; then he began to grin. "You'll do!" he said. "You'll do!"

"How much?" Gail drawled.

Beasley frowned. "I'll tell you Sunday night. I want to see you do your stuff, first. I pay straight salary. And listen, Red." He paused. "I'm running no Sunday school class, but a girl don't have to stand for any more than she wants to—and sometimes less! *Less!* Get me? Blondy, show her where to put her rags—and put her wise!"

Gail shrugged her lissome shoulders and tossed her copper-red head. "I'll tell papa if they get fresh."

CHAPTER XXI
Rehearsal

The door through which they emerged a moment later opened upon a narrow hall. No sooner had Gail closed it behind her than Blondy spun around, eyes dancing, caught the other in her arms, and executed a little jazz step with her.

"Great!" she whispered ecstatically. "You certainly put it over old Jim! Come on, Kid!"

Flushed with her minor triumph Gail followed Blondy up a flight of stairs to a corridor with doors on each side of it. Blondy indicated some of them, commenting:

"Rooms for private parties."

She stopped before a door at the upper end of the corridor, unlocked it, and entered. Gail followed her. The room was airy and prettily furnished. There were two single beds.

"This is my hangout, Red. Make yourself at home. The girl that left useter room with me."

"What a pretty room!" Gail exclaimed. "And what a view you have!"

She went to the window. It commanded a measureless stretch of blazing sea. The sun was dipping and there was in the atmosphere that warm tint which precedes the richer hues of sunset.

"Not so bad!" was Blondy's comment. "I'll be kind of sorry to leave it. I sit here sometimes when I get sick of the bunch."

"Do you really think I bluffed him?" Gail asked eagerly, as she turned away from the window.

"Do I!" Blondy grinned. "Never saw him take anything better. Oh, you'll put it over, all right. If you can bluff Jim Beasley you can bluff the rest of the gang, take it from me! I nearly died when you swiped his cigarette case!"

"That was an inspiration," Gail smiled. "What time do we go down?"

"About nine."

"Beasley said you would 'put me wise,'" Gail went on.

Blondy chuckled. "There isn't much to it. You just hang around the floor and dance with whoever wants you to."

"With or without introductions?"

"It doesn't matter. We are not particular, here. I'll give you a knockdown to one or two of the boys. That'll make it easier.

Treat 'em gentle and you'll get by. If they want to tip you, let them. It wouldn't seem right to refuse real money. Don't drink if you don't want to. You can always slop it into a palm."

"Isn't the place ever raided?" Gail inquired.

"Oh, once in a while, but Jim knows about it beforehand—usually. The Croc is kind of hard to get into."

They sat down by the window, Blondy chatting in animated tones.

Presently, the sun began to set. Soon it was gone into the fiery breast of the ocean, and the ocean, fiery no longer, began to darken until it seemed like a cauldron of molten metal aquiver here and there with sinister spearheads of light. Darkness gathered. Blondy began to tell Gail something of her married life with Kessler, of the brutalities and the infidelities of the man; and something of the varied and colorful and frequently vulgar experiences of her career.

Gail was intensely interested in the girl and she began to study her closely. The result was a revelation in character that astonished her. Beneath the surface artificiality of the girl she found something solid and clean and vital, something that held her a little breathless, as the discovery of a vein of yellow gold in a rock facing would have done. Moreover, she glimpsed an aspect of life that was quite foreign to her: a sub-world of dark shadows and brilliant lights, of hurts and heartbreaks and morbid despondencies. It amazed and awed her and left her, when Blondy had done, a little more tolerant of human frailty.

"If I'd had a man like that Kerry O'Neil of yours to love!" Blondy said, with a crooked grin. "Things might have been different!"

Gail pressed her hand gently. "You will have someday," she said simply. "You are too good not to."

Blondy's mood changed again. "I wonder where he has got to, Red. It don't seem possible that he could have got off the peninsula. I know them cops!"

Gail's face grew troubled again. "I don't know. I can't think. But somehow, I've got a feeling he is safe."

It was dark now. Blondy stood up, drew the shade, and switched on the light.

"Eight o'clock, Red. Time to doll up."

She went to a clothes closet and took out two evening gowns, a black chiffon and a green georgette, and laid them upon the bed.

"What a darling gown!" Gail cried, with her eyes on the green georgette.

"Slip into it, old dear. It is just the rag for you. Here's a green slip to go underneath."

Flushed with excitement, Gail tumbled out of her things, put on the slip, and stepped into the green gown. Nearly as excited as she, Blondy caught the snappers with trembling fingers; then she tossed Gail a pair of green chiffon silk stockings and dainty slippers to match. Gail drew on the stockings, rolled them, stepped into the slippers, and stood up, eyes shining. Blondy studied her with critical appreciation. Gail was on the point of starting for the mirror, when Blondy stopped her.

"Wait!"

Cosmetics, perfumes, and toilet articles stood on the dressing table. Blondy took up comb and brush, pressed Gail down into a chair, and applied them to her copper-red head. Then she took up chamois and rouge and lipstick.

"Not too much, Blondy!" Gail giggled.

"Leave it to me, old dear. You oughter have your eyebrows plucked, but I guess you'll get by."

She dabbed deftly at Gail's cheekbones. The contrast of the color against the white of her skin emphasized the tiny hollows below the cheekbones which the strain of the last few days had rather clearly defined. Blondy sprang back and with the critical eye of the artist inspected her handiwork. She nodded her satisfaction.

"You'll do."

Gail ran to the mirror. She saw a glowing, exotic figure with shining eyes and hair like a ruddy rippling flame rising white and straight and slender from a sheath of tender green. A sheath so scant and daring that Gail caught her breath.

"Oh!" she gasped. "Is it really I?"

"Sure is!" Blondy asserted generously. "You look like a queen. Wait till Nick sees you!"

Blondy began her own elaborate toilet in front of the mirror. She completed it swiftly and effectively and slipped into the black chiffon, drew on filmy hose to match, and stepped into black pumps with tiny silver buckles. Then she stood up, a slim and gaudy goddess as immodestly lovely as artful modesty could make her. Gail inspected her from twinkling buckles to mop of hair like ripe corn in the summer sun.

"You look stunning in that black chiffon, Blondy!" she cried warmly.

Blondy ran a critical eye down the scanty gown, which

terminated at the knee, and inspected her silken ankles.

"Uh-uh!" she admitted frankly. "This rag usually knocks 'em cold."

She picked up a silver cigarette case with a slender chain and slipped it over her wrist. Another, not unlike it, she gave to Gail.

"All set, honey. Come on."

They passed into the corridor and along a short hall which brought them onto a railed balcony crowded with dinner tables spread with snowy linen and agleam with silver. Dim green lights and potted palms lent an air of seclusion to each table. Here and there a waiter deftly perfected the spotless elegance of the tables.

Along the walls were booths built out onto the balcony. Curtains were hung to draw across them. Blondy directed Gail's attention to the booths.

"You and Nick will park in one of them tomorrow night," she said. "I'll fix it so that I can get the one behind. Leave that part of it to me."

Again Gail had a twinge of doubt as to the practicality of their plan. She put it out of her mind, however. Faith was half the battle.

A broad staircase led down to the first floor and as they slowly descended it Gail got a comprehensive view of the place. She saw a large and gleaming dance floor with a platform for the orchestra in one corner of it. Six musicians were already tuning up their instruments. Flowers and potted shrubs banked the platform. Many lamps, artfully suspended from the ceiling, shed a greenish shadowy light upon the floor.

Surrounding the floor were dozens of tables at which a few couples were leisurely dining. Palms were discreetly placed among the tables. Roses perfumed the air. The atmosphere of the place was subtle, exotic, enticing.

Gail took in the scene a little breathlessly. It was all new to her, tremendously fascinating and just a little disquieting. But she had that superb confidence in herself which is born of the knowledge of one's own good looks, and she was not afraid.

Easy chairs were placed here and there at the edge of the floor. Several of these were occupied by good-looking girls with an affected air of boredom. They were enticingly dressed and there was something about them that reminded Gail of Blondy. The latter seemed to sense her thoughts, for she waved her hand airily and said:

"Even as you and I, Red."

When they saw Gail their airs of boredom vanished and as the green georgette was recognized an eyebrow or two went up. Gail colored and held her head high. Blondy stopped by one of the girls.

"Meet my pal, Red Burns, Belle," she said, with a grin.

"Hello, innocence," the girl drawled. "How sweet!" Her eyes said: "Look out, you are dangerous!"

Blondy winked. "She's hard-boiled, Bluebell. Leave her alone." They passed on.

Blondy stopped by one of the vacant chairs.

"Better stick here for a while," she suggested. "I'll steer somebody easy onto you as soon as I can. He'll be good practice. Hang onto him and you'll be all right for the rest of the night."

Blondy went on and Gail sat down. She felt horribly alone and a trifle panic-stricken. But the feeling quickly passed and she began to take an interest in her surroundings again.

Friday is an off night for the roadhouses, and patrons came slowly to the Green Crocodile. Presently, there were a score of diners at the table and as the orchestra broke into a catchy fox-trot several couples began to gyrate around the shadowy floor. Others trickled in and soon a fair scattering shuffled to the strains of jazz.

Gail had completely lost her self-consciousness by this time. Letting her body relax, she assumed the lounging attitude and effected the bored air of the other girls. Two of them had partners and were dancing, and Gail began to wish that someone would approach her. Many of the women were smoking and Gail casually lighted one of Blondy's cigarettes and puffed on it leisurely, smiling whimsically at the ease with which she had fallen into the role she had undertaken to play.

Just then she saw Blondy bearing down upon her with a young man in tow and she began to feel nervous again. But as she got a good look at him she was reassured. He was an inoffensive looking young man with a patent leather head and an immature Bohemian air which he carried with indifferent success. When he saw Gail his mouth fell open and his Bohemian air vanished.

"Golly!" she heard him whisper.

Gail smiled, secretively.

"This is Eddie, Red," Blondy said affably. "He'll tell you the rest of it. Won't you, Eddie?"

"Lovatt," breathed the shocked young man.

"Treat him gentle, Red. He'll break."

Blondy departed and the young man stared at Gail abjectly,

searching his brain for something to say.

"Golly," he whispered again. "You are a peach."

Gail yawned. "I know. Let's eat. I'm hungry."

She hadn't had a bite since morning and for sometime had been unpleasantly aware of it. The young man seemed a bit disappointed at the callousness of the suggestion, but he quickly brightened and led Gail to a table, the most secluded he could find....

The evening passed not without incident. Eddie and Gail danced and dined and danced and smoked and danced again. Eddie forgot to be a Bohemian and fell madly in love with Gail: with her hair, her eyes, the whiteness of her arms, and the green georgette. He brought forth a silver flask neatly shaped to fit the hip, of which he was pathetically proud; but he quickly put it away again, when Gail yawned in his face. Presently, he wanted to hold her hand and Gail let him to keep him quiet.

Later, they went out into the grounds and Eddie led her into one of the discreet little arbors she had noticed on entering the courtyard with Blondy. It was on the side of the cliff, overlooking a fairy sea. There was magic in the moonlight and jessamine in the air. So exquisitely beautiful was the night, indeed, that Eddie very naturally forgot to be a Perfect Gentleman. He took Gail into his arms and tried to kiss her.

The moment was unfortunate. Gail was thinking tenderly of Kerry and when the touch of Eddie's warm hands broke the train of her thought she had to grit her teeth to check her anger. She was smoking a cigarette, and remembering Blondy's advice, contrived that it should encounter Eddie's ardent lips.

The young man howled.

"Cut it!" Gail said sharply. "I don't feel mushy tonight."

Eddie was contrite at once and earnestly, humbly begged her to marry him. He was so pathetic in his sincerity that Gail was sorry for him.

"Let's go in," she yawned. "I'm cold."

So they danced some more.

About one o'clock Eddie left in his roadster, with the cutout open. He went reluctantly and under pressure from Gail who had just declined again to marry him, or to go with him, or to give him any hope whatever.

"I'm coming back tomorrow night!" he had shouted. And then he had gone, engine roaring, to forget all about her.

The Green Crocodile was deserted of its patrons as Gail crossed the dance floor towards the staircase. It had not been as bad as she had expected, by a good deal. Things never were, for that matter, she reflected. But the Friday night crowd was not typical. The real test would come tomorrow—Saturday night.

She was aware of footsteps behind her. It was Jim Beasley. He looked at her critically.

"You'll do," he said approvingly. "But snap it up a bit! More speed. Get me?"

"I do," Gail drawled. "Watch me!"

Beasley nodded. Crossing to a door nearby, he opened it; but instead of entering, he stood on the threshold, talking to someone in the room beyond. Through the door steamed the odors of the kitchen.

Gail saw a long sink at which a man was washing huge stacks of dishes. She had to press her hands to her mouth to stifle the cry that rose to her lips. Her cheeks grew white and the floor rocked beneath her feet. Beasley passed into the kitchen then, letting the door swing to. Gail's hands fell to her sides.

The man at the sink was Kerry O'Neil!

CHAPTER XXII
Before the Crocodile Got Up

Gail stared at the closed door for a full minute, her eyes wide and her mouth open. She was aware of nothing but that lean dark face in the room beyond, which she still saw as clearly as if the closed door were transparent. Consciousness of her surroundings returned to her and she saw that the girl whom Blondy had addressed as Belle was watching her curiously a short distance away. Recovering herself, she affected a casual air and going to the staircase ascended it unconcernedly. She was relieved to find that Blondy had not yet come up to their room.

As she sat down by the window her amazement gave way to relief and joy and a chuckling appreciation of Kerry's resourcefulness. Bartlett and his men were as unlikely to seek Kerry in the kitchen of the Green Crocodile as they were to look for herself on the dance floor of the same establishment!

But soon these emotions were overshadowed by fear. What if Kerry should be recognized by any of the employees of the roadhouse? This was not unlikely for the affair at the Casa de Ayer had set the country by the ears and Kerry's face had become a daily feature of the press. She had another dismaying thought. Kerry might see her; might have seen her already, in fact. In either event his course of action was problematical; one could never tell about Kerry. So indignant might he be at finding her in such a place as the Green Crocodile that he would make a scene and ruin everything. She wondered what she had better do. Her mind was quickly made up. She would find him after dawn and forestall any action he might have decided upon by telling him everything and insisting on his cooperation.

Blondy came in just then.

"Well, old dear, how'd you make out?"

Gail smiled. "Not too badly. I had to correct him once or twice."

Blondy kicked off her black pumps. "Oh, Eddie's a sweet child. Lord! I'm tired, Red. Le's go to bed—big doings tomorrow night."

Gail was too troubled in spirit to sleep much and she got up at dawn, dressed quietly, and crept downstairs. The Green

Crocodile was as still as a tomb and Gail let herself out by a side door unobserved.

The sun was rising above the ridge of the peninsula. A silver sheen lay on the troubled breast of the ocean and the grounds were flushed and lovely with golden light. Gail walked in the gardens like Aurora, goddess of morning, and presently, by way of a cinder path, she came to the edge of the cliff.

The cliff fell steeply to a nest of ragged rocks and curling spray a hundred feet below. On the top of the cliff was an outcropping of rock with a little seat hollowed out of the face of it. A man sat on the seat with his head in his hands.

"Kerry!" Gail said gently.

His head came up with a jerk, he sprang to his feet and looked at her with eyes so sunken that they seemed deep hollows with dark fire in their depths.

"Gail!" he whispered.

He held his hands out towards her, but he did not move. The misery in his face hurt her and she went towards him with a tempest of emotion in her heart. She wanted to touch him; to draw his head down tight against her breast, to run her hands through his hair.

"You poor Kerry!" she found herself saying. "You mustn't look at me like that!"

He caught her almost savagely by the arms, and she saw a blaze of indignation in his eyes.

"My God, Gail! You've got to tell me what you are doing round this dump!"

She smiled secretively. "I've got a better job than you have, Kerry."

"Flirting with that pin-headed prune you had last night!" he stormed. "I saw you dancing with him! I saw him bring you out here!" All at once his eyes were wet and piteous. "What are you doing here, Gail? Who was he? You've got to tell me! I'll kill the beggar!"

Gail smiled. "Can anyone see us, Kerry?"

"No!"

"Kiss me and then I will."

He looked at her with his old grin breaking out all over his face.

"Golly! Do you mean it!"

Then he caught her to him, kissed her suddenly, soundly, and severally, held her apart, grinned rapturously down at her, and did it all over again. They clung to each other for a long minute, their hearts beating together. Time and place were forgotten; they lived in a world of illusion, a tiny golden sphere of light and love and song as remote from reality as star from star.

Kerry drew Gail down beside him onto the little seat hollowed out of the face of the rock. They could feel the rock tremble beneath the pounding of the tide brigades below.

"Tell me all about it, Gail," he said gently.

"How did you manage to get into the Green Crocodile?" she countered.

Kerry chuckled. "When I got out of the Casa de Ayer the other morning I knew they'd get me soon after dawn unless I got off the peninsula and there seemed mighty little chance of my being able to do that. I flipped that note up onto your balcony; then I sneaked down into a canyon I had hid in before—it was the best place I knew of.

"Pretty soon it was dawn and I got to glancing through that sheet of newspaper in which you wrapped those sandwiches. It was a Los Angeles paper, the classified section, and I stumbled across an ad in the help wanted column for a dishwasher at the Green Crocodile. There was my chance, I figured. The Croc was right under Bartlett's nose, so he wouldn't think of looking for me there. I applied for the job and got it. That's all. Your turn now, honey."

Gail was laughing. It was just the sort of thing he would do, of course! These quirks of character, these odd unexpectednesses bound him to her as with chains of steel. She told him everything that had happened since they had parted above the open trapdoor. When she had done he was silent for a moment. Then his hand tightened on hers.

"Golly!" he whispered huskily. "I'll never forget this, Gail! Doing this for me! I— Oh, Lord!" He grew incoherent with emotion. "That beast, Kessler! I'd like to wring his neck! When I think of you coming to a joint like this—for me!" He choked up again; his arm slid around Gail's slim shoulders and he drew her to him tightly. "You are the real thing, girl! I'll never be able to do enough for you." He paused again. "We'd better be getting back to the house. You are not going through with it, of course—I am going to give myself up."

"You are not!"

His arm no longer encircled a soft and pliant human form, but a quivering bundle of steel wires that whirled out of his embrace.

"You are not!" Gail said again.

She did not raise her voice, but there was a hard, compact

note in it that made him look at her in bewilderment. Her face was white; her lips were trembling; her dark eyes blazed with a quality of indignation that he had never found in them before.

"Gail—" he began.

She swept his protest aside. "I've started this thing, Kerry, and I am going through with it! Kessler saw Stark kill Dimity and he's going to tell what he saw. You can't stop me. Don't try!"

His dark eyes were anxious. "Look here, Gail. You can't stay in this place. I know what I am talking about. The Croc is the toughest 'high-class' roadhouse north of the Mexican border. Besides, this is the night of the 'Twenty-five Club.' They come down once a month and raise Cain. They are *wild*, let me tell you! Jim Beasley stands for anything they like to put over. If that bird Kessler comes you'll not be safe! You can't stay!"

"Do you really think I cannot look after myself?"

"It isn't that, Gail. The Croc is tough. It's no place for you. For any decent girl, for that matter."

Gail laughed. "Men like you are funny, Kerry. They always want to wrap their women up in tissue paper. It's no use, you old dear! I am going through with it."

Kerry's jaw set stubbornly. "You are not! I forbid it!" he said solemnly. "If you stay here another hour I'll give the show away. I'll tell Beasley who you are and I'll hand myself over to Bartlett. I'm going to do that, anyway."

Gail looked at him silently for a moment; there was an ominous flicker in her eyes.

"If you do," she said steadily, "you needn't see me again."

"Gail!"

"I mean it!"

His solemn front collapsed; he looked at her in consternation.

"Lord!" he groaned, running his hands through his hair. Then he sat up straight. "You've got to be reasonable, Gail! Dr. McEwan and this newspaper chap, Perrin, have turned up new evidence, you say. It points to Stark. I am just as sure as you are that he is guilty. What is the use of fooling around any longer? They can't convict me in the face of this new stuff!"

Gail shook her head. "I'm not so sure about that, Kerry. There is a tremendous feeling against you. I don't believe you realize how strong it is. A jury might acquit you—I am not at all sure that it would—but people would still believe you had had something to do with it. We don't want that. There mustn't be a breath of suspicion against you. Kessler can clear you. He saw Stark kill Dimity and he's got to tell what he saw! Besides, Colonel Conniston and old Dimity have been murdered in cold blood. I couldn't bear to think of that beast Stark going unpunished. It's got to be proven against him. Blondy is going to help me. I don't see why you should object. I am going through with it, anyhow, so please don't say any more about it."

Kerry saw that he was beaten. He surrendered gracefully.

"All right. But I am going to keep my eye on that bird, Kessler. Yell if he touches you and I'll break his neck!"

Gail diplomatically left it at that.

They parted presently and Gail went back to the room she shared with Blondy. The latter, sitting up in bed, greeted her with a yawn.

"Hello, dearie, where you been?"

"Out in the grounds," Gail said. "Do you know anything about the 'Twenty-five Club,' Blondy?"

"'Twenty-five Club'? Sure! This is their night at the Croc. Why?"

"Oh, I heard someone mention the name downstairs," Gail replied casually. "What kind of a club is it?"

Blondy winked, "A good time outfit, I'd call it. They are a wild bunch. They travel around the roadhouses a lot. Their main hangout is in Los Angeles. Quite a few of the movie crowd belong to it. They carry their own booze with 'em. It's a wonder to me the dry squad don't get them. My much-lamented ex-husband is a member."

"Kessler! Indeed!"

"Uh-uh. They'll make things hum tonight, take it from me! Jim Beasley is some entertainer when he starts and he always puts on something slick when the 'Twenty-fivers' come. Not troubling you, is it, Red?"

"Why, no, Blondy."

"Thought you might be worrying about Nick. Don't! Throw in the riot call if he gets sassy. Real sassy, I mean."

"Do you believe he will say what I want him to say, Blondy?" Gail asked tensely. She clasped her hands; her face whitened a little. "I am depending on it," she said earnestly. "It means—you know what it means!"

Blondy slipped out of bed and put her arm around Gail's shoulders. "Sure he will, Red! Feed him booze enough and he'll tell you everything he knows—and then some. Cheer up! You'll get what you want, all right. I'll steer him on to you as soon as he comes in. He'll want one of them booths on the balcony. I'll park myself in the one behind. Leave that part of it to me."

Gail nodded. "It's awfully decent of you, dear."

"Slush!"

But Gail had suddenly begun to doubt the practicality of their plan. There was something hasty and unsubstantial about it. Too flimsy a structure it seemed for the burden she had to put upon it. Would evidence got under such conditions have the authority a court would require? Had Kerry been right, after all? Was she complicating the affair still further to no purpose whatever?

Her misgivings made her wretched and she pulled herself together. She was going to put it over—somehow!

CHAPTER XXIII
The Saturnalia

That evening, from behind the mahogany rail which surrounded the dance floor of the Green Crocodile, Gail saw the "Twenty-fivers" descend in a whirlwind upon the roadhouse and take undisputed possession of it. They came in high-powered cars that made the night hideous with screaming horn and open cutout; and they entered with bursts of hilarious laughter that affected the tipsy atmosphere of the Crocodile as a draft of champagne would a bibulous elderly gentleman.

There had been a sizable crowd in the place before their arrival. But now the tables were thronged and out on the floor a mass of humanity as colorful as a regiment of rainbows slid and rotated and whirled to the musical gymnastics of the orchestra.

The uproar became deafening. Everybody talked and nobody listened. The blaring stridencies of the saxophone punctuated the slur of feet on the polished floor, the shrill laughter of the women, and the deeper guffaws of the men. And through it all ran a note unrestrained and daring; a little mad, perhaps, as if the more violent emotions were held in leash by the thinnest of threads.

Suspended from balcony and ceiling were hundreds of electric lamps enclosed in white shades emblazoned with dark green crocodiles. They cast a sinister tinge on the flushed faces of those who dined and danced below. Currents of air fanned them into motion and soon they were gyrating like imps on a gibbet. In the center of the floor had been erected a low square dais approachable on each side by a flight of steps. There was nothing on the dais.

Waiters hurried from table to table. The odor of foods mingled with the exotic perfumes of the women. An incredible number of teapots were brought from the pantry and received with a wink or a grin; and when their contents were poured into the teacups that had accompanied them they were sipped with relish or swallowed with gusto. Silver flasks began to twinkle on the tables. Bottles of spirits and wine, Scotch and gin, Burgundy and port and champagne emerged from the most unexpected places and were greeted with roars of approval. Ice tinkled in tall glasses and cocktail shakers flashed.

Convention and restraint were flung to the winds; liberty and license grew.

The scene was entirely new to Gail and she watched it, fascinated, as one watches a play on a theater stage. She was not yet a part of it, but her fingers were on its pulse, so to speak, and she felt the throb and beat of it. There was something else though. Something beneath the surface hilarity of the scene, not apparent to the eye. She did not know what it was—a presentiment, perhaps—but she sensed it dimly, as one would sense the presence of a naked electric wire in a bar of iron. Something impended. What was it?

Just then, a stout man with a round red face broke away from the boil of humanity on the dance floor and rolled towards her.

"'Lo, Baby!" he gurgled. "What you doin' all alone? 'Tain't right! A pippin like you. Come on—le's hop it awhile."

Gail stared at him languidly. "Beat it, Fats. I'm tied up already."

He swayed above her, moist and warm. "No, you ain't! Come on, kid!"

"Go 'way!" Gail blew a cloud of cigarette smoke into his face. "Go 'way and sit down or you'll fall. I'm not dancing with you."

The man's face, flushed with liquor, deepened in color. "Aw, come on, Red!" he whined. "Jim Beasley said I could have you. He said you'd dance with me. You got to!" He winked solemnly at her. "I got a bottle of real stuff. Come on, kid!"

His hot fingers touched her arm. For a moment Gail forgot herself.

"Go and sit down, you drunken beast!" she cried scathingly. "You are not fit to dance with anyone!"

"Drunken—beast!" the man echoed, in a slow rage, and his round red face swayed like a tipsy moon. "I'll show you—I'll show you—"

"What's wrong here?"

The voice came shrilly from behind the man and Gail was relieved to see Jim Beasley, resplendent in evening dress and diamonds. Her relief quickly gave place to fresh dismay, however. There was something in Beasley's crooked eyes that frightened her.

"Li'l' girl here won't dance," the fat man hiccoughed. "Says she's gotta date, but she ain't! Don't I know? Gettin' sassy, too. Hand it to her, Jim!"

Beasley gave Gail his up and down look. "What do you think I've got you here for, Burns?" he demanded raspingly. "What are you stalling for?"

"I got a date," Gail replied coolly. "A fellow I know asked me to wait for him."

"You are lying," Beasley snapped. "You are here to do as you are told. Either dance with Monty or get out!"

"Wait a bit, Jim. Wait a bit! This young lady is booked already."

Gail's emotions were varied as she saw Kessler's hard whitish face appear over Beasley's shoulder.

Blondy, grinning cheerfully, was behind him. Gail felt a sudden quickening of her pulses. Here was something definite! Kessler wore a dinner jacket, and that quality of sinister elegance, of breeding grown rank, was emphasized by his spread of white shirt front. As she looked at him she got an impression of strength and weakness. He reminded her of a tower of stone built on a bank of sand.

Gail laughed shrilly. "Hello, Nick! Blondy was talking about you. Didn't I tell you, Jim?"

Beasley was mollified. "All right," he grunted.

"You are too late, Monty."

The latter thought differently, however.

"Not on your life, I ain't!" he shouted belligerently, swaying a little. "I got here first! Come on, li'l' green girl!"

Kessler's eyes had not left Gail's face since first alighting upon it. They were small eyes, light blue in color, and shallow in expression. But as they fell on the fat man's round red face they dilated a little and a dangerous hardness leaped into them.

"Stand back, you fool!" he said thickly.

His arm swung out and the man called Monty collided with the nearest dinner table. There came the crash of crockery and a precious bottle of wine. Two men rose to their feet, cursing, and the two very blond women with them screamed. Those at the surrounding tables roared with delight: it wasn't their wine.

There is always a certain joy in being a bone of contention, the quality of the contestants notwithstanding, and Gail was human enough to feel the thrill of it. The next moment, she was swept onto her feet; a powerful arm encircled her shoulders and she was whirled out onto the dance floor. Gail caught a glimpse of Blondy nodding reassuringly and of the man called Monty picking himself up out of the wreckage of the dinner table; then they were swallowed up by the crowd.

While they danced and during the intervals Kessler emitted

a stream of conversational nothings to which Gail made the appropriate replies. He had been drinking and the intimacy with which he danced sickened her. However, it provided her with an excellent opportunity to study the man and she made the best of it. Her judgment of him was confirmed. He was all front; there was no carrying power behind. Her faith in Blondy's scheme was renewed.

Meanwhile, the revelry had risen to a shriller, wilder pitch. As she whirled around the floor Gail was reminded of a movie interpretation of a Roman Saturnalia. Many of the dancers were the worse for liquor and they reeled and spun in a frenzy of movement unrelated to the stridencies of the orchestra. One couple rolled on the floor, almost ripping the scant gown from the woman's back. A dozen others piled on top of them. Out of this tangle of silken legs and perfumed gowns rose a discord of tears and oaths, falsetto laughter and coarse jokes. Higher and higher shrilled the music. The musicians were like fiends fiddling at a dance of death.

Those at the tables were in no better condition. All of them had liquor. Gail saw a woman scramble onto one of the larger tables and execute a frenzied fandango to an accompaniment of clapping by her seven fellow-revelers. Glassware and china laden with food crashed right and left. A hullabaloo of applause burst forth from the surrounding tables. One girl with a fine touch of genius cracked crockery over the bald pate of her fatuously grinning companion. A second made castanets of cutlery. A third beat upon an ice bucket with the drumsticks of a turkey.

Upon another table was enthroned a movie star of dark, exotic beauty. Hand in hand, a dozen or so of her companions pranced around the table, emitting whoops that would have shamed a young Sioux chief. There were no protests. Grinning waiters cleared away the wreckage as fast as it accumulated. The mad "Twenty-fivers" would pay the bill.

The scene affected Gail curiously. She recognized its madness which, moment by moment, rose to fresh improbable heights. But there was something else. That presentiment of events impending had never left her. It was stronger now. She thought of it as an undercurrent of danger which, unsuspected by the revelers, ran faster and faster beneath the surface gayety of the scene; an acceleration of forces which would presently break forth with devastating effect. Catastrophe—that was it!

"There's something coming!" she whispered to herself.

Her presentiment seemed to gather confirmation when, a

moment later, Kessler whispered huskily in her ear.

"Beasley has locked the doors!"

The statement dismayed her. Why should Beasley lock the doors?

Kessler was becoming more intolerable with each moment. Gail looked up at him with smoldering eyes. His whitish face was flushed now. His eyes met hers with a fatuous grin and she forced herself to smile back at him. She must smile—smile—smile—until she had got—what she had come for! Ugh! How she hated the man!

The music stopped suddenly, and so did the dancers—those of them that had wit enough left to do so. Gail and Kessler were near the foot of the broad staircase which led up to the balcony. Before Gail knew what was happening to her, Kessler had caught her up in his arms and was reeling up the staircase with her as if she had no more weight than a bundle of feathers.

Gail kicked furiously and struck Kessler in the face. He was undisturbed, however.

"Take it easy, Red! Nobody's going to hurt you!"

The staircase was crowded with revelers passing unsteadily up and down. They made way for Kessler, grinning and exclaiming with delight at Gail's predicament. None of them interfered, reading into her violent protestations merely spirited acquiescence.

Gail abruptly ceased struggling and lay passive in Kessler's arms. If she was going through with this thing she must take the preliminaries easily. For a moment she had a vision of the Gail Hollister of a week ago—cataloguing antiques in a Los Angeles museum! The vision made it possible for her to smile up at him.

"Nothing slow about you, Nick!" she laughed.

His arms tightened again. "You redheaded witch, you!" he whispered huskily.

Kessler reached the balcony and picked his way between the crowded tables to one of the booths which bore a card with "Reserved" on it in prominent letters. The booth immediately behind it bore a similar card, Gail noticed. This would be Blondy's doings, she reflected, and drew courage from the thought. All of the others were occupied.

There were two chairs and a table in the booth. Kessler deposited Gail on one of the chairs. A waiter hurried up, menu card and order blank in hand. Kessler asked for cocktails by their given name, and with an air that proclaimed his contempt for the subterfuges popularized by the Eighteenth Amendment.

The liquor he had drunk already was inclining him to loquacity. He poked the bored waiter playfully in the ribs and introduced Gail to him as his "little green girl." When the man had returned with the order and departed again Kessler started to draw the thick curtains across the front of the booth. Gail stopped him.

"Leave 'em up for a while, Nick," she said, casually. "Beasley is staging something down below and I want to take a look-see."

"Sure thing," Kessler agreed. "Anything to please. Lots of time. Hot doings down below, eh? Have a cocktail, Red."

He pushed a glass towards Gail and took one himself. Gail let the glass stay where it was. There was a small potted palm in the booth. Whether it had got there by accident or design she did not know, but it would come in handy later on.

Her intimacy with Kessler during the last hour or so had been well-nigh unendurable. She wanted to adjust herself to the man by degrees. For this reason she had stopped him from drawing the curtains.

Just then Gail caught sight of Blondy picking her way towards the booth behind. Faithful Blondy! Kessler was busy with his second cocktail at the moment and Gail caught the girl's eyes. Blondy winked encouragingly and entered the booth. The curtains were drawn to.

Gail drew a deep breath. Could she go through with it to the end?

CHAPTER XXIV
The Dance of the Green Crocodile

As Gail had said, Beasley was staging something down below. The dancers were crowding back from the dais and the center of the floor, attendants of the roadhouse giving assistance to those who needed it. When the center of the floor was clear the lights were suddenly lowered and the hall was thrown into a semi-darkness that brought a ripple of surprise from the tipsy revelers. There followed a hush that contrasted sharply with the hilarity that had just ceased.

A minute passed. Then, with hair-raising unexpectedness, green flame burst out of the center of the ceiling and fell upon the dais below. Light of the same color flared up to meet it and in the twinkling of an eye the dais had become a lake of green fire. A clever arrangement of spotlights and reflectors created the illusion, but in the darkened hall its effect was weird and rather terrible.

Complete silence prevailed. Once again, Gail was aware of that acceleration of hidden forces. A climax of some sort impended, but whether it was merely in the affairs of Kerry and herself, or in something else as well, she did not know.

The dais was some forty feet square. The light revealed it as being different in character from the first general conception. In the center of it was an oblong hole or well, some ten feet in width by thirty in length, the bottom of which was in darkness. The attention of everyone in the hall, drunk or sober, was focused upon the dais and the oblong pit in the center of it. So quiet had the hall become that the silence could almost be felt.

Suddenly the whir of a motor was audible; and then the orchestra began to play a weird and haunting melody that somehow made Gail think of the chanting of an ancient people rising up through the dusty halls of time. It touched the spirit as with a ghostly hand. The tension mounted until it seemed as if the very atmosphere of the place must snap. A sudden "Ah-h-h-h!" of amazement breaking from the sobered audience relieved the strain.

Out of the pit was rising a monster of vast proportions. It was scaled like a reptile, dark green in color, and it had two red lamps for eyes. Apparently, the monster stood on a section

of the floor which could be lowered and raised like a stage in
some of the newer theaters. The section reached the top of the
dais, the elevation of the monster stopped, and the astonished
spectators beheld a gigantic and creditable reproduction of a
crocodile. It winked its red eyes, stamped its feet, and shook
its ugly snout.

A ripple of applause began, ascended in volume, then abruptly
ceased.

The snout of the monster had opened. Out of it slid a girl: a
lovely, fairy figure, straight from the garden of the gods. She
was clad in a scant jade green scarf and jade green shoes were
on her tiny feet. Her limbs and shoulders were dazzling white
and her hair was black as jet.

A thunder of applause shook the hall. Women screamed with
delight; men whistled and stamped their feet. Gail recognized
the girl as a noted New York dancer who had been on the
coast during the past month. She found a program on the
table before her. Opening it, she read:

JIM BEASLEY
Presents
ARLENE DEANE
in
THE DANCE OF THE GREEN CROCODILE

The music quickened and the girl began to dance. Her figure
was as light as the motes in a sunbeam, as liquid as quicksilver.
The dance had a sacrificial motif as intricately patterned as a
mosaic, and the girl floated through it with a scintillating
brilliance that held her audience spellbound.

Again the music quickened; so did the tempo of the dance.
The girl clapped her hands, a trill of joy broke from her lips,
and the green light turned blood-red, then gold, then brilliant
blue, and jade green again. Her fairy body personified the
youth and joy and beauty of all time. Sheathed and tongued
in colored flame it whirled into so riotous an ecstasy of
movement that the limitations of the flesh fell away from it
and she danced like one come from the gods to gladden the
hearts of men.

Meanwhile, Kessler had disposed of another cocktail and
Gail, on her own account, had fed one to the potted palm.
Kessler was quite pleasantly jingled by this. He had quickly
lost interest in the presentation below, his eyes returning
continually to Gail's copper-red head. Reaching out now, he

drew the curtain. Then he leaned across the table and put his hand on Gail's.

She met his swimming eyes steadily. Her hour had come and she was asking herself if she had the nerve to go through with it. His hands were cold and white, and hairless, like a woman's. His pale face swayed a little; the expression of his light-blue eyes frightened her. Then she looked at his mouth and jaw. No character! No strength! She felt comforted a little. The touch of his hand reminded her of Stark. Ugh!

The weakness of the plan she and Blondy had concocted between them was pitilessly clear to Gail now. Would Blondy in the booth behind be able to hear what Kessler might be persuaded to admit? Beasley's presentation had sobered the revelers, even their applause was withheld until the dance should end, and the partitions between the booths were thin; but Gail doubted the carrying power of Kessler's voice in his intimate moments. No! The whole scheme was impractical; a waste of time. She had been a fool to try it!

And then a curious thought came to her. It frightened her at first; then it gave her fresh hope. Hadn't Blondy been aware of this all along? She must have known that the din at the Green Crocodile would be deafening. Was it her intention to swear to anything she, Gail, said Kessler admitted, whether she overheard him herself or not? But that would be perjury! Was Blondy prepared to go to this length for the sake of getting back at Kessler? It looked like it. Was she herself prepared to go to this length for Kerry? She thought for a moment, Kessler's hand still on hers. Yes, she was! She would be a party to perjury for Kerry's sake. But could they make it stand up in court? Well, the only thing to do was to try it.

Kessler spoke in maudlin tones.

"She's not bad, but she's got nothing on you, little redhead."

Gail twinkled at him. "Think so, Nick? I wonder if you do?"

His ardent eyes distended a little. "Give me half a chance and I'll show you."

"What do you want?"

He leaned nearer. "You and I are going to be pretty good pals, aren't we?"

"Maybe, Nick."

"What's the matter with us going together, li'l' redhead?"

Gail withdrew her hand and lit a cigarette, coolly, deliberately. She was thinking swiftly. A glimmer of an idea broke through the fog in her mind. It promised well.

"Going together, Nick," she drawled. "What do you mean?"

Kessler winked. "You're not particular, are you?"

Gail pretended a vast indignation. "Aren't I? Let me tell you I'm an honest girl—and I work for my living!"

Kessler snickered. There was a hectic flush on his white cheeks now. A silver flask stood on the table. He poured a generous measure into a tumbler and swallowed it neat. Then he pushed the flask towards Gail.

"Help yourself."

Gail moved it aside; her eyes narrowed. "Come to the point, Nick. What do you want?" Then, in a louder voice: "Speak up, I can't hear you." This was for Blondy's benefit.

Kessler's eyes were like balls of fire. "I want you, you redheaded witch! And I'm going to have you!"

He sprawled across the table towards Gail. She whipped up her cigarette. Its red-hot tip stopped an inch or so away from Kessler's ardent eyes.

"Not so fast, old timer. Take it easy!" Then, in a slightly differently toned voice: "Can you hear?"

"Hear? Sure I can hear," Kessler grunted drunkenly.

But Gail was listening attentively for a signal of some sort from Bloody in the next booth. It came: a faint tap, tap, on the partition behind Kessler's head. Gail's heart gave a bound. Blondy could hear after all. If only Arlene Deane, the dancer, would hold her audience spellbound for another ten minutes! Kessler, apparently, had not heard Blondy's tap.

The orchestra was playing a tender love melody no louder than a summer breeze.

"The man that wants me," Gail stated coolly, "has got to come through."

"Thasso!" Kessler grunted. He made a vague gesture in the air. "Money, hey?"

Gail smiled and drew on her cigarette. "You bet your life there's got to be money." She paused and poured whisky from the flask into a tumbler and left it there. "But there's got to be more than money, Nick."

"Yea?" Kessler's head wagged from side to side.

His eyes strayed to the liquor in the glass. "Whaddoyou want, li'l' green girl?"

Gail looked down at her hands. "A ring, Nick," she said demurely.

He began to laugh fatuously, moisture drooling at the corners of his weak mouth.

"Marry you, eh! Tha's what you want, is it?"

Gail's hand rested lightly on his arm. She blew cigarette

smoke into his eyes and smiled at him bewitchingly.

"Don't you want to marry me, Nick?" she asked softly.

Kessler gulped down the whisky Gail had poured out. "Marry you! Sure I want to, you redheaded witch, you!" he cried in an exultant whisper. "Be a fool if I wouldn't! Ain't got a wife any moo-ore!" he chanted.

"Speak louder, Nick," Gail cried petulantly. "I can't hear you!"

He shot a look of suspicion at her; but his wits were fuddled and the girl's eyes were wide and candid, and whatever was in his mind quickly passed. He repeated himself somewhat incoherently; then he sprawled across the table again, his hands reaching for Gail.

"Aw, come on, li'l' redhead! Be a good li'l' sport!" he pleaded.

But Gail drew back with a tantalizing laugh and whirled her glowing cigarette in front of his face.

"Naughty, Nicky, naughty!" she cried lightly. "Burny burn. You haven't got me, yet."

He drew back before the cigarette and Gail pursued him with the glowing end of it until she had him at a safe distance. She was thinking with all the hard concentration her keen young mind was capable of. Her glimmer of an idea was leading her to light. She must stress the money motif. The rapt silence of the dancer's audience continued. If only it might last a little longer!

"But I'm not forgetting the cash end of it, Nick," she went on, deliberately. "That interests me as much as the ring. I want a name and I want the stuff to keep it up. And," she paused for emphasis, "and I don't much care how I get 'em!"

Kessler fumbled in the pocket of his dinner jacket, drew out a wallet, took from it a huge wad of bills, and slapped it down on the table.

"Eight hundred iron men!" he shouted thickly. "How zat?"

Gail turned up her dainty nose. "You'll need more than eight hundred to carry me, Nick."

Kessler grunted. "Tha's only chicken feed, ol' girl. Cig'rette money. I got—I got—" He was stumbling solemnly over his words now. "I got fifty thousand put where'll do the mos' good. And I got"—his voice dropped confidentially—"more coming!"

"Yea?"

The single drawled word was derisive. Its significance pierced the drunken fog clouding Kessler's brain.

"You don' b'lieve me, li'l' green girl, huh?"

"I didn't say so, Nick. Where'd you get it all?"

Gail casually poured out another drink of the whisky and

pushed it towards Kessler. He swallowed it neat.

"Never min' where I got it," he growled, wagging his head. "I got it—tha's 'nough, isn't it?"

Gail sniffed cynically. "Same old story, Nick. I heard it before." She half rose to her feet. In a flurry of drunken haste he was up, forcing her down by the arms. He tried to embrace her and Gail touched his hand with the end of her cigarette. Kessler reeled back with an oath and flopped down onto his chair.

"Sorry," Gail said, with a caress in her voice.

"Whaddoyou care how I got my money so's you get the spending of it?" he mumbled.

Gail lit another cigarette. "Oh, I like to know what kind of a man I'm tying up with. I like to know if he's got—nerve."

"Nerve!" Kessler echoed. "Nerve!" The word roused a storm of indignation in him. "Nerve's my middle name!"

"I wonder."

His face crimsoned and he pounded on the table with his fist.

"Yes—nerve!" he shouted thickly, and his wrath sobered him a little. "I'd be in a devil of a mess if I hadn't it! Nerve and a gun in my han'!" he added.

Gail's lip curled. "A gun! To peddle a bottle of bootleg! And you talk of nerve!"

Kessler was furious. He waved his arms in the air. "A bottle o' boo'leg!" he snarled. "I brought in two boa'loads las' month! An' I go' another coming!"

As he said this Gail felt as if fire were running through her veins. She could hardly hold herself still on the chair. A minute or two longer and she and Blondy would have it out of him!

"Bringing it in around here, Nick?" she asked, in a loud but casual voice.

Before he could reply a thunder of applause shook the Green Crocodile. It rose volume on volume until the ceiling rafters trembled. Gail stared at the man on the other side of the table, sick at heart, but still smiling. If the presentation was over, Blondy wouldn't be able to hear a word!

Kessler groped drunkenly for the curtains and parted them. Over the heads of the excited spectators Gail caught a glimpse of the dais. Arlene Deane, the dancer, was prostrate before the crocodile which moved its snout up and down and from side to side as if it were a deity considering the acceptance in sacrifice of the lovely figure in front of it. The audience broke forth into fresh expressions of appreciation and Nick dropped the curtain. Gail waited, shivering a little.

As quickly as it had begun the applause ceased. A hush filled the hall again. The orchestra began to play a plaintive melody that reminded Gail of the whispering of falling leaves on an autumn day. She had to clench her teeth to repress the sob of relief that rose to her lips. The presentation was not yet over!

"Bringing it in around here, Nick?" Gail found herself saying again, in the same hard and casual tone.

"Why?" Kessler's bleared eyes flickered a little, as with suspicion.

"Oh, I just wondered," Gail responded coolly. "They say stuff has been coming in around here. I thought maybe it was yours."

The suspicion faded out of his eyes; he snickered with tipsy boastfulness. "Sure it was, li'l' green girl!" he cried, slurring his words. "I go' a load out there now."

"Have you!" Gail exclaimed admiringly. "Why don't you bring it in?"

He solemnly wagged his head from side to side. "I'm gonna bring it in—soon's it's safe! I'll fool them sniff houn's yet, I will! They can't put it over Nick Kessler!"

"I'll bet they can't, Nicky dear!" Gail cried. She leaned nearer, blew smoke into his eyes, patted his hand, gave a little silver laugh. "Why isn't it safe?"

"Too much noshin' 'round."

"Nosing around, Nicky—what do you mean?"

"Whaddoyou wan' to know for?"

Gail's dark eyes seemed almost to melt into his. "Aw, tell me, Nicky. It isn't that I want to know—a girl likes to feel her man trusts her! That's all."

"You redheaded de'il!" he cried, in drunken ecstasy. "I'm comin' for you!"

He tried to scramble to his feet, but his legs were no steadier than his head was clear and Gail, perching herself on the top of the table, easily forced him down, and with the glowing end of her cigarette an inch or so from his ardent eyes held him still.

"You stay there, old dear," she cried, with a tinkling laugh, "until you've told me the rest of it. I don't go with any man that doesn't trust me. Get that into your old fat head."

He grinned up at her fatuously. She saw the beastliness of the man, his corruption, his cowardice, the intemperance of his desire, and she could hardly refrain from flinging herself out of the booth. No! she must go through with it. She could almost hear Blondy listening behind the partition.

"Daniels was sure you'd be afraid to tell me," Gail said softly.

"Daniels!" he mumbled, staring up at her. "Daniels—tell you what?"

Gail gave a little throaty laugh. "What he and you saw at the Conniston summer house the other night."

He stared at her with drunken incredulity. "Daniels tol' you—that!" he mumbled.

He shook his head as a dog shakes itself. His fuddled wits scented danger, but they were too far gone to grasp it.

Gail laughed lightly. "He knew you'd be afraid to. Joe's got nerve, Nick. Nerve! I like a man like that!"

Kessler's fist crashed down upon the table. "Like—that rat!" he bellowed, crimson of face and sobered. "'Fraid! The l-liar!"

"Well, what *did* you see?" Gail drawled.

She was swinging lightly on the edge of the table, puffing on her cigarette, laughing down at him, as lovely as Circe. But her heart was hammering against her ribs; she could hardly trust herself to draw breath. The plaintive melody the orchestra was playing came to her as from a distance.

"I'll tell you what I saw, li'l' green girl!" Kessler shouted in reckless maudlin tones. "The liar! I'll show you who's 'fraid! I'll tell you any ol' thing you wan' to know!"

He stopped to take breath. He meant what he said. Gail knew that he meant it, too. She had won. For a moment she experienced the ecstasy of victory. And then, in a flash, it was turned to the bitterness of defeat.

A whistle shrilled out in the hall below. It was followed by the crash of breaking windows. The effect upon Kessler was remarkable. His face went deathly white and he sprang to his feet with an oath. His eyes rolled in fear and his weak mouth fell open, giving his face an absurd, terrified expression. Gail had slipped down from the table with a little sharp cry of distress. She knew what had happened. Kessler flung her aside and swept back the curtains.

Those on the balcony were on their feet, crowding back upon each other, consternation in their faces. The air was thick with curses; a woman screamed. Down below the music had ceased. Arlene Deane, the dancer, shrank back against Beasley's grotesque crocodile. The revelers surged back and forth in terror, formed into little knots, broke apart again, swept back upon one another like sheep lost in a mountain fog.

Whistles pierced the odorous air again. Men in plainclothes, but bearing the unmistakable stamp of authority, ran to and fro, uttering commands in sharp, staccato tones. The revelers gave way before them like debris tossed on a rip tide. Other men poured in through broken windows, leaving guards behind them.

Kessler spun round upon Gail. He was sober now—sobered by his terror. His face had a purplish cast, his white hands shook, his big body quivered. Gail, herself in despair, nevertheless was appalled by the extent of the man's collapse.

"I got to get out of this! I got to get out!" he sobbed. "They've raided the Croc!"

CHAPTER XXV
Trapped

But Gail could think of nothing but her own defeat. Defeat on the verge of success. Before that whistle had shrilled out she had been sure of Kessler. Now she was sure of nothing but the ruin of her plans. She heard Kessler whispering hoarsely. "We got to get out, Red! Stick by me! I know a way. If the cops get me, I'm done! You'll stick by me, Red?"

Gail did not answer him. She wanted to get away from the man, to breathe the cool sweet air of the open night. Desperately she stared up and down the gallery, this end in view; and then all thought of her own escape was driven from her mind. Kerry O'Neil was bearing down upon them, his lean face white with rage. Gail was in terror. Kerry would clash with Kessler. That would be the end—if the end had not come already!

Kessler's hand closed on her wrist, then; he pulled her out of the booth onto the balcony.

Kerry bored his way through the panic-stricken multitude rippling and eddying around the tables. Kessler did likewise, drawing Gail after him. The two men were approaching each other. A dozen feet separated them. In a moment they would crash. Kerry's face was a mask of fury. They could hardly have met under worse conditions!

Half a dozen plainclothesmen raced up the broad staircase.

Kerry was upon them. He hurled himself at Kessler. The latter, completely taken by surprise, reeled back with an oath. And at that instant every light in the Green Crocodile went out.

The darkness dropped like a black pall. A nerve-racking stillness followed upon it. There wasn't so much as a glimmer of light anywhere. No one could see his neighbor's face. An audible shiver rippled through the roadhouse. A woman screamed; men gasped in a choking way. The interior of the Crocodile seemed to rustle with a hundred hidden terrors.

A sharp command rang out. Another. Beams of light from electric torches threaded the darkness.

Gail was listening for sounds of conflict between Kerry and Kessler. She heard none. They must have become separated in the darkness. Thank Heaven! If only she could get Kessler away before the lights went on. A hand closed on her wrist. It was Kessler's!

"Come on, Red!" he gasped.

She let him hurry her between the tables. A door opened. They sped down a narrow passage as black as pitch; through another door, and Gail found herself clattering down a staircase behind Kessler. The man went as surefootedly as a cat. Evidently this sort of thing was an old story to him.

Gail did not know where she was. So long as she could keep Kerry and this beast Kessler apart she did not care. They emerged into the cool clean air of the open courtyard. A round, golden moon was rising above the ridge. Kessler stopped, peered cautiously around.

"You are going to stick with me, Red!" he growled unsteadily in Gail's ear. "You know what I mean!" His hand tightened cruelly on her wrist.

"Yes, yes, Nick. Sure, Nick! We must get away—quick. Oh! you are hurting me!"

"I like you, Red—I'll hang diamonds on your ears if you want 'em. But I'll wring your neck if you turn me down!"

"Yes, Nick."

"Come on, then. Before they find the light switch. Step easy. My car's outside."

Kessler softly led her towards the main gate. A man was on guard there. They drew back into the shadow of a date palm. The green electric sign above the roadhouse and the lamps placed around the grounds were in darkness, as well as the building itself. If the lights went on they would be seen. Gail could hear Kessler muttering to himself.

"This way!" he whispered. His voice shook with fear.

A cinder path strange to Gail's feet brought them through banks of flowering shrubbery to a small door in the green board fence which surrounded the grounds. It was open. It was unguarded. They passed through the door. Before them on the side of the road were such of the cars belonging to the patrons of the Green Crocodile as had not been able to find accommodation in the parking space provided within the courtyard. Kessler hurried Gail towards one of the machines, a high-powered roadster.

"Get in! I'm taking the dirt road. They'd see us the other way!"

The engine purred and with darkened head and taillights the car slid into the highway, nosed around the county sign that blocked the condemned dirt road, and shot like a dark rocket into the emptiness of the night.

The lights in the Green Crocodile went on and the electric sign flashed out.

Kessler did not speak. His hands were glued to the wheel, his eyes to the dim ribbon of road ahead. His lips were drawn back, giving him an expression of ferocity; but his teeth were chattering and his face had that gray pasty look of one whose nerve is almost gone.

The cool night air beating on Gail's hot face cleared her brain, gave her a more exact understanding of her position. She had got Kessler away, but where was he taking her to? She found herself in terror of the man again. The roadster was doing forty miles an hour. How was she to get away from him? Yet she must! He intended unspeakable things.

Just then the car rose perilously on a bump in the road, rocked dangerously for an instant, and threatened to overturn. Kessler screamed, bent low over the wheel, swung to the left. The car righted itself, straightened out. Its speed lessened.

Gail looked at Kessler curiously. The man was shaking from head to foot and his face had gone a greenish tinge; he was muttering incoherently to himself. Her fear of him gave way to contempt.

Absently groping in the seat of the car, Gail's hand encountered a metallic object with a wooden handle. A small screwdriver! What was it doing there? Then she saw that one of the screws which held the speedometer in the instrument board was loose. Probably Kessler had been trying to tighten it. Gail found herself clinging to the tool tenaciously. She did not know why.

A moment later Gail became aware of a faint brilliance behind them. She glanced back and saw the headlights of another car. Her heart gave a bound. Was the car in pursuit of them? Or were its occupants patrons of the Green Crocodile, like Kessler and herself escaping the wrath of the dry squad along the condemned dirt road? She looked at Kessler surreptitiously. He was still muttering to himself. Behind, the headlights grew. The car was gaining.

Gail had an odd lightness of heart. No longer did she fear the man at her side. The screwdriver bothered her, though. She looked at it, frowning. Then she glanced up and saw the blackness of the cypress grove several miles ahead. It stood out against the sky line. Beyond it was the Casa de Ayer.

"The grove!" Gail whispered to herself. She had a queer and thrilling feeling of expectancy.

The roadster purred on like a contented cat. Kessler accelerated and its purr grew louder. Some of his nerve had returned to him, but his face still had that greenish cast.

Gail was astonished to find herself trembling with excitement and by an inward sense urged on to an undetermined course of action. She must do something! What?

"The cypress grove—the screwdriver—the car behind—Kessler's terror."

The phrases revolved in her mind as if they formed a part of the key to a secret formula. There was a link missing somewhere. She could not get the proper association of ideas.

The roadster rushed on. The headlights behind had swelled a little. Kessler must quickly become aware of them. Gail clenched her hands. What was this association of ideas that eluded her so persistently?

Suddenly, she had it!

Its daring and its promise thrilled her. She might yet turn defeat into victory. The cypress grove was some two miles ahead now. She had three minutes in which to execute her inspired plan. Her hand fell on Kessler's arm.

"Nick! There's a car behind—a police car! They are gaining on us!"

Kessler flung a terrified glance over his shoulder, gave a cry that was between a gasp and a groan, and dropped his head lower over the wheel. His white face was agleam with sweat.

"If they get me, I'm done!" he groaned.

The car hurled itself forward under the urge of fresh power.

"You can't beat 'em that way, Nick! Slow down! They're faster than we are!"

He took no notice of her. His lips were ashen.

"We can't beat 'em, you fool!" Gail screamed, digging her fingers into his arm. "Slow down! I know another way!"

He did not seem to have heard her. Ahead, the shadow of the cypress grove swelled like a thundercloud on a summer's day.

"Nick, you fool! Slow down! Do you want to see the inside of San Quentin?"

This got him. "God! no! It'll mean that, if they get me!"

"I know! It's a police car. They are gaining on us. They'll get us if we keep on! I know another way. We can beat 'em, Nick. Beat 'em!"

He checked the roadster a little. "Beat 'em, you say! How? Quick, Red! If the cops get me—"

"They won't if you trust me!"

"Maybe!"

"You'll do what I say, Nick?" Gail's voice was low, softly persuasive, charged with every bit of feeling she could cram into it.

"I'll wring your neck if you do me up!"

"Aw, Nick!" Gail stroked his arm. "How can you say that? Listen!" Her voice had sharpened. "That shadow ahead—see it?"

"Yes."

"It's a cypress grove. I know a road that leads into it. Know it well. Let me at the wheel, Nick. We'll slip into it."

"What then?"

"The cops'll shoot past. Never know we are there until it's too late. There's a trail down the cliff—"

"I know it!"

"Near the foot of it there's a cave. A secret cave, Nick—a swell place! You and me, Nick—we'll hide in it till dawn. They'll never find us. Let me at the wheel. Quick!—we are nearly there!"

Kessler turned his eyes full upon Gail. They were sunk deep in their sockets and they reminded her of living eyes in a death's head. They seemed to scorch her, so fierce was the heat of his terror of the law.

"All right—slip over!"

He held the wheel steady while Gail crawled over his knees; then he slipped into the other seat.

The bluff rushed down upon them like a dark monster of ancient legend. Gail riveted her eyes upon it; her hands were like iron on the wheel. The little road—she could not see it! For an instant she was tempted to switch on the headlights. Better not! Ah! there it was! But she could hardly distinguish it against the dark background of conifers. Could she do it? Touch and go if she did. And if they didn't— She could feel Kessler's hot breath on her cheeks. The shadow of the bluff enveloped them. Now!

Deftly she swung the car to the left, jerked it to the right. It rose on two wheels. A mudguard crumpled like matchwood against the trunk of a cypress. The machine shot ahead, tilted on two wheels again, threatened to overturn.... It straightened out between the whispering conifers, and with the scream of brakes came to a shuddering stop in the heart of the grove. Gail shut off the engine. Kessler's hand was clamped like a vise on her arm.

"Let go, Nick! You are hurting me."

He did so. Then he took a deep breath and drew his hand

across his gleaming forehead.

A streak of white and a dark shadow swept past on the road outside.

Gail knew that she would collapse if she permitted a slackening of the tension she was under before her end had been attained.

"Got a flash, Nick?" she demanded tersely.

"Yes."

"Let's have it. Quick!"

He fumbled about in the door pocket near him, took out a torch, and handed it to her.

"Come on."

He followed her through the trees in silence. But when they had come to the head of the cliff trail he seized her by the wrist.

"Wha' did you bring that thing for?" he demanded.

Gail looked at the screwdriver in her left hand and laughed lightly.

"Now aren't I the fool carrying that darn thing with me!" she cried. "I found it in the seat!"

He did not let go of her wrist. "Listen here! if you try any monkey tricks you'll not see daylight again! Remember that!"

Gail widened her eyes at him. "Why, Nick!" she exclaimed. "What makes you talk that way? Aren't I taking chances for you going down here?" Her voice softened; she let her copper-red head incline towards his cheek. "Nick, honey—I'd like to see the other man I'd do it for!"

He released her wrist, muttering to himself. "Go ahead!"

Gail swung the beam of the torch down the crooked trail she had ascended behind Kessler and Daniels some thirty-six hours before; she then commenced the rugged descent, Kessler following close behind her. Thanks to the torch, they got over the rougher bits without mishap and several minutes later stopped in front of the subway-like depression that led down into the cave of terror in which Don Silvestre Calderón had ended his life sixty years before.

And now, with the boom of the pit in her ears, the strength that had carried her this far deserted Gail. She began to tremble; her legs threatened to give way beneath her. She felt that the feat of opening the door of that pit of horror was beyond her. And then she felt, rather than saw, Kessler's eyes upon her again.

"What sort of a hole is this?" he growled.

His voice steadied her; strength flowed back into her body.

"Why, Nick!—you *are* queer!" she laughed, a little shrilly. "What's the matter? Don't mind the noise. It's the *swellest* place inside. Wait till you see it!"

His suspicions disarmed again, or partly so, Kessler followed her down the subway-like depression. Gail was careful to keep the light away from the brass plate on the door.

She found the padlock just as she had left it: the hasp thrust over the staple and held in place by the broken padlock. Gail unfastened the door with trembling fingers and let it swing open. She held the torch so that its flare did not illumine the interior of the cavern.

The reek of the place sickened the girl. Again paralyzing physical weakness threatened to overcome her, but she fought it down. Nick stood at her shoulder, peering into the cavern. She saw his eyes narrow upon her again.

"Throw the light inside!" he growled.

Gail gave a little laugh. "You are not *afraid*, are you, Nicky?"

He stepped closer, stood inside the doorway. Gail quietly stepped behind him. For a moment he stood still, peering into the dark and roaring pit ahead; then he must have sensed her intention, for he suddenly whirled around with a diabolical fury on his white face. As he did so, Gail summoned every ounce of her failing strength and hurled herself straight at his broad chest. He staggered back with a fearful scream, hands desperately clawing the air, lost his footing on the sloping floor of the tunnel, and went down into the darkness.

Gail had dropped the torch. She dragged the door to, groped for the hasp, and slipped it over the staple, securing it in place with the screwdriver. Then her strength gave out and she fell in a heap at the bottom of the door.

CHAPTER XXVI
The Death Pit

Success is an excellent restorative, however, and Gail quickly came to herself again. She climbed onto her feet and leaned against the side of the depression, clasping her hands together.

"Kerry!" she whispered exultantly. "I've got him!"

It certainly seemed so.

A fearful commotion was taking place on the other side of the door. Kessler was flinging his body upon it with tremendous force. The door shook and groaned and the screwdriver jumped and rattled against the hasp and staple. Would the staple hold? If it didn't—Gail shuddered at the thought. The possibility of it not holding was too horrible to contemplate. Kessler, bent on revenge, would be as merciless as a tiger. She felt at the fastening. It seemed solid enough.

"Let me out, you devil!" Kessler screamed through the small barred opening below the brass plate. "Let me out! I'll kill you! You—" A stream of unprintable obscenities followed.

Gail fumbled for the torch, but she did not light it. She did not speak. She just stood there in silence, smiling a little into the darkness. The staple would hold. Gail had a sort of intuitive confidence in it. There was plenty of time—now.

She heard the boom of the waters imprisoned in the cavern. The tide was low. At high water the pit would be an inferno. Indeed, it was that already.

A little while passed. Still Gail remained silent. Kessler continued to hurl himself at the door and to befoul the night with obscene vituperations through which there now ran a piercing note of terror. The rock at Gail's back quivered beneath the subterranean pounding of the incoming tide. She heard the snarl and hiss of the tortured waters. Gail waited, still smiling into the darkness.

"Red—let me out! This stinking hole—it'll kill me! There's things—alive—crawling in it!" A scream. "For God's sake!"

Gail waited a minute or two longer; then she turned the flare of the torch full upon his face, white and ghastly and terrible in the square opening in the door. There was foam on his lips and a frenzy of terror in his eyes. Gail remembered her reflection that a day and a night spent within this place might drive a man mad. She studied the wretched face before her.

No, Kessler hadn't come to the end of his rope yet. It didn't matter. There was plenty of time.

"Red," he whispered. "Let me out! I can't stand it! What do you want?"

"The tide is coming in, Kessler." She spoke as Gail Hollister now. "It should fill the cave in five hours." This was untrue, but Gail doubted Kessler's knowledge of the fact.

"What!—the tide!" His cry ended in a scream.

Gail extinguished the torch. In the depression the darkness was like a velvet curtain. She did not reply.

The man threatened, pleaded, blasphemed, by turns. Then he hurled himself upon the door again and rammed it until its ancient timbers creaked and groaned. But to no purpose. The staple held true. Kessler began to sob like a woman.

"Let me out! Let me out! Let me out!"

Ten minutes passed.

Gail shot the light into Kessler's face again. Its expression was pitiable.

"Whadoyou want?" he moaned.

Gail held the light steady for a moment, blinding him. His face, framed in the opening of the door, made her think of some unhappy wretch confined in a dungeon of the Middle Ages.

"Whadoyou want, Red? I'll do anything if you'll only let me out! It's killing me!"

"It will unless I let you out," Gail said coolly. "You can't break down the door. Your body will go out on the tide."

"God help me!" the man whispered. "I'll do anything you want, Red!"

"Do you know who I am?"

"No, no! Who are you?"

"Gail Hollister."

His eyes started from his head. "That—redheaded girl—O'Neil's girl—you!"

"Yes. I heard you and Daniels talking here yesterday afternoon. (It was not yet midnight.) I followed you up to the Green Crocodile. I lost out there, Kessler—but I've got you here!" Gail's voice rang with a note of cold fury. "You cowardly beast! You'd let an innocent man hang for a crime he didn't commit! Well, you are here and here you stay until you agree to tell Deputy Sheriff Bartlett what you and Daniels saw at the summer house the night Dimity was killed!"

The man's face convulsed with fresh rage. "By God!" he screamed. "I won't! I'll see you in—"

"The tide is rising, Kessler. I'll leave you to think it over."

Gail snapped off the flash, turned, and started up the depression.

"Come back, Red! Come back! Don't leave me in this hell-hole!" the man screamed.

Gail's purpose in leaving him was two-fold. If the man was going to "break," as she devoutly prayed, solitude would wreck him quicker than anything else. And if he did "break" she would need a witness. Her unsupported word would be worthless.

She believed there was just a chance that she might find a car going to or coming from the Green Crocodile along the condemned road. A police car, perhaps, or a stray reveler seeking to escape the consequences of his transgressions. If there wasn't, she would drive to the Casa de Ayer in Kessler's car and get Dr. McEwan.

But when Gail had come up the trail to the road she was relieved to see a pair of headlights bearing down upon her from the direction of the Green Crocodile. The car was traveling fast, but she ran out in front of it and waved her arms, a slender, gem-like figure in the green georgette. The machine, a roadster, slowed down, smothering her in dust, and stopped. A young man leaped out and ran towards her.

"Gail Hollister!" he shouted incredulously.

It was Perrin, the reporter!

"What are you doing here?" he cried, seizing her hands. He ran his eyes over the green georgette now sadly crumpled. "Lord!" he whistled. "What's all this? Where *have* you been? We've been looking for you all day."

Gail told him, in a hurried sentence or two. He looked at her in admiration, then with astonishment and wonder in his eyes.

"The Crocodile!" he cried softly. "You must think a lot of this man O'Neil, Gail Hollister!"

There was a note of pain in his voice which escaped Gail.

"I do," she said simply.

"I've just come from the Crocodile," Perrin hurried on. "I got word of the raid and I skipped the beginning of the inquest to get in on it."

"The inquest! I thought it was called for yesterday."

"It was. But you were missing and Bartlett had it postponed until tonight. The coroner was late getting down so it was delayed again. It's on now."

"You were at the Crocodile," Gail cried. "Kerry was there. Do you know—if he got away?"

"O'Neil gave himself up. The car he was in went on ahead of mine. He should be at the house now. Best thing he could do, too. He should have done it at first.... This man Kessler—pretty slick, getting him down there! Do you suppose he'll talk?"

"He's got to!" Gail asserted. "And he's got to identify Stark as the man who killed Dimity! Come on."

They found Kessler with his face framed in the opening in the door. As Gail flashed the light upon him she was reminded again of a death's head, so ghastly was the man's expression. For a moment she was tempted to pity him; then she remembered Kerry. Perrin stood close to the wall of the depression so that Kessler could not see him.

The man's lips were moving soundlessly. Then he began to whisper something. At first they could not hear what he was saying. Then his utterance grew louder.

"Let me out, for the love of God!" he was sobbing over and over.

Gail pressed nearer. "Are you ready to tell what you saw the other night?"

The wretched man fell silent. Gail kept the torch steady, its white beam full on his twitching face. Across it suddenly broke a tidal wave of hate and fury, and from his lips poured so scorching a stream of vituperation that Perrin started away from the wall with a low exclamation of anger. Gail restrained him with a touch of her hand.

This outburst was abruptly silenced. During the last minute or two the waters imprisoned in the cavern had been comparatively quiet. But now they broke forth into a snarling, hissing, booming tornado of sound that shook the cliff. Through the opening in the door poured the stink of corruption, and Kessler whirled around as if he feared some foul hand were reaching out to drag him down into the pit behind. Gail shot the flare of the torch past his head so that he might fully realize the nature of his prison. He gave a scream and flung himself upon the door again, beating at it with his fists.

"Yes—I'll tell—anything! I saw him do it! Let me out!"

"You'll make a statement?"

"Yes! Yes!"

Gail uttered a cry of thankfulness. Perrin, at her shoulder, gave a little sharp "Ah!" of delight.

"I want to know what you and Daniels were doing at the summer house the night Dimity was killed," Gail said clearly. "I want to know what you saw. Tell me everything."

"Let me out—first!" Kessler whispered.

"No."

Kessler moistened his lips with the tip of his tongue. For a moment he seemed to have lost the faculty of speech. Then, in low and sullen tones, he began:

"Joe Daniels and I were to bring in a boatload of bootleg liquor early Wednesday morning. We had a pile of driftwood heaped up near the Casa de Ayer. If we lighted it, Swanson was to run into a cove down near the Crocodile. If we didn't, he was to stay out.

"Around midnight we went up to signal Swanson to come in. Just as we got near the place where the driftwood was, we saw three men running along the beach with flashlights, as if they were looking for someone. They were flashing every shadow and cave along the cliff and Joe and I were so caught that we couldn't get up or down the beach without being seen. The men looked like cops and we knew we'd have to talk if they found us—the last thing we wanted. There was a trail near us. It led up the cliff. We didn't know just where it went to, but it was the only way out and we took it. The moon had gone behind a cloud so they didn't see us.

"There was a summer house at the top of the trail. At first we thought there was nobody in it; then we saw an old man sitting there. He looked as if he were waiting for someone. We were just going to sneak off along the cliff when another man came out of an olive grove behind the summer house. He looked around as if he wanted to be sure nobody was watching him. We were in the shadow of a cypress, so he didn't see us. Then we saw that he had a piece of iron pipe in his hand. Well, he walked into the summerhouse, the old man started up, and the other man cracked him over the head with the pipe. Then he sneaked off and so did we. That's all."

"You saw the man's face?" Gail asked tersely.

"Yes. We were pretty close to him."

"You could identify him?"

"I s'pose so. I don't know his name. Aren't you going to let me out of this hole now?"

"Not yet, old-timer," Perrin drawled, coming forward. "We want a written statement from you, signed and witnessed."

Gail saw the blood rush to Kessler's haggard face; his teeth bared. It flashed upon her that he had hoped to deal with her alone. But Kessler was beaten; his flare of defiance died.

"All right," he gasped. "You've got me."

Perrin took notebook and fountain pen from his pocket and while Gail held the torch so that he could see what he was doing, wrote swiftly.

"Listen to this, Kessler," he said presently.

"I, Nick Kessler, declare that Joe Daniels and I planned to bring in a boatload of bootleg liquor some time Wednesday morning, August 26th, and that towards midnight, Tuesday, August 25th, we went up to a beach near the Casa de Ayer to light a signal fire. I further declare that to avoid questioning by deputy sheriffs who were then on the beach, we climbed the cliff trail which leads to the summer house, in the grounds of the Casa de Ayer, and that there we saw a man whose name we do not know club an old man on the head with a piece of iron pipe. I further declare that we withheld this statement from the authorities to protect our own interests, and that I now make it of my own free will without the coercion of anyone."

"How's that, Miss Hollister?" Perrin asked pridefully.

"Splendid!" Gail cried. She was too overjoyed to say more.

Perrin thrust the notebook and the fountain pen through the opening in the door.

"Sign it, Kessler. And make it legible. Hold the light so he can see, Miss Hollister."

Gail did so. Kessler sullenly wrote his name and handed the book and pen back to Perrin. The latter then witnessed the statement. Gail followed his example, her fingers trembling so that she could scarcely hold the pen.

Her task was done! She wanted to laugh, to shout, to dance, to make some extravagant demonstration of her happiness.

Perrin tore out the statement and pocketed it.

"I don't suppose you have a gun, Kessler, but you'd better stick your hands up and keep 'em up." Perrin opened the door.

"Come on—your hands up!"

Kessler stumbled out into the beam of light from the torch, eyes on the ground. Gail thought of a whipped dog as she looked at him. Perrin went through his pockets, but he was unarmed. The young man shut the door.

"Kessler," he said sternly, "you are going to the Casa de Ayer with us. And when you get there you are going to stand by this statement you have made—every word of it—and you are going to pick out the man you and Daniels saw kill old Dimity. He'll be there. Understand, Kessler?"

The man nodded sullenly.

"Up the trail to my car.... March!"

CHAPTER XXVII
"There He Is!"

When Perrin drove up to the Casa de Ayer some fifteen minutes later, Gail saw that every window was ablaze with light. A dozen or more cars were parked in front of the house. How different it looked from when she had first seen it six nights before! Atmosphere being largely a quality of the imagination, she supposed that once they had settled this matter of Conniston's and Dimity's death much of its dark glamour would vanish.

The front door was ajar and they entered, sending Kessler, sullen and passive, before them. Voices came from the library, the door of which stood open. They passed down the hall and paused outside the library. The room was packed. The inquest was not yet over. A dozen staid and earnest men were seated along one wall—the coroner's jury. Their tired faces expressed their weariness of the formalities of the law. Behind the library table sat an elderly bearded man with shrewd eyes—the coroner. Besides the coroner and his jury, nearly a score of people were packed into the room: Mrs. Wessels, Stark, Dr. McEwan, Conrad Gill, the diamond merchant, and his son, Victor; Bartlett, Decker, several reporters, and half a dozen other men.

Kerry O'Neil was there, also, a look of defiance in his dark eyes. He was handcuffed and a deputy stood at his side. Gail was furious. She wanted to announce their presence at once, but Perrin restrained her.

"Wait!" he whispered. "Something doing. Let's hear it."

The room was quiet—strangely so. Something tense and expectant was expressed in every face. Gail thought of the man who had died within its somber walls. His spirit seemed to brood down upon the gathering from the shadowy beams above. Her heart began to race. She felt Perrin's hand tighten on her arm. A rustling of papers was audible; then a voice called:

"Dr. Wallace McEwan."

The scientist came forward. The oath was administered and he took a vacant chair near the table, facing the jury.

"You have been investigating the death of Colonel Conniston independently of the sheriff's office, Dr. McEwan?"

"I have."

"On whose behalf?"

"Miss Gail Hollister's."

"Do you know where Miss Hollister is?"

"I do not."

"You have discovered evidence bearing upon the death of Peter Dimity?"

Dr. McEwan fingered his neat brown beard. "Not directly. My information has to do with the motive which resulted in the death of Colonel Conniston. It is connected with the death of Dimity only in so far as the two murders are related. They are related, of course."

"What is the nature of your evidence?"

"Well, I believe I have discovered how the combination of the vault came into the possession of the man who brought about Colonel Conniston's death and who, I presume, killed Peter Dimity."

Silence again.

Gail crept a little nearer the open door. Her eyes fell on Stark. His heavy face was white and tense. She guessed what emotions were rioting in his heart. Well, his hour had come! Then her eyes fell on Kerry and they grew humid with tenderness. Dear Kerry! *His* hour had come, too! Their hour! Her heart was singing.

"Let us hear your evidence, Dr. McEwan," the coroner said.

"My evidence is rather disappointing," Dr. McEwan began, in his clear, cultured voice. "It is interesting as an explanation of a puzzling angle of the case, but it does not indicate who killed Colonel Conniston and Dimity—though it may be of value in that respect later on. Let us consider the arrangement of the room. Colonel Conniston had *at least* three visitors on the night he was killed. They were Mr. O'Neil and Messrs. Victor and Conrad Gill." Dr. McEwan inclined his head towards the latter and Mr. Gill bowed blandly in return. "They will remember the arrangement of the room as it was then, no doubt. With your permission, Mr. Coroner, I shall make one or two changes."

Dr. McEwan turned his chair towards the table, drew up another chair and placed it alongside the one on which he had been sitting. The table had not been moved, so the position of chairs and table was now the same as it was when Conniston was killed. McEwan drew the attention of his audience to this fact; then he sat down on one of the chairs.

"We shall assume that the man who murdered Conniston

sat in one of these chairs chatting with Conniston and that he asked the latter to let him see the famous intaglios. Conniston consented and went to the vault. The vault is some six or eight feet behind me. I cannot see it."

Dr. McEwan now went to the vault. Its door was in shadow. He turned on the droplight and the combination dial stood out in sharp relief. McEwan went back to the table.

"I must disturb you, Mr. Coroner," he said. "There are two articles in that drawer which I require."

The coroner drew back his chair. McEwan opened the drawer and took out of it the Venetian hand mirror and the powerful lens, both of which had been on the table when Gail found Conniston's body. McEwan closed the drawer and sat down on one of the chairs on the other side of the table. He then took up the mirror in one hand and the lens in the other.

"We shall assume that Conniston is at the vault. Very well. My back is towards him. I cannot see the vault, so I hold the mirror thus,"—suiting his actions to his words—"and the combination is reflected in the glass. I can see the numerals, but I cannot decipher them—so I use the lens. It is a powerful instrument, my eyes are fairly keen, and I can just make them out. Still assuming Conniston to be at the door, I see him turn the combination to the right to 32, left 71, right 49, left 18. The combination of the vault, gentlemen! I drop the mirror and lens—take out my fountain pen—this scrap of paper—I write the figures down—blot them on the corner of this writing pad—thrust the paper into my pocket—so!" (Still suiting his actions to his words.)—"All this while Conniston is opening the door. It is done! Conniston turns around and I am casually examining the workmanship of this excellent Venetian mirror. That is all, gentlemen."

The library might have been empty, so still was it when Dr. McEwan had done. For perhaps ten seconds everyone in the room stared at him with blank astonishment in their faces. This moment of silence was a fitting prelude to the scene that followed. Perrin, with an eye for the dramatic, chose it for their entrance into the room, and propelled Kessler before them.

"Pick out the man who killed old Dimity!" he shouted, in a ringing voice.

The command cracked like a pistol shot in that surcharged atmosphere. But it was the appearance of Gail in the green georgette that brought everyone in the room up standing—save the coroner, who alone maintained his sense of dignity.

Kessler's sullen eyes swept the group.

"There he is!"

Involuntarily, Gail's eyes sought Stark's white, tense face. And then, with feelings of amazement to which she was incapable of giving any expression whatever, she saw that Kessler was not pointing at Norman Stark.

Kessler was pointing at Victor Gill, son of the diamond merchant.

Gail never ceases to look back upon the climax of that hectic night with the sensations of one who has passed through a sort of earthquake. Certainly, her feelings at the moment were those of one beneath whose feet the earth is rocking!

For half a minute or so there was dead silence. A pin might have been heard to drop. Even the function of breathing seemed to have ceased.

Victor Gill had become the target of every eye. But strange as it may seem Victor Gill, outwardly at least, was less disturbed than any of them. His pale, hawk-like face neither colored nor whitened; his dark eyes were as hard as flints. He stood as still as a marble statue....

Gail has only a vague recollection of what immediately followed. Pandemonium broke loose in the library. Bartlett, his men, the jury, and the newspaper reporters swept down upon her and Perrin and Kessler in a tidal wave, flooding them with cross-currents of questions, demands, exclamations. Somehow, Kerry O'Neil found his way to her side, put his handcuffed hands upon hers. The coroner pounded for order.... At last the room grew still. She heard Bartlett request a twenty-four-hour adjournment of the inquiry. The request was granted. And then Bartlett, a little grimmer than ever, took charge of the situation again; and when Perrin and Gail and Kessler had had their say, of Victor Gill....

For three hours, alone with Bartlett in one of the bedrooms, Gill withstood the deputy's merciless cross-examination. Bartlett had ideas of his own upon the gentle art of extracting confessions from tight-lipped malefactors, and he tried every one of them upon Gill. But the man's composure was adamantine. Bartlett could get nothing out of him. And then the deputy played his trump card.

Perrin had suggested that Joe Daniels be found and that he be "persuaded" to support Kessler's statement. Bartlett had leaped at the suggestion, and not being quite himself yet, had humble-mindedly complimented Perrin on it. To Decker had been assigned the task of finding Daniels. Kessler had then sullenly admitted that Daniels had been at the Green Crocodile and Decker had got in touch with the dry squad. Daniels, it turned out, had been arrested on general principles. Needless to say, Decker tackled the job of getting a statement out of him with gusto.

Thus it happened that towards dawn the door of the room in which Bartlett was attempting to "break" Gill was flung open and Joe Daniels was propelled inside. Decker followed, closing the door behind him. The little man was trembling from head to foot; his face was ghastly and his lips were twitching. Decker looked pleased with himself.

"That's him!" Daniels croaked. "That's the man we saw kill Dimity!"

There was dead silence for a moment. Daniels, pointing a shaking finger at Gill, was like an accusing specter risen from the tomb. Bartlett and Decker watched and waited.

The expression of Gill's face changed curiously. The skin seemed to whiten and tighten over the bony structure as if someone were drawing it from behind. His face was like a mask that hid all the devilish emotions of the human heart. He took a step forward, his eyes smoldering, his clenched hands upraised.

"Back there!"

Gill stared at the weapon that had leaped into Decker's hand. Then his arms dropped; his face grew composed again.

"All right," he said coolly. "You've got me. I did it. I'll make a statement."

The exultant detectives hurried him downstairs to the library. The stenographers were still there. Indeed, so intense was the interest of those who had heard Kessler's dramatic accusation that every one of them had remained. Perrin, Gail, Kerry, and Dr. McEwan were together on the little balcony; they reentered the room. The hum of conversation had ceased as Bartlett and Decker thrust Victor Gill into the library.

A little dapper figure stumbled towards them. It was Conrad Gill. The diamond broker had lost every shred of his amazing conceit, of his bland complacency. He looked old and broken. His white hands fluttered out towards his son like frightened birds.

"Victor!" he whispered.

Bartlett pushed him aside and led his prisoner to the chair in front of the table at which sat the coroner. "Let's hear it!" he said curtly.

The stenographers fluttered the leaves of their notebooks. For a moment the room was quite still. And then, in a flat monotonous voice, Victor Gill began his statement.

"I saw the Conniston intaglios for the first time at the Panama California Exposition in San Diego ten years ago. But I had read of them and I knew the history of every one of them long before that. And—I wanted them. My father did not know—he could not have understood. My father is a merchant, not an artist. None of you, for that matter, can understand what those stones meant to me. They were food and drink, body and soul, life and death; they had more beauty in their green hearts than anything else in the world. They had living fire in them. I wanted to hold them, to press them to my lips, to worship them. You think I am mad: you do not understand.

"Conniston said he would sell them, but I knew that he was lying. I knew that no man who had possessed those divine stones as long as he had could ever sell them. I determined to have them for myself—somehow. I had not enough money to buy them and my father, as I have said, is a merchant, not an artist. We came down last Sunday, only to find, as I had expected, that Conniston had changed his mind. But he said he would let us see the stones, and he went to the vault and began to turn the dial. And then, I saw my chance.

"This mirror was lying on the table in front of me. Conniston had received it from Hart & Company, the antique dealers, that day. Dr. McEwan has described how I used it to get the combination. My father was examining those curtains at the window and he did not see what I was doing.

"When Conniston showed us the divine intaglios I could hardly control my desire. Nothing could have kept me away from them now! But of course you cannot understand. We got up to go. I made a pretense of examining the curtains and drew back the bolt which held the window, hoping that it would not be noticed before I returned. We left, then. That fool O'Neil held us up—as if I should have let him take the stones had we had them! We registered at the hotel in the village and went up to our rooms.

"About one o'clock I came down and went out. There was no one around, but I found an old Ford car parked near the hotel. It was just what I wanted. I drove out here and entered by that window which was still unbolted. I started to open the vault. And then Conniston came into the room. Perhaps he had seen the desire in my face; perhaps he had seen me draw back the bolt. I do not know. We struggled and his body went limp in my arms. I thought he had fainted and I began to tie him up. And then I saw that he was dead. That is all, except that I heard the man Dimity tell Miss Hollister that he knew who had killed Conniston. A lie that, for Conniston died of heart failure. But—it was necessary—to remove Dimity."

The monotonous voice ceased and Victor Gill stared casually around the room; his dark eyes calmly met the accusing faces about him. There was no emotion in his expression—merely a vague regret, and something furtive and calculating. Not so much as a whisper of sound broke the stillness of the room. And then, suddenly, Norman Stark's voice cracked like a whip.

"The intaglio emeralds—where are they?"

Victor Gill smiled thinly. "I don't know where they are. They weren't in the vault. Somebody got there before me."

"What!"

The cry came simultaneously from Stark, Bartlett, and Kerry O'Neil.

"You are lying!" Bartlett shouted.

"I am not lying!" Victor Gill said evenly. "I never lie. The intaglios, I tell you, were gone. Somebody got there before me. Moreover, I left the vault *open*, not closed, as you found it. Somebody opened it before I got there. And somebody *closed it after I left!*"

There was in this extraordinary statement a ring of truth that convinced against their wills everyone in the room. Nobody spoke. Even Bartlett was at a loss for words. The tension slackened; they were off guard.

Victor Gill saw his chance and took it.

Decker stood near him, his arms folded across his chest. The bulge of his automatic showed at his hip pocket. They had not handcuffed Gill and he suddenly flung himself upon the man, wrenched the pistol from his pocket, and put it to his own head. There was a crack, a scream, and a curling feather of smoke. Victor Gill pitched to the floor, writhed, and lay still.

The case for the state was complete.

CHAPTER XXVIII
The House of To-Morrow

When Kerry had taken Gail up to her room immediately after the suicide of Victor Gill she felt as if she could never sleep again. But towards ten o'clock she found herself opening her eyes; they had been tightly closed in slumber for nearly four hours. Curtains were drawn across the window, but pencils of sunlight crept in here and there and it was one of these, falling upon Gail's eyes, that had awakened her. She was rested; her mind was clear.

So Stark hadn't killed Conniston and Dimity, after all, and Victor Gill had! was her first thought. It had seemed too fantastic for belief; but now she knew that it was true. Gill had demonstrated its truth in a manner that left no room for doubt. She had a vision of that still figure on the floor, that upcurling feather of smoke. And then the vision faded out of her mind, as an evil dream does, and smiling a little she began to think of Kerry. Surely it was a miracle, this tender thing that had come to pass! She lay quite still, bathed in the radiance of her thoughts, her body seeming to float on a sea of illusion.

There came a gentle knock on the door. Mrs. Wessels put in her round and shining face and followed it up with the vast bulk of her body.

"'Ow are you, dearie?" she inquired commiseratingly.

Gail was all right, but she didn't say so. She was staring at the graceful bronze vessel in Mrs. Wessels' arms.

"Where on earth did you get *that?*" she exclaimed.

Mrs. Wessels sniffed. "Another of them Dimity urns, Miss 'Ollister. I found it in 'is room. 'E must have 'ad one for 'is wife and one for 'imself—when 'e needed it. No wonder there's deaths in a 'ouse when them as lives in it keeps corfins and corpses by them! Will you 'ave your breakfast in bed, dearie? A nice bit of bacon and a fried egg."

Gail was thinking, but she answered swiftly, "No. I'll come down."

She slipped out of bed and Mrs. Wessels left the room.

Gail dressed quickly in white and green. The crumpled georgette gown lay on a chair and she hung it up in the clothes closet. It had served her well, but she never wanted to see it

again. Or green georgette, either, for that matter: it would
always remind her of Kessler. She must get Blondy a new
gown. In the future she was going to see a lot of Blondy. Her
experiences during the past week had given her a contact with
life which she would never have got in the rarified atmosphere
of the Westcoast Museum. Her life was full, rounded, and
complete. Kerry had completed it.

She went downstairs. Kerry and Dr. McEwan were at
breakfast in the dining room. There was no sign of Stark.
Kerry ran to meet her and promptly kissed her once, twice,
thrice, and made no bones about it, either, though Gail was
properly embarrassed. Then he sat her down at the table
between himself and Dr. McEwan. Mrs. Wessels appeared with
fruit and cereal.

"I suppose congratulations are in order," Dr. McEwan
murmured with a twinkle.

Gail blushed; or rather her blushes deepened. "I don't know.
Kerry takes so much for granted."

"Dr. McEwan has promised to be best man," Kerry observed
complacently.

Gail changed the subject. "Have you found the intaglios?"

McEwan sipped his coffee. "No, we haven't, my dear."

"What about Stark?" Gail went on. "I still am sure it was he
that Mrs. Wessels and I saw in the moonlight."

"So am I."

"Do you think he took the intaglios?"

"No. I think they were taken before Stark got here. And
before Gill got here, too. Stark was after something else."

"What?"

Dr. McEwan laughed genially. "We have evidence to show
that Stark was here the night Conniston was killed; you and
Mrs. Wessels saw him in the moonlight; that man in the village
saw a Druid sport roadster speed by in this direction; we know
that Stark owns a Druid such as this man saw; and we have
the carbon paper impression of the letter Colonel Conniston
wrote to him. Very well. We decided from the wording of this
letter that its subject matter was Conniston's will, though it
did not actually say so. Stark was on bad terms with his uncle,
we assumed that Conniston had expressed this antagonism
in his will, that he had notified Stark to this effect, and that
Stark intended to plead his cause in person on the 23rd or the
24th.

"Very well. Stark, Mrs. Wessels informed me, has a liking for
night driving. Some people have. Perhaps he couldn't get away

earlier. Anyhow, I am going to assume that Stark drove down from Los Angeles on the evening of the 23rd, that he got here about three A. M. on the morning of the 24th, saw a light at the library window, found the window open, entered, and discovered his uncle dead on the floor—just as Victor Gill had left him. I don't suppose he was greatly concerned. He went to the vault which Gill had left open, found the will, and read it. The document didn't favor him as he thought it should, and since it was a holograph will, he decided that it must disappear. And disappear it did. So did the correspondence he had had with his uncle concerning it.

"Stark then closed the vault, bolted the French windows, and left the house by way of the trap in the cellar. I suppose he followed this course to divert suspicion from himself, should the police discover that he had been on bad terms with his uncle. Perhaps he intended to give the impression that the crime was an 'inside job.' He ascended the cliff by way of the summer house trail. You, Gail, and Mrs. Wessels saw him in the gardens as he made his way back to his car."

"It must have been Stark who phoned the sheriff's office," Gail declared.

McEwan nodded. "I imagine he wanted to get back here as soon as he could. He would be anxious to know what conclusions the police had come to. But he knew he would have to explain his appearance if he came before they notified him what had happened, so he invented that story about the telephone call and phoned the sheriff's office himself to support it. Rather clever, I thought. The move tended to turn suspicion away from him, too. Fortunately, you and Mrs. Wessels saw him in the moonlight, Gail."

"Pretty good!" Kerry O'Neil cut in. "But how are you going to prove it—about the will, I mean?"

McEwan smiled. "I had a little talk with Stark early this morning and I indicated to him pretty much what I have said to you. I asked him if he preferred that the will should reappear or that certain evidence which we possess—the carbon and the statement of the man in the village—should be turned over to Bartlett."

"Great!" Kerry exclaimed. "We've got him there!"

"It seems so," Dr. McEwan agreed. "He gave me the will two hours ago. He said he 'found' it between the pages of Mather's *Ancient and Medieval Antiques*—a book Conniston used a good deal."

McEwan took a document from his pocket and passed it to

Kerry; his brown eyes were twinkling. "Apart from bequests
to Dimity and Mrs. Wessels," he went on, "the estate—some
eight hundred thousand dollars, including the intaglios—is
equally divided between Stark, you, and the Westcoast
Museum. 'To the son of my good friend, John O'Neil,' Conniston
puts it. A handsome wedding present, young people. I
congratulate you heartily."

"Wasn't that awfully decent of him!" Kerry exclaimed, as he
glanced through the will.

"I knew he meant to do what was right!" Gail cried, over his
shoulder.

"This," Dr. McEwan went on, "brings us to Dimity. We have
still to account for that fragment of his coat sleeve which
Decker found on the door of the vault. If we are to understand
Dimity's part in the affair we must remember that he was
abnormal and that his behavior might deviate sharply from
that of a normal person at any time and without warning. As
soon as this becomes clear to us Dimity's conduct is
understandable.

"Apparently, Dimity became obsessed by the idea that Colonel
Conniston and his valuables were in danger, and that he was
their protector. He was always 'listening and watching.' I gather
that Colonel Conniston was more amused than angry with
him. One cannot resent an old man's faithfulness. From what
you tell me, Gail, he was listening at the door while you were
talking with Colonel Conniston; and he was there while you
were kneeling by Conniston's body the next morning; you, Mr.
O'Neil, tumbled over him when you rushed out of the library.
This delusion of Dimity's, in my opinion, explains the
disappearance of the gems.

"Dimity, I venture to say, was at the door when Victor Gill
got the combination of the vault. He must have seen him write
it down and blot the figures. Here his abnormality crops up
again. Instead of telling his master what he had seen, as he
would have done if his poor muddled brain had been clear, he
later on read off the combination as you did, opened the vault,
took out the intaglios, and hid them away. I can almost hear
him chuckling at the disappointment of the thief when he
should come. The gems hidden, and his master safe in his
room, he relaxed his pathetic vigilance when it was really
needed. Poor Dimity! When he found that his master had been
killed, I imagine that he was too grief-stricken and terrified to
tell what he knew. Or perhaps he wanted to work it out in his
own queer way.

"This is pure theory, of course, but it seems to fit in with Dimity's mild insanity. If we find the gems, and they are where Dimity could have put them, I think my theory will be proven; if they are not where he could have put them, it will be disproven."

There was a sound at the door just then and they all looked up.

"Come in, Stark," McEwan called pleasantly. "I thought I heard you there."

For a moment there was silence; and then Stark's bulky figure filled the doorway. His heavy face was red with anger.

Kerry airily waved the will. "Congratulations, old man! We are companions in good fortune, I see."

"Mr. Stark!" Gail exclaimed, before he could reply. "You offered ten thousand dollars' reward for the recovery of the intaglios. Is the offer still good?"

"Since you know so much you ought to know where they are!" Stark said thickly.

"I imagine we shall find them," McEwan responded evenly.

Gail stood up, laughing, her hand on O'Neil's shoulder.

"Come on, Kerry. I am sure Dr. McEwan and Mr. Stark have much to say to each other."

Kerry required no persuasion and Gail led him past the raging Stark. They went out into the patio, along the cliff path, and down the summer house trail to the beach.

"Where to, Gail?" Kerry wanted to know.

Gail put her fingers on his lips, whereupon Kerry, promptly kissed them.

"Wait and see."

Ten minutes later they stood in the shadow of Cathedral Rock.

It rested upon them like the shadow of a benign presence, and even the importunities of Kerry O'Neil were silenced. They stood in front of it for a moment; and then Gail led Kerry to the tiny steps that were like an approach to a pagan altar. They scrambled up them and knelt by the font in which Gail had buried the urn two days before.

The abalone shell was still there and Gail began to scoop out the font. Kerry helped her, using his bare hands. Gail was trembling with excitement and Kerry was on fire with curiosity; neither of them spoke until the abalone shell struck the urn and the top of the vessel was uncovered in its bed of sand.

"What's this?" Kerry whispered.

"Lift it out."

He did so.

"It isn't sealed—open it, Kerry! Open it—quick!"

Kerry pried at the lid, got it off, and thrust his hand into the bronze vessel. For a moment he kept it there, his dark eyes blazing incredulously into Gail's; then he slowly drew it out. The Conniston intaglios were in his hand and they spilled through his fingers like fire: green fire, liquid fire, the cold fire of starlight on frosty nights. Their beauty held him still and breathless as once it had held Victor Gill who had followed it into the pit of madness and death.

"How did they get here?" he whispered.

Gail laughed unsteadily. "I buried the wrong urn, Kerry. Dr. McEwan was right about Dimity. It came to me—in a flash— this morning."

She told him the story of Dimity and his two urns.

There was silence between them for a little while and they sat side by side on the sun-warmed rock. Then Kerry picked up the urn and they started up the beach, hand in hand. Presently, they came within sight of the Casa de Ayer and they stopped and looked at it. The hot sun shone on the bright red tiles and it seemed to Gail that the shadow beneath which the house had stood this last week was there no longer.

Her hand tightened in Kerry's.

"If we could only live there always!" she whispered.

"We can," Kerry said, with a grin. "There'll be plenty of money. I am going to buy it for you."

When they started up the beach again the Casa de Ayer, house of yesterday, had become the Casa de Mariana, their house of to-morrow.

THE END